STRESSED!

Ogre's Assistant
Book One

DJ Martin

Stressed! Ogre's Assistant Book One

Copyright © 2013 by DJ Martin

Published: 1 March 2013

ISBN: 978-0-9888547-0-3 (e)
978-0-9888547-8-9 (sc)

Published by The Herby Lady, LLC

ACKNOWLEDGMENTS

Every single character in this book is loosely-based on someone I have known in my life. I won't name names except to say that Fudge is an amalgamation of several cats who have owned me over the years. If anyone happens to recognize themselves, I won't apologize for making you look better!

Laura Perry, editor extraordinaire, did a bang-up job of correcting all my writing faux pas. When you get all wrapped up in your story, it's difficult to see grammatical, punctuation and formatting errors.

My thanks to my beta readers (you know who you are) for being a cheering section. Without friends like you, I wouldn't have had the intestinal fortitude to actually go public!

Finally, head cheerleader and husband, Pete, is the best support a woman could ask for. Without his prompting, my off-the-top-of-my-head short story would have stayed just that … and buried on my computer.

CHAPTER 1

An ogre, a vampire and a werewolf walk into a bar ... Someone more creative than me could make a joke of my life.

My boss, Evander Angelich, is an ogre. No, really. Not just a grumpy person but an ogre. He stands a little over seven feet tall; weighs somewhere around 500 pounds; has a very large, round head; small eyes set too close together; a caterpillar for eyebrows; a mop of brown hair on top; and doesn't have the best personal hygiene. Think sewer backup. Yeah, that bad at times. Unlike Shrek, his skin isn't green; it's sort of puce. He also wears beautifully-tailored, custom-made suits instead of too-small breeches and vest. But like Shrek, he's pretty much a nice guy. I guess Hollywood gets some things right.

Ev owned the largest personal security business in the Midwest and the bulk of the client list would make the paparazzi go ape if they could get their hands on even one itinerary. Most of the guards were ogres or dwarves (short but tough little bastards with no sense of humor) with a couple of wizards thrown in for good measure. Ev chose these species because they can't truly be harmed by vampires, weres or other predators. Although wizards are human in the greater sense of the word, there is something about their aura that makes bloodthirsty species either not want them or be unable to seduce them.

He owned the company, I ran it. Ask any executive and if he's telling the truth, he'll admit his secretary does nearly all his work. Going into the office at 7:30 a.m. gave me a chance to read the reports from the previous night and start wading through all my paperwork before the phone started ringing off the hook around noon. Everyone knew Ev hated rush hour traffic so they waited until later to call him. (That was a lie. Ev didn't even have a drivers' license. He had a limo with a driver. He just wanted an excuse to sleep late.) By that time, I had a list of things for Ev to know about and/or do and when the agents and managers started calling, he could play the all-knowing big shot. It was a comfortable relationship that had lasted something over seven years.

My day started out normally. The sun woke me up at 6:00am as it shone through the bedroom window of my garden-level apartment. I originally had room-darkening drapes, but they were expensive and didn't stay intact for long. My cat, Fudge, climbed anything he could reach and since the window was at waist height, he shredded anything hung there. The curtains were as cheap as I could find – just enough to prevent any Peeping Tom from getting an eyeful. I replaced them about every two months, which was about how long it took Fudge to rip them to the point they were see-through instead of opaque. Everything in my apartment was geared towards a "me first" cat. Instead of the usual ceramic or glass knickknacks most of my female friends had around, the window ledges only held my collection of stuffed animals. They didn't break when Fudge swept them off to make room for basking.

I made the best of the situation by being a quasi-morning person. The timer on the coffeepot was set for 5:50 a.m. so when I was rudely awakened by so much light, there was at least an immediate infusion of caffeine to make the morning bearable. Although I hate needles, I always wished someone could figure out how to inject caffeine intravenously. I needed the morning jolt. After a half-pot of coffee inhaled while checking email, Facebook and Twitter, I was awake enough to do my stretching. I showered and headed off to work, just three blocks away.

Living in the heart of the city had its advantages. I didn't have to own a car. Most everything I needed was within walking or biking distance, or a fairly inexpensive cab ride. Although my building was an older one, it had been completely renovated just before I moved in. It was still considerably less expensive than the high-rises a mile or so away and I didn't need all the fancy stuff like a concierge service, anyway. I have twice the space for half the cost. My building came with a bonus: unlike those high-rise buildings, the owner had also put up good wards – something I needed due to the people I worked with on a regular basis. Magic just isn't my forte.

The same advantages turned into disadvantages when my boss figured I was always available since I was very single and lived so close. After about a year of him calling me on a Saturday or Sunday morning to come in for one "emergency" or another, we compromised. I'd get no more weekend calls and he wouldn't sing soprano.

Anyways, as I was saying, my day started out normally enough. Ev's odor preceded him into the office shortly after eleven. Mario, one of the wizard guards, was waiting to see him. He was unhappy with his current assignment – a pert blond movie star who thought she was a witch but in reality hadn't a clue about magic. Mario's comment was, "She has every episode of *Charmed* and all the Harry Potter movies on DVD. Therefore, she thinks she knows everything there is to know about magic." He was pretty much over being dragged into "rituals" and then being whined at when nothing happened. My notes suggested switching Mario with one of the dwarf guards currently following a foreign author around. She wouldn't be dragging a dwarf into anything!

Noon saw my lunch delivered from the deli downstairs. I had a long-standing friendship with the witch who ran it. She could really cook, whether in a cauldron or on a stove! Apart from anything containing peas, she had carte blanche to send up whatever she wanted. This day, lunch was a pastrami-on-rye sandwich with a side of some of the yummiest potato salad I'd ever tasted. The paper that wrapped my sandwich had a note: "Watch your back. I've got a bad feeling." Cassandra wasn't often wrong with her feelings but when I looked at the mound of paperwork and my calendar, I didn't see anything that could go any more haywire than usual.

Things went fairly normally until a phone call came in about 3:30. When I answered the phone, the voice on the other end sounded like it was coming from the bowels of Hell. I was used to the echo sometimes generated by cell phones but this positively vibrated through the wires.

"May I speak with Mr. Angelich, please?" growled the voice.

"May I tell him who's calling?" I answered back.

"Just tell him Happy is on the line. He'll speak with me."

Happy? With a voice like that? I buzzed Ev on the intercom and after a pregnant pause and a sharp intake of breath, he told me to put the call through. Tempted though I was to eavesdrop, I had other things I needed to do before I called it quits for the day so I went back to my own work.

Ten minutes later, the light for that line winked out. Ev slammed his office door open, stormed straight past me without a word and out the door. I didn't think anything of that. Ev often had temper tantrums and went for a walk to cool off. He usually returned after about a half hour, much quieted.

One of the benefits of starting work early is I got off early, too. Ev took the late shift, often working until nine or ten at night to keep track of all the guards who were out on assignment and be available if anything went awry. Although he hadn't yet returned, I assumed he would and at 4:00 I shut off my computer, locked up the office and headed home for my standard two-hour nap. It made up for getting up so early. Sort of.

I had just put my pajamas on and snuggled into bed, Fudge deserting his spot on the window ledge for a piece of my pillow, when the phone rang. Damn and blast! I'd forgotten to turn it off. Caller ID said it was Ev's cell phone. "This had better be good," was my not-so-cheerful greeting.

Without so much as an "I'm sorry to disturb you", Ev hurriedly said, "I need you to go to John's party for me tonight". In that split second where all sorts of stuff goes through your mind before you answer, I was thinking he sounded out of breath, whiny, and what the hell? I had a nice evening planned with a decent dinner, maybe a bottle of wine and my word processor.

(I forgot to mention: I write paranormal romance novels on the side under a pseudonym. Don't tell Ev. He'd never let me hear the end of it.)

"Ev, it's Wednesday. I had plans for tonight and besides, you know I can't go to one of those sorts of parties and be into work early the next morning," I replied.

"Whatever your plans were, you can change them. I'll cover the morning. Just do this, OK? Gregory will pick you up in the limo at 9:30. Stay for a couple of hours, schmooze folks the way you know how and leave. It's not like you've never done this before."

Guys, ogres in particular, really have no idea what a woman has to go through to get ready for an upscale party – especially if we aren't in the mood to do so. But he sounded like this was a real emergency. I sighed, said yes, hung up the phone and determined I could at least get my nap in before I'd need to eat dinner and start to get gussied up.

I set my alarm and settled back down. I had to move Fudge – he'd spread over the entire pillow during my conversation. He resettled himself and started kneading in my hair, making it entirely possible it would take another fifteen minutes just to comb out the snarls he was creating. I was used to it and had built an additional quarter-hour into my routine after he came to live with me.

It was getting dark in the apartment when the alarm went off, which suited my mood. My dreams had been off-kilter for some reason and the thought of having to go to a party, much less a late one, didn't improve my disposition. Still in my jammies, I padded into the kitchen, flipped on the light and started rummaging through the fridge for the makings for a quick dinner. I settled for a salad with leftover shrimp as a garnish. There was enough shrimp for Fudge and me to share without argument. An argument, I might add, that I invariably lost.

Two hours after that, I was as gussied as I was going to get. My dress was a full-length emerald green satin that fit well in all the right places and complimented my waist-length copper-red hair. I wasn't pleased with Fudge's coiffure attempt but it had only taken ten minutes to comb out his snarls before washing my hair. I was, therefore, five minutes ahead of schedule. Matching shoes and clutch completed the ensemble that wasn't quite *au courant* but still looked good. While silently thanking the fashion maven who declared pantyhose unnecessary, especially in summer heat, I watched out the window for Ev's limo.

CHAPTER 2

Gregory pulled up right at 9:30 and we headed for the 'burbs, where the uber-rich had transformed rolling farmland into fancy estates. During the ride, I mentally reviewed what I knew about this party:

It was being thrown by John Minton, agent-to-the-stars. Even though it was common knowledge in the paranormal circles that he was bisexual, he put on one of the straightest acts I've ever seen. The guest of honor was one of his clients and if the rumors were to be believed, his current paramour, an actor who was the latest heartthrob of several million teen girls. He *was* handsome, if you liked the type: tall, nicely built, dark hair and eyes, pale skin and a very full mouth. Although he looked to be in his early twenties, little did those googly-eyed teenagers know this particular actor was almost a hundred years old. Both he and John were night people. Vampires to you; which should explain why the party started so late. Ev provided security to some of John's clients and was always hoping to get a few more into his fold. Hence the attendance at the party.

Gregory let me off at the door of a Tara-wannabe mansion. I don't know how many acres John owned but there was an expanse of lawn to either side of the drive large enough to hold a couple of soccer matches on, with room for at least one more out the back before you got to the pool. (I always wondered what his monthly landscaping bill was. Astronomical, I'll bet.) White columns framed a large swath of shallow steps, which led to ten-foot high mahogany double doors.

Instead of the usual guard or butler greeting the guests and taking coats, John was doing the duty himself. After all, it was summer so there were no coats to be dealt with.

"Amy, what a pleasant surprise!" he greeted me, taking my hand in his in an attempt at old-fashioned gallantry. "Are you on your own or is Evander showing up at some point?" When I explained that something had come up for Ev and I was filling in, he smiled and his look turned from cordiality to one closer akin to lust.

"None of that, John," I said, retrieving my hand from his grasp and moving so he'd be outside my personal space. "You know what happened the last time you tried to sink your fangs into me and we don't want a repeat in front of all your guests, do we?"

John coughed, told me to enjoy the party and turned his smile to the next arriving guest. I smiled inwardly at the memory. The first party I had attended at his house was with Ev, a little over a month after I'd started working for him. No one knew who I was so I was fresh meat (literally, in some cases). Ev escorted me around the room, introducing me to everyone I needed to know. It was a veritable Who's Who of the entertainment industry … agents, managers, producers, and even a couple of up-and-coming actors I'd heard of.

John had immediately appeared by my side the moment Ev excused himself to use the restroom. I guess he was good looking: tall, athletic body, dark hair, grass-green eyes and sharply chiseled features. A little on the pale side for my taste, though. It was obvious from his demeanor that he was used to women falling over their tongues and assumed I would do the same when he turned his charm on me. He took my hand in his and tried to be seductive. (I am apparently immune to vampires' bedroom eyes because I have never swooned when they give me The Look.) I knew he was important to Ev so played along as best I could, despite the fact that his hand was like ice. But when he tried to get cozy and started eyeing me as if I were the blue plate special, I pressed my great-grandmother's silver cross into the exposed portion of his wrist below his sleeve. He screamed like a little girl with the pain. Although vampires normally heal almost instantly, it was a month before he could wear short-sleeved shirts again. That cross was on a charm bracelet I wore every day. I may be a mundane but I certainly am not stupid.

After leaving John at the door, I headed for the bar and grabbed a glass of chardonnay. Although I really prefer a nice, dark red wine, I didn't want anyone thinking the flute contained something else. With my Irish ancestry and its accompanying pale skin, I'm sure some thought I was a 'night person', as well.

I saw many people I knew, clients and business acquaintances alike, and headed for the nearest group to do what Ev wanted me to do – schmooze. I said hello to those I knew, introduced myself to those I didn't, and basically made nice to everyone. I always avoided being alone with any vamps but with the advent of spray-tan booths, it was getting more and more difficult to tell many from normal humans. (Some disdained the 'healthy, alive' look and you could spot those across the room.) Once I got into a group, though, I could always pick them out. Blood is a lot thicker than wine and leaves a coating on the goblet. You just have to look for it.

About an hour later (it seemed more like four – my face was hurting from the continuous smile) I felt a tap on my shoulder. I turned to find His Honor the heartthrob smiling at me. "I don't believe we've had the pleasure of meeting. I'm Andy and you're beautiful," he said. Spare me.

"Hello. My name is Amy," I replied. "If you're looking for someone gullible, I suggest that blonde over there. She doesn't know who you are." I refrained from saying "what you are". Calling someone a vamp to their face in mixed company isn't polite. He must have missed my point.

"I prefer sultry redheads and you fit the bill. May I have your drink freshened?" Sigh. Ev would consider Andy Deland a real catch for a client and be seriously pissed if I didn't at least try to bring him into the Angelich Security fold. I kept the smile plastered on my face as we meandered over to the bar. I got a fresh chardonnay, he had his B positive topped off from a wine bottle mysteriously missing its label. Like I couldn't tell the difference between cabernet sauvignon and blood.

He steered me to the patio where it was easy to get lost in shadows created by pillars and torchlight. Andy naturally gravitated away from the torches. Vamps and fire don't get along. He chose a cozy spot, out of view from the rest of the guests – even those wandering on the wide expanse of lawn stretching off the patio and leading to the pool. Warning bells went off in my head.

"So, what brings you to John's party?" he asked. I launched into my standard spiel about Ev's company, downplayed my role in it and tried to gush a little about some of the clients. The latter was always the most difficult part. It's tough to be awed by anyone who calls you when hungover, whining about the fact that their bodyguard insisted they leave a party when the guard saw something that could damage either the client's body or reputation, breaking up the client's fun. It happens more often than you might think.

Andy moved closer into my personal space. "Now I know about your work. I want to know about *you*. First tell me why you smell so good, then tell me what makes Amy tick." He reached around my waist and tried to pull me towards him. I saw his fangs drop a little – not a good sign. I'd had enough. Although he was trying to be normal, referencing the Guerlain Samsara I was wearing, to him my 'perfume' was blood, as he well knew. Vamps could smell blood a mile off and naturally, it was an aphrodisiac to them. Especially fully-human blood.

I pulled his arm away from my waist and, moving backwards, said with a glare, "What makes Amy tick is nothing I want to share with you. Please do us both a favor and go find someone closer to your own age to bother."

He moved back closer to me. "But I like older women," he pleaded. "I *prefer* them. Girls my own age are mostly airheads." Talk about playing a part! Maybe not Oscar quality but he knew his lines.

"Girls your own age are no longer girls. Unless they're not human, they're either dead or close to it. I'm going to be polite and excuse myself, now. Believe me when I say I can quite easily cause a scene that won't harm *my* reputation in the least." At that, I turned. It was definitely time to leave and head towards my bed, populated only by myself and Fudge.

I found John, said my goodbyes and was half way to the door when I heard a roar. Andy had apparently decided I was going to be his conquest and/or snack for the night, whether I wanted it or not. He came flying through the room and probably would have bowled me over had John not stepped into his path, effectively blocking me from my pursuer's sight. John grabbed Andy by the collar and brought him up short. "See you soon, Amy," he called as if everything was normal. "Folks, Andy apparently had a little too much to drink. I'll be back as soon as I put him to bed," he said to the rest of the guests as he dragged the vampire toward the archway that led downstairs. I unclenched my fist around the dangling charm, continued my path to the door as leisurely as I could with quaking knees, and gratefully climbed through the car door Gregory already had open.

About half way home, my phone rang. Ev again. Without preamble I said, "I'm on my way home. Everything went fine."

"I believe you but that's not why I'm calling," came the reply. "I'm in trouble and need your help."

An ogre in trouble. Right. "Ev, it's nearly midnight and I've been smiling so much my mouth needs its sleep to recuperate. What in the hell can't wait until I get in tomorrow?"

"I'll explain when you get here. Tell Gregory to bring you to Club Tread." With that he rang off.

I sighed again. I was going to pay myself triple overtime for this night. I told Gregory to change direction and checked my appearance. Club Tread was a very exclusive membership-only nightclub catering to non-human species. I had to look good and confident or the patrons would view me as either an unwanted human intrusion or food.

Gregory pulled up to one of those steel-and-glass multipurpose buildings just on the edge of downtown. You know, the kind that has shops and restaurants on the ground floor; offices on the second, third and maybe fourth, and fancy condos above that. Club Tread took up the entire second and third floors, and was accessed by a grand staircase that took up about a third of the lobby. No elevator … if you couldn't walk up the staircase in style (all the better to see and be seen), you didn't need to be here. Although I'd been here before (with Ev and a client, naturally), I was always impressed at the soundproofing. Not a decibel penetrated to the lobby. Maybe it had something to do with the ultra plush carpeting that my heels caught in, nearly making me stumble. I climbed the stairs, wondering how in the hell I was going to get in.

Ev met me at the door but instead of escorting me inside, turned me down the balcony overlooking the lobby.

"I'm ready for bed, Ev. What's this all about?"

"You know that call I got from Happy this afternoon? I had some dealings with him in the long-ago past and thought I'd never see him again. I need you to act like my wife, just for an hour or so, OK?"

"*Act like your wife? Are you out of your fucking mind?*" I hissed back. You just don't yell in a posh atmosphere like that, although it took everything I had to keep my voice down. Humans and ogres weren't the first thing that came to mind when one thought of "two people made for each other". Size was the first issue, hygiene another and I don't even want to think about sharing a bed!

"Please, Amy, I really need to be married right now. It was an, um, wager that I never thought Happy would check up on. Please?"

"Why me? You've got plenty of female friends to chose from. Some of them are even your own species. There must be someone who owes you a favor!"

"Believe me, I tried. I've been calling everyone I know since this afternoon. I can't get anyone to pretend, not tonight anyways. Please?"

As I said earlier, Ev is basically a good guy. And despite all my complaints, I actually liked him. Also, pale puce isn't a very attractive color and Ev was so pale with nerves he was close to being an albino for his species. I guess it couldn't hurt to pretend to be his wife just for an hour or so to get this Happy guy off his back.

"OK, I'll do it. But I get the rest of the week off and I don't want to hear a peep out of you until Monday morning. Otherwise, I'm out of here and you're on your own."

"I knew you'd help me out. Deal. I promise I won't call, even if the building blows up." With that, he produced a wedding ring that even J-Lo would drool at. I was surprised I could hold my hand up once I got it on my finger. It was heavy. About fifteen carats of diamonds twinkled from a platinum setting probably designed by Tiffany. I was better off not knowing where he'd gotten it on such short notice. He turned me back towards the club's doors. "Just so you know, you *do* work with me at the agency; he knows you've been to a party on business tonight; and we've been married two years. No kids." I thought I could remember at least that much, put my arm through his, plastered my fake smile back on and we walked into the club.

As soon as we walked through the huge double doors, my eyes and ears came under assault. Lights flickered and flashed, and whatever music was blaring seemed to be nothing more than its bass beat. If the dance floor was any indication, I was the only one who wasn't pleased with the sound. Variously sized, shaped and colored bodies gyrated together, looking like a sardine can that had popped open to reveal seriously deformed fish. Ev led me around to a booth on the upper level overlooking the floor. Soundproofing was somehow at work here, because although we could look down on the dancers, the music was muted enough to carry on a conversation. (I found out later that Club Tread has a wizard on staff to do nothing more than keep the soundproofing in place. Cushy job!)

"Amy, I'd like you to meet Happy. Happy, this is my wife," Ev said. It was a good thing I'd had a lot of practice smiling when I didn't want to. Did you ever see the cartoon, "God, the Devil and Bob"? There, the Devil looked more-or-less human with purplish skin, blond hair and a couple of little horns. I was looking at the cartoon's prototype. As Happy stood to greet me, I saw a moderately tall, well-formed man. Blond hair and purple skin were set off by a perfectly-tailored *red* suit that looked very much like Gucci styling. Two horns, just little nubs, were indeed peeking out of the Greek curls covering his head.

Happy's voice was just as gravelly in person as it was on the phone. "I'm very pleased to meet you, Amy. Please, have a seat. May I order you a cocktail?" I definitely needed one and something a little stronger than wine. "Yes, thank you. I'll have a gin and tonic, preferably Tanqueray, extra limes," I said to the waiter who had mysteriously appeared at my elbow. With that, I slid into the booth and Ev sat on the edge of the bench. (He didn't fit all the way into standard-sized booths and had obviously chosen this one so Happy wasn't dwarfed by the ogre-sized booths scattered throughout the club.)

"So, Happy, how do you know Ev?" I asked, trying to make small talk when all I wanted was for that drink to arrive so I could down it in one gulp.

"Ev and I go back a long time," he chuckled. "I'm surprised he never mentioned me. We spent a lot of time together when we were both in LA." I looked at Ev, who swallowed a little hard and attempted a smile.

"Oh yes, those were my wild days. I've never mentioned you because all that is behind me and has no bearing on my current life. I don't think I've *ever* said much of anything to you about my days in LA, have I darling?"

"No, Ev, you haven't. It seemed like something you didn't want to talk about so I didn't press," I smiled at him. That was really the truth. I knew Ev was born in Los Angeles and had lived there for quite some time prior to moving to Minneapolis, but he didn't talk about it and I had no interest in his past.

My drink arrived. "A toast to the happy couple," said Happy. We clinked glasses and I made a conscious effort to just sip instead of chug it. "Tell me, how do you like being married to Ev?" Happy continued with his interrogation.

"It was an adjustment, I'll admit. My first husband was human so there were species differences I had to get used to. But he's a great guy." I didn't lie again, except for implying the marriage part. Working with an ogre *did* take some getting used to and my first (and only) husband *was* human.

The banter continued. I was guessing Happy was trying to figure out if it was all real. Thankfully when you worked closely with someone over a long period, you got to know most all their foibles so I was able to easily answer all the questions. But it finally came my turn. There was only one question I really wanted answered.

"So tell me, is Happy your given name or a nickname?" I asked.

"It's a nickname I got a long time ago. I tend to be an acquisitive sort and in my younger days when I got something I wanted, I did a little happy dance. There was a time when I was getting *everything* I wanted and I danced a lot. My friends picked up on that, started calling me 'Happy Dance' and then just shortened it to Happy. It has stuck with me all these years." If he was who I thought he was, 'Acquisition' was probably his middle name and 'Of Souls' his last.

With this, I smothered a yawn. Sneaking a peak at my watch, I could see that it was something past 1:00 a.m. "My apologies," I said. "I am not used to being up quite this late. Although I'd love to continue this conversation, sweetheart, I really do need to get to bed." This last was directed at Ev, who looked at Happy.

Happy nodded and said, "On the contrary, it's I who owe you an apology. Ev, I'd really like to continue catching up if you're up to it."

"Sure," Ev replied – through slightly clenched teeth. "Just let me walk Amy out. I'll be right back." We rose; Happy kissed the back of my hand, effectively dismissing me from his presence. Ugh. I was glad to leave.

Once we were back in the lobby, Ev hugged me. If you've never been hugged by an ogre, I suggest you avoid the event. "Ev, I can't breathe," I said into his none-too-nice-smelling waist. "Sorry," he said, releasing me. "I keep forgetting about the size difference. Thank you for this. I don't think he suspected a thing. I owe you big time."

I started walking down the staircase, Ev right behind me. "Yes you do." I said over my shoulder. "I'll start collecting this morning when I don't go into the office. Since it looks like you won't make it in early, either, I'll change the voicemail to say we're opening at noon. You'd better be there to handle everything because I certainly won't. Good night, Ev. I'll see you Monday morning."

Once again I climbed through the door Gregory was holding open for me. Five minutes later I was at the door of my apartment with Gregory watching me go inside. (Although Ev knew about the wards on the building, Gregory had instructions to ensure I was inside them before leaving. He did double-duty as driver and extra-pair-of-eyes for Ev: Gregory was a wizard, too.)

I hit the locks, freed my feet from the heels, fed a pissed-off Fudge (three-plus hours late), called in to change the voicemail, put the coffee together but turned off the timer and headed for the sack. What a night! If Ev ever put me into a situation like this again, I *would* emasculate him. Wife indeed. I was seriously considering what it would be like to work for a normal person again. Maybe I'd check the employment sites on the 'Net when I got up. There had to be a better – or at least easier – way to make a living.

However, I had four days to do nothing but sleep in, play with my cat and write. (Laundry had to be done somewhere in there, too.) I think I'd even managed some fodder for a new book this evening: an out-of-control bisexual vampire in a love triangle with Satan waiting in the wings. Could be interesting!

CHAPTER 3

Six o'clock comes early anytime but especially if you're wanting to sleep in after a long and stressful night. Just like clockwork, the sun shone through my bedroom window. I groaned and pulled the pillow over my head to blot out the bright light, dislodging Fudge in the process. He readjusted himself against my back and we both went back to sleep. I opened my eyes the next time to see the clock ticking its way to seven. Still too early but damn it, I was awake. Would I ever get back to being a night person? I missed being able to sleep until noon without any difficulty!

Since I hadn't set the timer, the coffee wasn't waiting for me. Ten minutes is a long time to kill before your first caffeine fix of the morning. I distracted myself by scooping Fudge's litter box. It's not the most pleasant chore in the world and best done while still half-asleep. That way you don't remember much of the odor.

Odor. That brought Ev and the previous evening back to mind. I pondered everything while sipping on my elixir. How in the hell did I get myself into these situations? Ah yes. I remember now. Stupid girl.

I was in my first year of college when I met the man who would become my husband. I thought it was love at first sight. He was handsome in a rugged sort of way, athletic but not a jock and an art major. The man could definitely draw and had dreams of becoming an anime artist for a major company. He had a nice combination of brawn and sensitivity that I found very attractive. We dated for about six months, broke up for almost a year and then picked up where we'd left off. When he proposed, I immediately accepted with the typical dreams of a house with a white picket fence, 2.5 children and a dog. I would quit school and become the bestest housewife in the world – call me June Cleaver, Jr. At twenty, you don't think much about practicalities and my folks weren't around to remind me of them – they'd both died in a car accident when I was seventeen. I was on my own.

What I failed to realize is that there are a *lot* of people with dreams of being an anime artist. Try as he might, Ted could never make it to the top of the heap of applicants for the few job openings. He made a living as a carpenter with his dad's remodeling firm. Since I'd learned to type in high school, I got a job as a secretary. Neither of us was happy.

Our marriage broke up after two years and I was back on my own. I had a not-much apartment and a not-much job in a not-much city. I decided it was time for a major change. I updated my resume and started perusing the help-wanted ads online in cities other than the one I lived in. Nothing seemed any different from what I had until about three months into my search. One morning an ad in the Minneapolis Star-Tribune caught my eye:

Administrative Assistant needed. Must be well-organized and people oriented. Experience with non-human species a plus. Bookkeeping skills a must. Starting salary commensurate with ability. Health insurance and 401(k) provided. Send resume to …

I couldn't look up the company because the email address was at Yahoo. Nice and anonymous, that. Experience with non-human species? In what way? Face it, Iowa wasn't a paranormal Mecca. There weren't a lot of non-humans to interact with. I knew several weres from my college days and there was one dwarf in my high school class. We weren't friends but I got along with them. I didn't know if that counted. However, I fulfilled all the other requirements and I'd heard the Twin Cities were a nice place to live, so I fired off my resume hoping to hear something.

A couple of days later there was a message in my inbox asking for a telephone interview. If that went well, it would lead to a personal interview at their office – travel expenses paid by them. A bonus: the writer, Evander, asked if I minded if the phone conversation happened in the evening, which was when he did the bulk of his work. No skin off my nose. I'd rather I didn't have to excuse myself from work since they didn't know I was looking elsewhere. I replied with some convenient times for me (like, every night after 6:00 p.m.) and within minutes, we had set up an appointment for the following evening.

I don't remember the entire conversation but Ev told me he was an ogre and he had non-human employees and clients. Did I have a problem with that? As long as no weres or vamps bit me, no, not really. He asked whether I followed celebrity gossip. It's really unavoidable these days but honestly, I paid little attention to who was marrying or divorcing whom, who got picked up on a DUI and the like. I found it boring. I was asked about moving. I thought my sob story would come off as a little self-pitying, so I just told him I was looking for a change and had heard the Twin Cities were nice. I didn't say but I implied I wasn't willing to move without a guaranteed job. I had a little money left from my parents' estate but certainly not enough to live off of indefinitely. I preferred to keep that invested for emergencies or better yet, retirement.

Apparently I said all the right things because Ev asked if I could come to Minneapolis for an interview. He was used to working weekends so if I wanted to come that Saturday, he'd be able to see me then. There was a hotel a short distance away from his office. He'd make a reservation in my name for Saturday night, arranging for a late checkout Sunday morning so I didn't have to rush; and he would be sure to have gas and food money for me when I got there. It was about a four hour drive so we set up a 2:00 p.m. appointment.

His office was on the south side of downtown, in an older area that up-and-comers probably considered 'quaint'. It was a mixed neighborhood with residences, small shops, and small offices. Everything was well-kept, fairly quiet if you discounted the fact that it was on a main thoroughfare, and there didn't appear to be any riff-raff on the streets. I liked it. His office was on the second floor of one of those buildings, with a deli downstairs and another, currently-unoccupied office on the floor above.

The place was tiny compared to the large corporate offices I was used to. Ev greeted me at the door and gave me the nickel tour. There was a reception area with a desk, a couple of comfortable chairs sized for larger people, and a coffee table replete with the latest Hollywood gossip magazines. Beyond that were two offices: one obviously used and the other empty except for what looked like cast-off home furnishings. The rest of the space contained a half-bath, a small kitchen and a storage room with file cabinets and a copier. He pulled Cokes out of the fridge for both of us and we sat in the reception area to talk.

Although I'd heard of ogres and seen a photo or two of them in the newspaper, I wasn't prepared for how large they really are. Especially compared to me. I stand 5'4" in my bare feet and weigh about 110. Most humans are bigger than me and Ev is considerably larger than most of them. I felt a little like a bug that could be squashed if I wasn't careful to keep out of his way.

His body odor was another thing I wasn't expecting. You'd think in today's age of television commercials for *everything* smelling sweet, he'd have picked up a hint or two. But he had a separate office from where I'd be sitting so I thought I could handle it, as long as I had a *lot* of scented candles burning the whole while.

I asked what happened to whoever it was I would be replacing. Surprise, surprise. I wasn't replacing anyone. Ev had been trying to do it all himself for the last two years and had been a miserable failure at it. He needed someone to keep the office straight while he dealt with the clients. That made sense. (I found out several months later that I had been the only applicant for the job. Apparently I was the only one who didn't mind non-humans.)

Obviously, the in-person interview went well or I wouldn't be here today. But what sealed the deal from my end was the salary offer. It was four times what I was making back home. (Little did I know the excess was 'hazardous duty pay'.) Although cost of living was a little higher in Minneapolis than Waterloo, I would still be sitting pretty. We shook on it (well, he enveloped my hand in his and pumped my arm up and down a few times) and agreed I would start work a month later. That would give me enough time to give my notice at the old job and the old apartment and make the move. Ev said he'd been going it alone so long now that another month wouldn't matter. I hoped so but based on the piles of paper lying around, I knew I would have my work cut out for me when I finally dug in.

I had dinner in the hotel restaurant that night and grabbed the early-edition Sunday paper from the rack. The news wouldn't be quite current but the ads would be. I curled up on the bed with a glass of wine (a freebie courtesy of the cute bartender) and started looking for a place to live. My phone rang. It was Ev.

"I think I may have found you an apartment. The building is owned by an acquaintance of mine and is close to the office. I can give you the phone number of the super if you're interested." I didn't have anything to lose so took the number. Nothing in the paper looked truly promising, anyways.

The next morning after breakfast I called the super and he was amenable to me coming right over. It was only a mile walk and the spring weather was gorgeous, so I left the car in the hotel's garage and hoofed it.

I fell in love with the place, even before I heard the rent and 'bonus'. Like the rest of the neighborhood, the building was older but well-kept. It was a basement apartment, but rather than being only the width of half the building to either side of the interior staircase and extending to the back, it spanned the entire width of the building and more than half the depth, making it larger than the other apartments and almost twice the size of the place I was currently in. Also because it was on the lower level, it had its own entrance from the street, with a second one into the back hallway. The laundry room was right across the hall. No hauling stuff up and down stairs! The boiler room was also across that back hall but the super assured me the tenants were the quiet type and everything was well soundproofed, so I wouldn't hear anything. Large windows let in a lot of light.

The bath was in the process of being retiled and would be getting all new fixtures. The same would be done to the eat-in kitchen, new appliances brought in and then they'd put down new carpeting in the bedroom and living room. Although anyone passing by could look in the windows, it was on a side street without a lot of foot traffic. Sheer curtains would hide me during the day and heavier ones over those would hide me at night and block out the morning sun. It was perfect.

Then he told me how much rent was: $100 more a month than I was currently paying. With my hefty increase in salary, I thought I could manage. Then came the surprise. "Mr. Owens, who owns the building, is a wizard. He doesn't like anyone messing with any of his belongings and also takes an interest in his tenants' well-being because it's good for business. This building has been heavily shielded against unwanted attention. If you decide to take it, you'll have to give Mr. Owens a strand of your hair. That way he can key the wards to you, too."

I opened my mouth to protest. I'd heard what witches and wizards could do with someone's hair, nail parings, skin, anything of a *very* personal nature. "I know what you're about to say," the super pre-empted my objection. "Mr. Owens will do what he does in front of you and destroy your hair right there and then. It just takes something with your DNA to key the wards." I decided I could live with that.

I signed the lease and wrote a check for both the security deposit and the first month's rent. I was assured all the renovations would be completed by the time I was ready to move in. We exchanged phone numbers and I walked back to the hotel. I don't think my feet touched the ground the entire time. I'd found a job that paid an insane amount of money and a really cool apartment in less than a 24-hour time span. Things were looking up!

I wanted everything to happen immediately but unfortunately, life doesn't work like that. I drove home, already mentally packing up my apartment. My boss wasn't too surprised when I gave my notice the next morning. "I knew you were unhappy. It was just a matter of time before you tried greener pastures," he said. I gave him three weeks instead of the usual two. He was a nice guy and I didn't have to be back to Minneapolis for a month, anyways. That would give me a week to pack and move. It wouldn't even take that long.

So I hired a moving company, made the move, met Mr. Owens (quickie spell and my hair went poof!), got settled in the apartment and my new job. Within a month I realized I didn't need a car at all so sold it and invested most of the money. I splurged a little on a good bicycle and some things I wanted for the apartment.

My neighbors had to be some of the best in the world. The four apartments above me were occupied by retirees … two witches in one, a dwarf in another, and two mundane men who, like me, had something to do with the paranormal in their working lives. Edward, the super, was one of the mundanes. I was greeted with mounds of food the day I moved in and offers to help me unpack. They were all very friendly and as I was so young (in their view), they vowed to keep an eye out for me. Over the years, I became the daughter none of them had ever had and they, in many ways, were my surrogate parents. I could talk to any of them about anything and loved them for it.

It didn't take long for Ev and me to form a comfortable working relationship. As he'd admitted, he was an abject failure when it came to the paperwork end of business. At this, I excelled. Within a month, the piles of paper had vanished and within six months, I had the

Internal Revenue Service off his back by ensuring all the taxes were deposited on a timely basis. His accountant was profoundly grateful for my presence and even sent flowers after the first quarter passed without a nasty notice from the revenuers.

Ev, on the other hand, reveled in the people end of things. Given his temper tantrums, I was always surprised when he was able to sign another client. I'd never been in on any negotiations but whatever he did, it worked. Over the years I learned how to smile and be polite, even to some of the grossest people I'd ever met. Ev said having me around to 'charm' folks was a bonus. If that's what it took for my steady rises in pay, I'd smile at the devil himself, who was probably least among the … interesting … people I met.

First and foremost, there was Ev: an ogre with a fairly sweet disposition – at least towards me. Sure, we butted heads but all I had to do was remind him why he'd hired me in the first place and he usually calmed down. He threw a temper tantrum at least once a day but he got over it and things got back to normal quickly. He was single but then again, still fairly young – only a hundred and fifty-four. The business appeared to be successful – he lived out in the 'burbs, had a limo with driver and enjoyed partying at some of the more exclusive clubs in town. I couldn't find anything wrong with the books (once I set them up, that is) so I don't think he was skimming. Just paying himself a nice salary – and me, too.

Then there were the various bodyguards. They were all ex-military or ex-law enforcement so on the outside, they were all toughs. However, there were a few ogres who, despite their size and training, were pussy cats – as long as they or their charge weren't threatened. All the guards were associated in some way with the paranormal. If they weren't non-human, they wielded magic as well as a sidearm. Ev's was the only paranormal security firm in the country, which made him quite popular in some circles. Most of the security was provided on a contract basis. Clients didn't want to take on the exorbitant expense of the workers' compensation insurance. Too, there were always times personalities didn't mesh; it's easier to switch contractors than fire an employee. On occasion, the guard/client relationship became permanent. In this case, Ev took a finder's fee of one year's salary. Let me tell you, personal bodyguards make a *lot* of money.

We usually had about 20 contracts out at a time, so it wasn't too difficult to juggle schedules. Most of the clients were actors or at least someone really famous but once in awhile, we got a rich nobody who was just a Nervous Nellie. Ev didn't discriminate when it came to taking people's money.

Because you had to have *money* to have a bodyguard, Ev ran in some pretty stratified circles. That meant parties hosted and attended by the glitterati. At first, I was thrilled when Ev asked me to accompany him or play hostess at one he threw at his house. I was in my mid-twenties, just an administrative assistant, and I got to rub shoulders with the rich and famous. After a time the glitz of the parties wore off and I decided I'd rather stay home. I didn't attend *every* party to which Ev was invited but one or two a month, if the situation warranted for some reason or another.

Not to mention that Ev gave me some money so I could buy appropriate evening wear. The only fancy thing I had in my closet up to that point was my wedding dress in its plastic cover. Being the thrifty person that I am, the money he gave me went a *long* way. I found all sorts of nice outfits at thrift stores, consignment shops and on sale racks. All I had to do was shorten them, something I had to do with a lot of clothing, not just the glam wear.

When I first started working with him, Ev gave me a rundown on the most prevalent non-humans I was likely to meet and how to deal with them. Ogres I already knew and was getting used to. Dwarves, too. Witches and wizards were pretty much like other humans. They were just able to wield magic and lived longer than mundanes.

Vampires were really everything I'd ever read: pale, fangs (if they *chose* to show them or got pissed or lusty); couldn't handle direct sunlight, fire, silver, crosses, holy water, or stakes through the heart. The thing books got wrong, though, was vamps *could* be out during the day as long as it was overcast or they had heavily-tinted car windows; and they could see their reflection in a mirror. (Good thing. Most of the ones I met were so vain they probably would have staked themselves if they couldn't see what they looked like.)

Weres looked and acted normal unless it was around a full moon but there was something of a predator in both their appearance and mannerisms. I probably wouldn't meet any elves since they didn't often mix with anyone outside their race but if I did, I'd know one. They looked like humans but *perfect* in every way, with the Spock ears. They were also haughty and would look down their nose at me. I shouldn't take it personally – they were like that with all non-elves. There were others, of course, but none I'd likely run across in my normal dealings, like various forms of fae, pixies, brownies, dryads … the list went on.

With information arming me and my normal attitude towards people, I thought I could handle just about anything. I had my great-grandmother's cross added to a charm bracelet I purchased, and made sure I stayed off the streets around the full moon.

CHAPTER 4

I've already mentioned the first party I attended at John Minton's house and the ensuing confrontation. Countless parties later, Ev introduced me to a current client's agent and immediately after the introduction, left us with a wink. Ev was trying to fix me up but it didn't look like his taste in men was too bad. Tony Wellington was the first person I'd met at one of those parties who wasn't entirely full of himself. Instead of yammering on about his current client roster and who wanted to hire him, he could talk about literature; enjoyed going to museums and the theater; and a plus: he looked like Hugh Jackman's 'Wolverine' but without the muttonchop sideburns. I managed to contain the drool in my mouth and didn't even hear those little warning bells in the back of my head. Or if I did, they sounded like wedding bells. Or something. At least screwing bells.

Tony was in town for a few days seeing to some things for his clients. He asked me out and I accepted. Two days later, he took me to a wonderful restaurant on the top floor of one of the downtown buildings where there was a lovely view of the skyline. Even with my newfound 'wealth', I couldn't have afforded to dine there on my own. My clue? It was one of those places where the lady's menu didn't have any prices on it. I didn't think restaurants like that existed anymore. I mean, what if I was picking up the tab, not him? Women are liberated, now!

Anyways, dinner was fabulous, the wine excellent and conversation scintillating. We even saw eye-to-eye on most political issues. Between the dining, wining and conversation, I was more than ready to hop into the sack with him, which happened in his hotel room a few hours later. It was fun and I hoped to repeat the experience many, many times but maybe with a little more advance planning on my part: I had to crawl out of a very comfortable bed, shared with a very attractive man and go back to my lonely apartment to feed the damned cat.

Tony left town but called every day and sent flowers several times. Ev was snickering and calling me "Lovey". I thought it was nice to be romanced so ignored the remarks.

Less than a month later, Tony arranged to return to the Twin Cities for an overnight, just to be with me. I was thrilled and flattered and made sure Ev knew I wouldn't be available even if the world came to an end. On the night in question, I remembered to put down food for Fudge before leaving and on the off chance that evening went as well as the first, carried some overnight necessities in a larger-than-normal purse.

Tony sent a limo to pick me up and we went to another fancy restaurant. More good food, wine and conversation and naturally, we ended up back in his hotel suite. Our night was just as much fun as the first one and coffee-cum-breakfast the next morning was delightful. I was sorry when he left for the airport, dropping me off at my apartment on the way.

The romance continued for several months. I received a lovely bouquet of flowers at least once a week and long phone calls were a twice-a-week occurrence. Tony would arrange to come to town for a weekend or even just overnight. When time permitted, we'd go to a Broadway show at the State Theater, a play at the Guthrie or an opening of an exhibit at one of the museums. Even if it was the wrong time of the month for me, we enjoyed cuddling with each other late into the night. I was beginning to think that I'd met Mr. Right.

Our last date wasn't *quite* as fun. We were getting cozy on the couch in his hotel suite with a glass of bubbly when the clouds parted and the moon shined directly through the sitting room window and straight into our faces. Any other night, I would have said it was gorgeous. It happened to be a full moon. Right in front of me, Tony's face elongated into a snout (with "the better to eat you" teeth), his fingers became claws and as his clothing ripped, I could see all sorts of hair starting to sprout where it shouldn't on a man. Before his face completely turned, he managed to growl out, "Shit, I am going to kill that wizard. His potion didn't work!"

Needless to say, I made a beeline out the door. Thankfully, we hadn't gotten to any point of undress so all I had to grab were my purse and shoes. I didn't want to wait for an elevator so I virtually flew down fifteen flights of stairs to the lobby, out the door and didn't stop until I was several blocks away and too out of breath to run any farther. Not to mention that my bare feet hurt. I hailed a cab and got inside my apartment behind Mr. Owens' wards before I took any sort of normal breath.

A full bottle of wine later I calmed down enough to go to bed. Although I knew I was safe in my apartment, I really didn't sleep much that night. The scene of Tony changing and imaginings of those teeth taking a chunk out of me kept running through my brain. If the timing had been any different, he would have given new meaning to eating a girl. "Let that be a lesson to you," I told myself. "No more dating anyone you meet at Ev's fancy parties."

My phone starting ringing about noon on Saturday. Caller ID told me who it was and I had no interest in talking to him. I turned it off after the fourth call in ten minutes. I also didn't answer the knock at the door mid-afternoon. When I finally ventured to open it maybe an hour later, two dozen red roses in a Lalique crystal vase stood on my doorstep with a note that simply said, "I'm sorry." I gave the roses to the two witches who lived in my building — they'd enjoy them. I packed the vase away to use as a gift for someone at a later date.

I spent the weekend curled up with a good novel and by the time Monday rolled around, felt more like myself. When Ev walked in the door Monday morning, the first thing I did was reach up and slap his face, but good. It left a greenish mark on his puce-colored skin in the exact shape of my hand.

"Ow. What did I do?"

"Didn't bother telling me Tony was a were, that's what you did."

Ev looked confused. "But I didn't *know* he was a were. I would never have thought to fix you up if I knew, or I'd at least have said something. Honest! What happened?"

Without going into any gory details I simply told him Friday evening had been ruined when Tony changed and then mentioned his comment about a wizard's potion. "I've heard of those and always wondered if they worked. I guess not, huh?" Ev said.

"I thought non-humans could sense other non-humans but it looks like I thought wrong. From now on, no more trying to fix me up, Ev. I'll make my own choices in men and I can guarantee they won't be anyone from your side of the tracks. Now, we have some business to talk about." With that, I picked up my notes and we got to work.

Naturally, Tony called that morning. He knew I'd have to answer *this* phone. He started out with "Amy, I'm truly sorry. I'd like to see you again, at an appropriate time of the month."

I *really* didn't want to date a were. With both of us having our 'times of the month', I could envision all sorts of problems, especially if they coincided. I blew him off with, "I don't think we're right for each other. Please don't call again unless it's business-related," and hung up. He got the message and never called the office phone again. If he needed to speak with Ev, he called Ev's cell phone. I saw him occasionally at parties and we always managed to stay on opposite sides of the room from each other.

That was almost five years ago. I hadn't exactly been celibate in that time but seeing as how my work and social life sometimes blurred together, I didn't meet anyone I really wanted to get serious with. I decided only true humans or wizards were safe but none lasted more than a few dates. If they were fully-human, they had an ego the size of China. If they weren't mundane, there was always something niggling in the back of my mind about how the relationship could go majorly wrong in a short period of time.

OK. Enough reflection. I was half way through my pot of coffee and it was time to do something productive. I showered and sat down at my desk. I decided against perusing the want ads. I knew in my heart that despite everything, I liked my job. I also knew that there was no way I'd be able to replicate the income and benefits I currently had. So, it was time to start writing.

Fudge bestirred himself to come off the window ledge and curl up on my desk as close to the keyboard as he could get without actually doing the typing himself. I initially found this arrangement unsatisfactory but after several attempts to get him to lie elsewhere, I gave in and as long as he didn't touch the keyboard, we worked together – me typing and him supervising.

On further reflection (I seemed to be doing a lot of that this day), I started writing about the time Fudge came to live with me. Was he my Muse?

I'd been in the apartment almost two years and in that time, had convinced Mr. Owens to put screens on my windows so I could open them in nice weather without worrying about being bug chow. Don't ask me how, but he'd managed to put a spell on the screen so when I had the windows open, the view from the street was obstructed. So I was able to have privacy along with airflow. There were perks to having a wizard as a landlord! (For some reason the spell didn't work when the windows were closed so I still needed drapes. Nonetheless, I'd take the tradeoff.)

I was sitting on the couch with my nose stuck in a book one lovely spring night with the windows open when I heard some caterwauling outside. This was really nothing new: the neighborhood cats occasionally had an argument about territory. What *was* different was the proximity. When I said 'outside' I meant 'right outside my window'. It was loud. I was about to yell for them to take it elsewhere when the screen came tumbling into the living room followed immediately by a dark brown streak that after a pause with a crazed look around, headed down the hall to my bathroom.

When I looked out the now *really* open window, I saw a large orange tabby staring in. He made one attempt to come into my apartment and stopped cold, as if he'd run into a brick wall. He did some more staring, tried again and again was rebuffed. The only thing I could think of was Mr. Owens' wards were doing their thing but against a cat? I'd have to ask about that. I closed the window and slid the drapes back into place until I could get the screen back on and decided to deal with the interloper.

I looked in my bathroom to see a kitten huddled behind the commode. He looked pitiful. I didn't have a lot of experience with cats but he looked to be six months old at the outside and so skinny, he could have been the proverbial thermometer. His coat wasn't in the best shape, either, but that could have been from lack of food, too.

"Well, if you got through the wards, you must be OK," I quietly said to him. When I moved to pick him up, he didn't try to fight me, bite or anything. "Let's see if I can find you something to eat and drink. Then we'll worry about the rest of you, huh?"

He stayed cuddled in my arm as I walked into the kitchen. The only thing I could find in my cupboards that might appeal to a cat was tuna, so I put down an entire can plus a bowl of water. He promptly devoured the food and looked at me as if to say, "More?"

"That's all I have and it's too late to go to the store tonight," I answered the unspoken query. Then I remembered that the two witches upstairs had a couple of cats. Maybe I could borrow some food from them. I picked up the phone and when Elinda answered, I described my predicament. She came right down with a large plastic container of kibble.

"Aw, what a sweetie!" she said. "Do you want to keep him? If not, we can try to integrate him with ours, although the age difference may be a problem." I thought about it. The last pet I'd had was a dog that had died a year before my folks. He'd made the mistake of trying to cross a busy street at night and didn't survive an encounter with a car. I wasn't averse to pets. I just had never gotten around to getting another.

"Sure, I'll give it a try," I replied. "As long as he stays indoors, that is. I don't want the heartbreak of losing him to traffic or one of the neighborhood bully cats."

"Wonderful. I always like to see strays get good homes. We'd probably have twenty if we had the space. Over the years we've collected a *ton* of cat stuff. I'll go get one of our spare litter boxes and some litter to tide you over. I'll also bring back the phone number of our veterinarian. He needs to be looked at." Elinda left and was back in less than five minutes with everything. We decided my bathroom was large enough to handle the litter box, too, and put it down.

"You're a witch. Maybe you know the answer," I said as we arranged everything to my satisfaction in the bathroom.

"What's that, darlin'?"

"How did the kitten race through Mr. Owens' wards and his tormentor run into a brick wall?"

"Ah. I'm not *exactly* sure because witches and wizards go about their spells differently, but I've got a good idea. This building is spelled to be a safe haven. It's supposed to be for the residents but maybe the Universe decided the kitten was supposed to be a resident here. As for the bully, he had bad intentions, even if it wasn't against a human resident, so the wards naturally wouldn't let him in.

"Now, you and he get acquainted. You'll have to find a name for him, you know." She left and with a promise to check in the next day, went back upstairs.

While the kitten was chowing down, I went outside to put the screen back on. There was no sign of the tabby, for which I was grateful. There had been enough drama for one night. I tried to go back to the book I'd been reading but couldn't get back into it, so I turned the television on just to have the noise.

After the kitten had eaten about a cup of the kibble Elinda had brought down, he used the litter box without even having to be shown where it was, and then hopped into my lap. It must be a reflexive thing. With him in my lap, I automatically started stroking him. He started purring. "Name, huh?" I said to him. "Well, you're a beautiful shade of brown – like a good chocolate dessert. How does 'Fudge' sound?" The purring intensified and he started giving himself a bath. I'd heard somewhere that cats only bathe when they're content and somewhere they feel safe. I guess that was my clue. 'Fudge' it was.

The next morning I woke to find him curled up in my hair. Apparently straight hair isn't an acceptable bed because when I looked in the mirror, I saw the worst case of bed hair I'd ever had. It was a good thing there were no birds around. They'd have happily adopted the nest for their own. It took fifteen minutes to comb out the snarls and I was almost late for work.

I made an appointment with the vet for that afternoon. Because the referral came from Elinda and Fudge was a stray, she squeezed me in. Ev wasn't too happy about my leaving the office early but didn't bitch too much because I rarely did so. Dr. Evans was a witch, one who could speak with animals. She gave the cat whatever shots she felt were necessary, and she gave me instructions on feeding, getting rid of the ear mites and the like. At the same time she told me 'Fudge' was a good name coming from a human – he liked it. (Cats do have their own names. We just can't pronounce them.) "For the moment, allow him to eat however much he wants. He's a couple of pounds underweight. We'll adjust his diet once he starts looking really healthy." I had to bring him back in two months' time for a checkup.

It didn't take long for Fudge to declare himself master of the house. He altered my routine so he ate at appropriate times. I had to scoop the litter box every day. He was even more fastidious than what I imagined cats to be. If I forgot and left it too long, he used the bathtub to remind me that I was shirking my duties.

Then there was the issue of the drapes. Within two weeks my lovely room-darkening damask drapes were in shreds. I sighed, thinking kittens did climb a lot, admonished him when I caught him hanging from them, and bought some replacements. A month after that the new ones looked like a lot of modern jeans: artfully ripped here and there. For some reason the sheers didn't suffer the same injustice as the heavier curtains. I resigned myself to not having fancy drapes and purchased cheap ones that didn't block the sun but did provide some privacy.

Because of the drapery issue, I became a morning person in the summer months when the sun shined directly into my windows at an insanely early hour. Since I had an altered routine already, I kept it up even in the winter when my bedroom was dark until almost 8:00 a.m. (Getting up and into the office early also gave me an excuse not to go to as many parties as Ev would have wished. There are benefits.)

As a young single woman with effectively no love life, I had started reading romance novels in between the literature I'd never read in school. I made my way through some fantasy, too, laughing at how much the authors got wrong about non-human species. Burying myself in the romance, I could at least enjoy the pleasures of a man's company vicariously. But after the tenth one, I got to thinking that I could probably write as well, or even better.

Just to see if I could do it, I sat down at my computer one Sunday afternoon and started writing. It wasn't too difficult to create characters and then get them into bed, with a few hiccups along the way. Fudge did his part by ensuring that once I got going, I stayed at the computer for at least a couple of hours. If I tried to procrastinate, he batted at my hands, implying I needed to get back to work.

It didn't take long to turn my experience with Tony coupled with an inventive imagination into a full-length novel. Once I'd written it, though, I had to know if it was any good. I turned to my closest friend, Cassandra, for her opinion.

CHAPTER 5

I'd met Cassandra on my first day of work. I was used to running out for lunch, picking up something at a drive-through, bringing it back and eating at my desk. However, on this particular day, I had walked to work and the closest fast food joint was about a mile away. I decided to check out the deli downstairs to see if their food was edible.

I walked through the door that opened on the stairs, rather than go outside and enter by the front door. I was greeted by lovely smells: fresh-baked bread, spices, cheese, meat, everything I associate with an old-fashioned deli. It was fairly small: five bistro-type wrought-iron tables with glass tops and four chairs each were the only seating. A glass-fronted case held various meats, cheeses and breads with the usual machines on a counter behind the case. One door behind the case led into what I presumed was a kitchen and another at the far end led to the bathrooms. All the tables were full with five people in line, waiting to order. All-in-all, a brisk business.

The lady behind the counter appeared to be about my age (she's actually five years older). She was tall and skinny with long, coal black hair coiled underneath a hairnet, and bright green eyes. No tits to speak of meant the amethyst spear she wore on a chain swayed all over the place when she moved but it didn't appear to bother her at all.

"Hiya. What can I get you?" she asked when it came my turn.

"I just started working upstairs and I've got more work than I even want to think of. How about a sandwich of some kind that won't drip anything on the papers?"

"You mean Ev finally broke down and hired someone? I've been trying to convince him to do that since he opened the agency two years ago. No ogre I know has any sense of organization and he's the poster child. D'you think he'll finally pay the rent on time? My name's Cassandra, by the way."

"I'm Amy. I knew I had my work cut out for me when I saw the mounds of paper on his desk at my interview. Is there anything else I need to know?"

"Nah. Ev's a good guy, especially for an ogre. Just stay assertive and you two will get along fine." Her eyes went kind of blank for a moment. "As a matter of fact, you're going to get along well for quite some time."

"Excuse me?" I said. "How do you know about this 'quite some time'?"

"Oh, sorry. I forget sometimes. I get visions and forget to think before opening my mouth. Did I say something to worry you?"

"No. I've just never had any part of my future blurted out quite like that. However, it's good to know the job will work out. I hate to cut this conversation short but I really do need to get back to work."

"Of course. Do you have any preferences for a sandwich, or any allergies I should be aware of?"

With the exception of peas, 'No' to both questions yielded a BLT on homemade wheat bread with homegrown tomatoes and lettuce; and homemade mayonnaise. The mayo was so thick there was no danger of it dripping out of the sandwich. She paired it with fresh, hot potato chips only lightly salted, and a glass of iced tea with a sprig of fresh peppermint served in a hard plastic tumbler with a plastic lid.

"Bring the glass back and I'll refill it anytime. I hate using anything that can't be recycled or composted. Consider this lunch a welcome to the neighborhood. I have a feeling I'm going to be making enough money off you that I can afford to give away a freebie the first time," she grinned.

I took my meal back upstairs and the first bite told me she was right: I decided I'd be having all my lunches from her. That girl could cook!

It only took a couple of weeks for us to become fast friends. Cassandra was a witch from a long line of witches. (*Do not* shorten it to Cassie unless you want to experience what it's like to be a frog for an hour or so, and 'Cass' will get you the retort that she is skinny and can't carry a tune.) She had grown up around the deli and inherited it and the house next door just a few years earlier from her grandmother, who had died when a spell when horribly awry. Her parents lived in Arizona, enjoying the sun and fun that came with retirement from the mundane world.

Cassandra owned the entire building, actually. The floors above the deli used to be her grandparents' living quarters. When the house came up for sale they bought it and after moving, renovated their old apartment into offices. There was a large garden in the backyard of the house which was what her grandmother wanted. It's where she grew most of the vegetables and herbs she used at the deli during the warm months and Cassandra carried on the tradition with her sickeningly green thumb.

She and two helpers ran the deli. With two employees she had enough time to tend to that garden and still deal with other things. The deli was closed on Sundays and Mondays, effectively giving her an entire weekend, and leaving her free to do things on a Saturday night. We had our first girls' night out within a month of meeting and over the course of several months, she and her friends showed me all the places a single girl could go without having to worry about fending guys off … and some where you could go if you *didn't* want to fend guys off.

She was also an avid bicyclist and in addition to helping me buy my bike, took me on my first tour of all the lakes. Thankfully, there were plenty of places to pause since I wasn't quite as in shape as I'd like to be. The ice cream shop just a step away from one of the bike paths became another one of our hangouts in the summer months. From their patio you could watch all the other cyclists and rollerbladers go by. I had no idea just how tight an ass rollerblading gives a guy until that point.

Naturally, when I wanted a girl's opinion about something, Cassandra was the one I called. So one Saturday evening I called to make sure she was going to be home, printed off a hard copy of the manuscript and headed over with a couple bottles of wine.

"You didn't tell me you were writing!" was how she greeted me.

"I didn't want to say anything until I knew whether I could or not. I kind of like it but want another opinion. You up for a read?"

"Of course! I love romance novels. You pour the wine – I want to dig in right away!"

I poured us each a glass of wine and turned the television on low. Her cat, Merlin, jumped into my lap and settled there. She looked up once at what I'd turned on and grimaced. "Baseball?"

"I happen to like baseball. Go back to reading."

Two hours later, the Twins had won their game, we'd gone through almost a full bottle of wine and she'd used up a half box of tissues. "This is *wonderful!* I don't know how but you managed to turn a were into a sympathetic being. I've never read anything like it!"

I blushed. "Now the question is: will any publisher like it? I guess I have to do the regular 'Here's my book, wanna publish it?' thing. I'm not sure I'm any good at writing stuff like that."

"We'll do it together. I write all the marketing copy for the deli and ain't so bad at it, if I do say so myself. But not tonight. Let's celebrate you finishing it and do the serious stuff Monday night, huh?"

Celebrate we did. I staggered home about 2:00 a.m., glad I didn't encounter any of the local constabulary who probably would have taken me in for public drunkenness. Fudge, of course, wasn't at all happy that his dinner was so late. I told him he should be glad I came home at all and only slightly missed the dish with his serving of kibble before falling into bed completely clothed.

I missed most of Sunday. The sun naturally woke me up early but instead of heading for the coffee, I gulped down two large glasses of water and a couple aspirin before crawling back into bed and pulling the covers completely over me. It had been a very long time since I'd had that bad of a hangover but then again, I usually managed to control my intake and drink plenty of water in between glasses of alcohol.

It was starting to get dark when I finally emerged from my hole, vowing not to repeat the previous night for quite some time. I shared some soup and crackers with Fudge, showered and headed back to bed.

Monday after my nap, Cassandra and I ate leftovers from the deli and then started doing research on the Internet about romance publishers. There were plenty to choose from but I wanted one who'd be willing to take on the paranormal aspect of it, too. That narrowed it down to three. Paranormal romance was just beginning to take off and there were only a handful of authors writing it. Cassandra did a marvelous job of constructing the inquiry, which I sent off when I got home via an anonymous Gmail account.

Here's where having a witch as a friend comes in handy. Before I left for home, Cassandra took my manuscript back into her workroom. I followed, really curious.

Her workroom used to be a porch at the back of the house that her father had converted into a four-season room for his mother. It had a lot of windows (with drapes unmolested by cats to block out curious eyes); the longest side looked out on the garden. He'd taken out the original outside door and enlarged the doorway to a lovely archway. He also added a door to an attached greenhouse, which opened to the outside. Dad had even added a fireplace at one end so if not for the shelves, a workbench and one rather large étagère that doubled as an altar, it would have made a cozy family room. The dried herbs hanging from the ceiling gave it a wonderfully-scented atmosphere.

Cassandra made one concession to convenience and summertime heat: she'd installed a small, propane-fueled camping stove next to the workbench.

She started pulling jars off shelves with Merlin's close supervision. A pinch of this and a pinch of that went into a mortar and pestle. After grinding all that a bit, she pulled out an old cast-iron pot (oops, cauldron), lit the flame on the stove, put the pot on the stove, added the contents of the mortar and some liquid out of another jar. As she stirred, she said something under her breath. After there was a 'poof' sound and some smoke from the cauldron, she drew some liquid from the pot into a pipette and dropped it on the first page of the manuscript, muttering some other things as she did.

She cleaned up her mess, putting the now-used herbs into a plastic tub I knew she used for kitchen waste that would eventually end up in her compost pile in the back yard. "There, it's done," she said as she handed the manuscript back to me.

"So, what did you do besides make the first page look and smell funny?"

"I did a spell so your manuscript would find the right 'home'. Keep it on your desk next to your computer and when you send those inquiry emails, ask the manuscript to find a home."

The three publishers we'd chosen wanted all submissions sent electronically. I thought spells would only work if someone held the manuscript in their hands but she assured me that wasn't the case. How that transmitted through the wires, airwaves, however the Internet works is beyond me, but however foolish I felt, I did as she instructed. It worked.

Within a week I had three responses. All three publishers were interested in reading the first couple of chapters, so I did a cut-and-paste and sent the new document along. One of the three sent me a publishing contract. I'd never had to handle anything heavier than an apartment lease and really didn't want to involve Ev's attorney. As a matter of fact, I didn't want to involve Ev at all.

Cassandra had her lawyer look it over for me and he declared it OK for me to sign. We had another 'celebration' night but this time I took it easy and only got a little tipsy. That's when we came up with the idea for my pseudonym so even if anyone in Ev's circles read books like that, they'd have no idea who the author was.

She also did her 'thing' over the contract before I mailed it back. I got a wonderful editor (who, I learned years later, was also a witch still in the broom closet) and a year later, *Full Moon, Dark Moon* hit the shelves.

I took Cassandra out to dinner at a really posh place out by the airport with my first royalty check. I could afford to. I'd sold nearly 10,000 copies in the first six months and the check was a nice one.

The next two books also sold well. The characters were always loosely-based on people I'd met working for Ev. At that point I probably could have given up my job and written full time but then I'd lose my pool of characters. Besides, I was building up a nice nest egg that I only wanted to see grow. I didn't have any problem sitting at my computer a couple of nights a week and one weekend day, knocking out a book every nine months or so. Hey, a girl has to have a hobby!

Damn, I needed to stop thinking about the past and get on with the present! I must have looked like I was procrastinating. I was sitting at my desk, Fudge doing his usual sleepy supervising but all of a sudden, I felt paws batting my hands. It was time to get back to work. I'd just finished the final editing on my fourth book and here I was, ready to go on another, this time basing a couple of the characters on Andy and Happy. The words flowed from my fingers.

I wrote until nap time and spent my evening engrossed in a movie on television. I didn't usually watch television except for the occasional baseball game but I was on 'vacation' and could indulge myself a little. Friday was a repeat of Thursday. I could get into lazy mornings!

Saturday I decided maybe I'd better be practical so instead of lazing around in the morning, I hit the market. Both Fudge and I needed food and it was time to do laundry but I was out of detergent. I usually shopped during the week and regretted not doing so this time. *Everyone and their brother* were out shopping. The aisles were crowded, checkout lines long and children screamed their frustration at not getting whatever it was they wanted off the shelf. I got back to my apartment with groceries *and* frayed nerves, and vowed to go back to shopping on weekdays only.

Although I love writing and could probably do it most of my waking hours, I'd never met a cleaning fairy so I spent a very practical Saturday working out my frustrations from the market … doing laundry, scrubbing the bath, slinging a dust rag about and Fudge's least favorite activity: vacuuming. He didn't emerge from under the bed until it was nap time.

I'd just laid down when there was a pounding on my door. Throwing on a caftan so I wouldn't answer the door in my bathrobe in the afternoon, I looked through the peephole to find Ev standing there, his skin a deep purple – he was seriously pissed about something. When I opened it, he pushed his way in with, "Why haven't you been answering your phone? I've been trying to get hold of you since noon."

"Ev, if you recall, I am *off work* until Monday. I turned the phone off to have some peace and quiet. It's also

Saturday and I thought we agreed a long time ago that I didn't work weekends."

"Yeah, I know all that but this is an *emergency*. I need your help bad." Ev paced around my living room which was an interesting sight. At over seven feet tall, he just about grazed the ceiling and had to duck to avoid the ceiling fan with each pass.

"So what's the *emergency* this time?" I asked. "And it had better be good. We had a deal, if you'll recall."

"Happy is throwing a party at his hotel tonight and has insisted that I *and my wife* attend. I tried to get out of it by saying we had another party to go to tonight but he told me to cancel our plans and come to his. I *have* to go and I need you with me."

"Ev, sit down. You're going to break my ceiling fan if you don't. Now, I want you to tell me *exactly* why Happy has such a hold over you and if you don't tell me the truth, not only will I *not* go with you tonight but I'll tender my resignation effective immediately."

While he plopped down on my couch, causing the springs to groan, I poured him a glass of water, which he immediately gulped down and handed back to me for a refill. He really was upset. Ev usually disdained anything healthy like plain water, instead opting for can after can of full-sugar soda. I tried to get him to drink the diet version early in our relationship but he spit out the first sip of the first can. I gave up at that point and grimaced at the weekly delivery of cases of soda. We had an open account with the local Coke people.

"As you learned the other night, Happy and I met when I lived in Los Angeles. I hadn't even turned 100 yet, was full of myself and randy as a bull. [The thought, *"So what's changed?"* flashed through my mind.] I met him at a club similar to Club Tread when I was working as a bouncer. He was one of the members. Yes, I know how he looks but I just assumed he was a species I hadn't yet come across. Since he was always polite and didn't treat us bouncers like we had nothing between the ears, I liked him.

"Well, we sort of became friends. We played golf on occasion, ran across each other at the different clubs and if he met a girl he thought could handle someone my size, he made sure to introduce us. I liked the girls he brought to me and we had fun so obviously, he knew my taste in women.

"Ten years or so after we met, I was working as a bodyguard for one of John's clients. John was a member of that club, too, and had offered me a job that paid three times what I was making as a bouncer. Sure, the hours were irregular but I couldn't turn down the pay. On top of it, the guy I was looking after went to all these fancy parties and I got to meet even more girls. As a matter of fact, my life was so busy that when Happy wanted to introduce me to someone, I told him I simply didn't have time for any more girls.

"For some reason, Happy didn't like the fact that I wouldn't see one of 'his' girls. He threatened to curse me but as you know, spells just bounce off ogres so I wasn't worried. I laughed. Happy got even madder and said, "Do you have any idea who and what I am?"

"No, but it doesn't really matter, does it?" I replied. "I don't know why you're so upset. If you wanted more than friendship you wouldn't want to curse me over something as trivial as a girl, so I'm not interested."

"He spit back at me, 'I had your life all planned out for you but this is just a detour in the journey. Eventually you'll want to get married but I bet you can't find the right girl. You'll come crawling back to me in fifty years, begging me to find you a girl to settle down with. At that point, you *will* be mine.' With that, he went 'poof' and I didn't see him from that point until the other night.

"A few years after that, I found out just *what* Happy was. Although he is usually described as a devil, he's just a demon. [*Good. No souls involved. Or maybe that was just my Christian upbringing speaking.*] I still wasn't bothered until my Grandpa told me that these guys can be really irritating – he had one dogging him for a couple hundred years until he married my grandmother. They're immortal so they can pop back into your life at any time and bug you until you're miserable. I really don't want him popping in and out over the next five hundred years, so the easiest way to get him off my back is to be happily married.

"I thought I'd solved everything Wednesday night but something must not have sat right with him. I know it probably seems trivial to you but he's well-connected and if he wants, could easily muck things up on the business end as well as in my personal life. *Please* Amy, be my wife again one more night. Whatever was bothering him from the other night we'll figure out, huh?"

I should have gone out of town instead of staying home. A friend owned a cabin up north and I could have borrowed it, rented a car, taken my laptop, and written there as easily at home. Fudge would have liked the change of scenery. But no. I had to think I'd be just fine at home and Ev wouldn't bother me at all.

On the other hand, I really didn't like bullies or pests. And unless the issue of Happy was resolved, I'd probably hear about the trials and tribulations he caused until I decided to quit my job or retire. But … what could I get out of Ev for saving his butt one more time?

"I'll go but what you owe me has just skyrocketed. I haven't yet figured out how you're going to repay me but you will – with interest," I told him. "To start with, you're going to take me to dinner at McCarthy's before the party. Now scoot. I expect you and Gregory back here at eight." (McCarthy's was a *very* exclusive, *very* expensive restaurant downtown.)

"McCarthy's? I can't get reservations there on just a couple hours' notice."

"Sure you can. I've seen you do it before when you wanted to impress a girl. Impress *me*. Now *go!*" I pushed him toward the door. Not that I could really make him go if he didn't want to (that size thing, again) but he was already on his cell before I got the door closed.

CHAPTER 6

I wasn't really too put out at having to go to a party. Honestly? I'd had enough of my apartment for the moment and had seriously considered walking over to the local pub for dinner and a drink that evening.

Murphy's Pub was about as Irish as you could get: corned beef and cabbage on the menu, Guinness on tap, Irish jig music playing quietly in the background. It was catty-corner across the street from the office and had become my hangout when I didn't feel like staying at home but didn't want to go partying. It was also one of the places Cassandra had shown me where I didn't have to worry about fending off guys. Most of the clientele lived within staggering distance and were pretty equally split between human and non-human. Cork Murphy was part giant and didn't tolerate any kind of bull. He'd throw you out if you looked wrong at any of his customers. It was a comfortable joint.

Instead, I grabbed a granola bar and went to comb my closet for something that would say "rich, happily married woman". (Was there such a thing?) I finally pulled out a dress I hadn't worn in several years. Can't figure out why. I loved it. It was a deep purple one-shouldered silk thing that flowed like a Greek goddess' gown. I always felt like I was about six feet tall when I wore it. In the strappy heels I wore with it I maybe hit 5'7". But it was the thought that counted. Maybe it was the color? I know purple is the color of royalty and is considered to be a power color. Anyways, I always felt *good* in that dress.

Since I had a little time, I took the pains to curl my hair and put it up *á la* that Greek goddess with ringlets hanging halfway down my back. A heavy application of hairspray ensured it would stay curled, even in summertime humidity. By the time I'd put the 'wedding ring' back on and added a rhinestone necklace and earrings, it was damned near eight. There *were* times I wished I'd have been born a man. About all they had to decide was black, blue or brown suit; then which tie went with whichever suit they'd pulled out. Run a comb through their hair and they were ready to go.

Knowing I was going to be coming home late, I put Fudge's food down so he wouldn't rip my dress to shreds when I came back in. I'd just slipped my shoes on when Gregory knocked at the door.

I climbed into the back of the limo with Ev and immediately started choking. The smell of patchouli was overwhelming. "What in the hell did you put on?" I asked.

"You always complain about how I smell so I thought I'd cover up whatever bothered you. Did I use too much aftershave?"

To hell with privacy and to hell with my hairdo. I hit the buttons that would roll down both windows and open the sunroof. "That would be a slight understatement," I told him. "Hopefully by the time we arrive at the restaurant, it'll have dissipated enough that I won't be tasting patchouli instead of food, nor will the people at the surrounding tables."

Ev looked sheepish. "I was just trying to help."

"Next time, use about a quarter of what you did this time, OK?"

Within fifteen minutes, Gregory pulled up at McCarthy's. "See, I *said* you could get a reservation if you really put your mind to it," I said. "Hang on. Let me see if I can do something with the mess that is now my hair." *Everhold* is indeed a wonderful product. All I had to do was finger-comb everything back into place. If you have really straight hair and want curls, I'd highly recommend it. Just be prepared to shampoo your hair several times to get it all out.

Dinner was, as I had anticipated, marvelous. I'd have to figure a way to eat there more often. My steak was done to perfection, the wine delicious, the chocolate mousse scrumptious and Ev was on his best behavior. He made use of his napkin and even used the correct silverware for each course. I didn't know he had it in him.

We left McCarthy's, Ev a couple of C-notes lighter, and Gregory drove us six blocks to the Hotel Centrale. Happy went in style, I must say, staying in the penthouse suite of one of the most exclusive hotels in the city. The view wasn't much, just the river (too many buildings downtown overshadowed the Centrale) but you couldn't argue with the four diamonds or the accoutrements that earned them those four diamonds.

Happy didn't greet us at the door. A butler-type did. I had to make an effort not to stare. The guy was dressed in breeches and a tailcoat, wore a powdered wig and held a staff in one hand. Ev hadn't said anything about it being a costume party!

He asked Ev who we were. He pounded the floor twice with the staff and then boomed, "Mr. and Mrs. Evander Angelich," announcing us to a room which didn't even seem to notice. Now I knew Happy was definitely older than he looked. No one did that anymore, unless it was a royal thing. Was it? Looking around the room, the rest of the guests were probably used to those types of introductions, royalty or not. I think I was the only mundane (read: youngest by far) there.

After that loud introduction, I got a little nervous. What if someone we knew was there? I didn't want to have to pretend to be Ev's wife *all* the time! But all I saw were demons, obvious from the variously-colored skin and horns sprouting from their heads, a few pale-as-death vamps, and some who were probably older witches and wizards – old enough to have gray hair, anyways. I didn't know any of them and doubted they'd know anyone we knew to spread the rumor.

Happy detached himself from a group and came over to greet us. He was wearing that red Gucci suit again. "Amy, you look positively radiant tonight." He kissed the back of my hand and then shook Ev's. "I'm so glad you could come to my little get together on such short notice. May I offer you a cocktail?"

Now that I knew what to expect, a glass of merlot did just fine for me. Ev had a beer. I was accustomed to seeing Ev hold a tiny human-sized mug in his hand but Happy had managed to get larger ones that would have served me as a pitcher. Happy thought of everything, it seemed. We both made an effort to sip, not gulp. Our host took us around the room, introducing us to some of the other guests. I noticed a pattern: we met every single demon in the room and none of the others. Ev got a little paler with each introduction. It looked like Happy was trying to intimidate him and I think it was working.

When we had a moment alone, I tugged on Ev's sleeve to get him to lean down to my level. "Why are you so nervous?" I asked. "We don't know anyone here and I doubt they run in any of your circles. Relax! We can make our excuses in an hour or so."

"Some demons can tell if you're lying. I think he's trying to fish us out by using the gifts of some of his friends," came the strained reply.

"No one has specifically asked if we're married. We've worked together long enough that unless someone asks you what brand toothpaste I use, we should be safe. And the more nervous you get, the more you sweat. Cassandra tells me predatory types can tell when you're nervous by the changes in body odor. These are *definitely* predatory types so cool it!"

Ev took a deep breath and his color started turning a little more normal. "You're right. As long as we don't lie, we should be good. Let's get fresh drinks and try to mingle a little more. Maybe introduce ourselves to that wizard over there who looks a little lonely." How did we know he was a wizard? Think *Gandalf* and you get the picture. I'd never met anyone who dressed in such a stereotypical fashion!

We got fresh drinks and moseyed over to where the wizard stood staring out the balcony door, holding a glass that looked to be all melted ice and stroking his beard as some do when deep in thought. He didn't look too happy. I touched him on the shoulder and he turned to face us. "Excuse me, I don't believe we've met. I'm Amy and this is Evander," I said to him.

"Good evening," he replied with a voice almost as deep and gravelly as Happy's, with a slight Eastern European accent. "I'm Adamo. Are you friends of Happy's?"

"Acquaintances would be more like it," answered Ev. "How do you know Happy?"

"I have known him for a couple of centuries. I don't usually come to his parties but I could find no reason to say 'no' to this invitation. So, here I am until I have been here long enough to make polite excuses."

"Ah, you, too!" Ev got excited. "We, too, are waiting until we can politely leave. How is it we find ourselves unable to say 'no' to his invitations?"

At that, Adamo and Ev started comparing notes. Seems Happy had tried essentially the same thing with the wizard as he had with my boss, only a couple of centuries earlier and hadn't gotten the memo that Adamo preferred his own company to anyone else's. Every thirty to fifty years, Happy popped back into the poor guy's life and tried to fix him up. It was much easier to come to a party and hang around the fringes for a couple of hours than it was to argue. It got Happy to 'go away' faster.

Adamo was just waiting for the current introduction so he could say 'not interested', leave and get back to his solitude. He assumed it was the witch Happy was currently talking with. "Even if I liked her, I'd say no," Adamo said. "I hate to think what strings would be attached to any relationship Happy set up. But I've yet to find anything interesting in any of his picks, so I think I'm safe."

"I wonder why he tries so hard to fix people up," I mused. "Is there perhaps a Mrs. Happy at home that makes him Mr. Unhappy? Or maybe it's a punishment from one of his higher-ups for something he did in his younger days. But it's ridiculous all the same."

Happy broke up our tête á tête by saying he wanted Adamo to meet someone, and did indeed bring the old wizard over to the witch he'd been speaking with. Ev and I gravitated to a group of vamps and tried to engage them in conversation but all they wanted to talk about was flavors of blood. After a polite interval, curiosity got the better of us and we headed over to Adamo to see who the newest 'suggestion' was. She appeared to be around Adamo's age (at least she had gray hair) but unlike him, was dressed in a normal evening gown.

"Thank you," they both said in unison. "We were trying to be polite but neither of us wants to be here," Adamo said. "This is Bella, by the way. Bella, Amy and Ev."

"Listen, I have a suggestion," Ev said. "Why don't the four of us leave together? Happy will probably think he's made his match. We can go over to the Foursquare Bar, have a cocktail and laugh at his expense."

"What a wonderful idea," Bella smiled. "I never mind making new friends. It's when Happy wants me to get a little closer than 'friend' that I start getting upset. At my age, I'm quite happy being single. What do you think, Adamo? Shall we beat him at his own game?"

Adamo nodded and, looking at Ev, jerked his head in Happy's direction. Both men went over and apparently said all our goodbyes. The four of us left, trying very hard to contain our amusement until well out of the hotel.

The Foursquare Bar was right across the street. Although it was a popular place on weekends, we were able to get a table just as it was being vacated. Immediately after placing our drink order, we all burst out laughing.

"I know he'll probably check up again in another thirty years or so but to make him think for even a decade that he'd made a match will be worth the next visit," Adamo said. "Thirty years? I get them every twenty or so," laughed Bella.

"I'm lucky then. I haven't seen him in almost fifty years," Ev said.

"Yes, but you live longer than we do," was Adamo's answer. "On the other hand, this should be the last time you see him since you're married and not to anyone he chose."

I looked at Ev and he nodded. "Actually, we're not," he explained. "Amy is my assistant and I talked her into acting like my wife to get Happy off my case. I hope it worked but if it didn't, by the time he comes around again,

I'll either *really* be married or tell him we're living apart because of her age."

"You're a mundane?" Bella was confused. "How did you get mixed up with our crowd?"

"I answered an ad in the newspaper for a job. Although Ev wrote straight out that it entailed working with non-humans, little did I suspect I'd get dragged into something like this. I hope this is the last of it," I said, elbowing Ev hard enough that he grunted.

We enjoyed our drinks and the conversation. Bella and Adamo were fairly reclusive but managed to meet some interesting people when they did come out in public. They regaled us with stories of these folks and it really was a pleasant time, at least for me. Both of them dismissed Ev's stories, saying they had no interest in the rich and famous. I think he was a little put out but gracefully took the unspoken criticism.

About an hour later, we were ready to leave. Ev asked the other two if we could drop them anywhere. Adamo lived a short distance away and preferred to walk but Bella took him up on the offer. Turns out she lived only a half-mile away from me and when I said as much, she replied, "Give me your phone number. If I get the urge to get out of the house, I'll call, OK?"

When we reached my neighborhood, we swapped numbers and she went into her house. Ev and Gregory let me off at my door and after ensuring I was in safely, pulled away.

I put my dress in the pile to take to the cleaners and crawled into the shower to wash all the crap out of my hair.

An hour later, my hair was dried and I crawled into bed, pulling the pillow over my head to stave off the early-morning sun that would be shining in my face in just a few hours. (It didn't work. I'd thrown off the pillow during the night. I woke up to sunlight and re-pulled the pillow back over my head.)

I spent Sunday afternoon working on the outline of the new book and making notes for future reference. (I work very unconventionally. I start writing a book and about two or three chapters in, quit the actual writing long enough to do an outline. Then I go back to writing. Strange, but it works for me.) Happy had given me even more interesting characters at his party the prior evening. The butler, for one!

Monday dawned bright and early as it always did. By the time Ev and his hygiene problem wafted into the office, I'd already gotten the majority of the over-weekend work handled. It included talking with Ev's (and my) investment manager (a were with a keen nose not only for meat but money) about moving some funds to a place with a higher yield and handling a complaint from Blondie about Max, the dwarf we'd assigned to her. She didn't like the fact that he didn't have a sense of humor *and* that he wouldn't participate in any of her little rituals.

I had explained to her that Mario had been personally requested by another long-time client (not true) and that our one other wizard was already working on a long term contract (true). We'd be happy to engage the services of another wizard bodyguard just for her but it would take some time to find an appropriate person and that special replacement would cost considerably more than she was currently paying us. Would she like me to send a revised contract to her manager for his signature? All of a sudden, Max and his quirks didn't seem quite so bad to her. She may be a ditz in other areas but she knew her manager would scream at her for needlessly spending money.

"Mornin' Amy," Ev said with a smile. "What do I need to know for today?"

I filled him in on the morning, especially my conversation with Blondie. "When the current contract is up, let's not renew it, OK?" I asked.

"OK by me. She's a real pain and I think we've got enough other business that we can be solidly booked when her manager calls," he answered.

"So, have you heard from Happy since Saturday night?" I changed the subject to the one that *really* interested me.

"No, but he's usually not around on Sundays. I'm sort of holding my breath for the next couple of days. If I haven't heard from him by the end of the week, I'm guessing I'm good for awhile."

"What do you suppose makes him want to fix people up all the time? And what happens to those he actually succeeds with? Do you know anyone we can find out from? It might be worth having that information."

"Why are you all of a sudden *this* interested in my personal life? You've never paid a whole lot of attention before."

"I guess maybe because you dragged me into it, huh? I *really* don't want to have to play your wife again. By the way, here's the ring for you to return to wherever you got it. I'm not comfortable having to be responsible for a piece of jewelry like that."

Ev took the ring and put it into his pocket without a thought, like it was nothing more than a piece of five dollar costume jewelry. "I don't know anyone to ask and frankly, I don't want to put my nose into his business. Hopefully he'll go away again and like I said Saturday night, the next time I see him, either I'll be really married or you won't care."

Ev went into his office and got on the phone. We honestly were trying to recruit more wizard bodyguards. There were mundane clients out there who didn't like non-human guards but would happily take one who appeared fully-human but could wield more than a fist or gun. If we had more wizards on staff, we could probably expand the number of clients we served.

CHAPTER 7

Just as I was about to leave for the day, John called. He had an office set up in the basement of his house so he could work even on bright, sunny days. "I tried calling last week but Ev said you were out of the office until today. Amy, I'm really sorry about Andy's outburst last week. I thought I had trained him properly but he's still relatively young. Apparently the stress of an audition that afternoon coupled with too much to drink tore down his self-control."

"It's not you who should be apologizing, it's Andy," I retorted.

"I know but I'm having some difficulties with him at the moment. I just wanted to make sure you had *my* apology and assurance that it wouldn't happen again. I do want you to continue to attend my get-togethers."

"Apology accepted. I do need to go. Thanks for the call, John." I hung up and went home, thinking that whatever problems John was having with Andy, I was glad not to be involved.

I was about to hit the sack that night when Fudge stared at the window, arched his back and hissed. He continued hissing when I heard, "Amy, which apartment is yours? I need to talk to you," from outside. It was Andy's voice! How the hell did he find out where I lived?

I opened the door, careful to keep every part of me inside. Fudge followed me and stood at my side, eyes ablaze, fur on end. He'd stopped hissing but a low growl escaped his throat. Andy was standing on the sidewalk looking up at the building, just at the top of my stairs.

"I have no wish to talk to you, Andy, especially not now, when I'm about to go to bed."

He made a move toward the stairs. And stopped cold. "Ouch. Your building is warded?"

"Of course. Go away, Andy. I'm going to bed."

I shut the door, turned off the lights in the living room and crawled into bed. Fudge hopped on the bed but maintained his vigilance, looking toward the window. Just as I was about to turn out the bedside light I heard, "Amy, please invite me inside. I really want to talk to you."

Was he nuts? There was no way I was inviting a vamp into my home! I picked up the phone and called John's cell. "It's Amy. Come get your boy toy," I said without preamble when he answered.

"He's *there*? Oh shit, Amy, I'm sorry. Where do you live? I'm on my way."

I told him where I lived (not something I really wanted him to know but this was an emergency) and hung up, resigned to the fact that I would not be immediately going to sleep. Nor would Fudge. Nor would the rest of the neighborhood. Andy kept whining, "Amy, please. I'd like to talk to you."

My phone rang. It was Elinda. "What the hell is happening down there? Do you need any help?" I explained that it was a vampire, apparently lovesick and that I had called someone to come get him. "I can dump some garlic water on him from up here if it'll help," she said.

"I don't want to hurt him, I just want him to go away. His friend should be here shortly."

"OK but if he doesn't go away, I *will* pour garlic water on him. We may not have to get up in the morning but I don't find his mewling pleasant." I assured her I didn't either, and she had my permission to drench him if things didn't calm down shortly.

I sat on my bed, fervently wishing my life was different. First the damned demon and now this. I couldn't call the police. They knew better than to confront a vampire. Of course they'd come if I called to report a stalker disturbing the peace, but they'd leave when Andy dropped his fangs, which he would as soon as he saw the squad car. As a matter of fact, the cops didn't have a whole lot to do with the paranormal community. They preferred that particular section of society deal with its own problems; they had enough on their plate in the mundane world.

Andy continued his plaint. Fudge continued his vigilance. I continued to get angrier by the minute.

John made it to my place in record time. He must not have been at home. Less than ten minutes after I called, I heard him say quietly, "Andy, what the hell do you think you're doing? It's sleep time for all these people and it's obvious Amy doesn't want to talk to you. Come home with me. We'll talk it all out, OK?"

"But …" Andy sputtered.

"No buts, Andy. You've already pissed Amy off more than once and I suspect unless you leave with me now, she'll find a way to make your life even more miserable than it currently is. Come home, boy, or I'll leave you to her."

I parted the curtains just enough to sneak a peek. They were standing on the sidewalk, John with his hand on Andy's shoulder. A Jag was parked along the curb, engine running and both doors open. So I didn't get caught looking, I closed the curtains again and listened.

"She's not the only one pissed," Elinda hollered out her window. "I've got a bucket of garlic water sitting right here. Go home with him or I'm dumping it on you."

I heard Andy hiss. I'll bet his fangs had dropped, too. "You don't scare me, witch. If I want to talk to Amy, I'll talk to her. Ow, damn you!"

I peeked again. Andy's head was wet and steaming just a little.

"That's just a cup of what I've got a whole bucket of. Go away, boy!"

"C'mon, Andy, you're causing entirely too much trouble," John said. I heard some scuffling, then a car door slamming shut. "My apologies, ladies. I will sort this out and it will never happen again."

I heard the car pull away and it was finally quiet in the neighborhood. I hoped this wasn't going to cause any problems for me. I liked my apartment and my neighbors. Fudge and I settled on my pillow and I gratefully turned out the light. It was awhile before I fell asleep, though. Various scenarios of staking Andy or shoving him into sunlight ran through my mind. I hated the fact that my quiet life had been so disrupted!

Ev was out on the left coast on Tuesday, doing some recruiting, so I had the office to myself. It was pleasant until Andy called late in the afternoon.

"Amy, I really do want to talk with you. I wasn't lying when I said I preferred sultry redheads, especially one that doesn't care who I am. [I didn't care *who* he was, just *what* he was.] Can I buy you a drink this evening?" He sounded like a little boy who hadn't gotten the toy he wanted for Christmas – very whiny. I was waiting to hear him lie down on the floor and pound his fists in a temper tantrum.

"As I told you at the party and again last night, I have no wish to talk with you, much less share a cocktail," I growled back. "Unless you leave me alone, I will ensure the media knows what an ass you're making of yourself with me. I doubt all those little girls will be as excited to watch your movies when they find out what a child you are."

"You wouldn't do that. John would make sure the rest of his clients quit using your service," he said.

"Wanna bet? Rather than ensuring his clients drop us, how about him dropping you? He didn't sound too happy with you last night."

"John would never drop me. I make him too much money."

"Andy, I don't know how many ways to say it but listen carefully: I am not interested in you. You are not my type, in more ways than one. I have no desire to see you again, unless it's on a professional basis. Excuse me but I have work to do." With that, I hung up, sat there for a moment shaking with rage and decided that work could wait. I needed to vent.

"You looked majorly pissed," Cassandra said as I stalked into the deli. "How about a cup of mocha latte? Will that take the sting off?"

"You know I'll always drink a cup of your latte but I just need to vent." I told her about Andy while the espresso machine hissed and gurgled.

"Honestly. You say this guy is almost a hundred?" she said, handing me the steaming mug, which smelled like heaven and came complete with the sprinkle of cinnamon I adored.

"That's what Ev says, although he's acting about twelve at the moment. I don't know what to do to get him off my back, apart from staking him."

"Yeah, the smell of garlic doesn't exactly translate through the telephone, does it? Let me ask Mom if she's got any suggestions. I think she had a run-in with a vamp before she met Dad. She might know of some way to redirect his attention. Take the mug with you. I know you need to get back to work."

When I got back upstairs, there were four messages on voicemail, three from Andy and one from John. I ignored the first three and returned the fourth.

"Amy, I do think it would be helpful if you met Andy for a drink," John told me.

"John, I really don't know how to tell him or you. I would have no interest in him, even if he weren't undead. As you should know by now, I don't do actors, no way no how. I don't want to deal with all the drama that comes with dating someone constantly in the limelight. That's not even addressing the fact that he acts like a child."

"I understand that, but I think the issue is only going to be resolved face-to-face. I tried talking with him last night but all he could say was, 'I know she'll like me if I can just talk to her.' Please, Amy, for both our sakes. Meet us for a drink this evening. I promise we'll both be on our best behavior."

"No, John. I have plans for this evening and as far as Andy is concerned, for every evening from now until eternity. He's your boy. You're going to have to figure out how to deal with this whole mess."

"If I can get him off your back, will you promise not to go to the media? He recounted your conversation to me. It would hurt me if this business with Andy got out."

"I doubt I would make good on that threat," I said. "It would just pull me into the spotlight and I don't want that. However, I don't want this to be a continuing headache and I will find a way to hurt him if he doesn't back off. Figure it out, John." I hung up. This was getting ridiculous.

Ev got into the office about noon on Wednesday and after regaling me with his recruiting exploits, asked me how the previous day had gone. Nothing of consequence had happened on the business front but I recounted Monday night and Tuesday's Andy-headache.

"Until it's settled, I'm going to have Omar shadow you," he said. (Omar was a retired guard, an ogre who was a pussycat unless something threatening came up. He helped Ev out on occasion.) "I don't like the sound of the way things are going. I've heard of vamps going crazy before and the consequences aren't pretty."

"Shit, Ev, I don't want a guard. It'd just make me even more uncomfortable than I already am. You're in town for the next week or so and can keep an eye on me at the office. I won't go anywhere except home, where I'm behind wards. If I need to go out for groceries, I'll call Cassandra. OK?"

"No can do. I have to go back to California tomorrow for some follow-up meetings. Although Andy may not want anything to do with Cassandra, there's not a lot she can do if he makes a play for you, except throw something on him, which may or may not incapacitate him. Omar is yours until John tells me the situation is under control." With that, he went into his office, picked up the phone and shortly, I heard him talking with Omar.

Lovely. Now I had a shadow – figuratively and literally. Omar was larger than Ev and even standing a few feet away from me, made an effective sun block. Big he may be but fast he definitely was. I'd seen him run and catch a client's cat when it got out of the hotel room and went streaking down the hallway. He was definitely fast enough to block a vamp from getting into my personal space.

Omar showed up about a half hour later and grinned. "I'll just hang out here until you're ready to go home. If you need to leave your apartment for any reason, call me. I'll only need ten minutes to get to your place. OK?"

Great. Now I had two ogres' stench to deal with. I got as much work done as I could before the scented candles were overpowered, which was only about a half-hour before I'd normally leave work. I told Ev I was going home and motioned Omar into action. The two of us made an odd looking couple walking down the street. More than one car slowed and I know people were staring at us.

"Are you planning on going out tonight?" Omar asked as we got to my door.

"No," I sulked. I didn't like having to let someone know my plans.

"Good. Call me ten minutes before you're ready to leave in the morning. I'll hang out until Ev gets to work." He turned on his heel and walked back in the direction of the office.

I changed into my pajamas and climbed into bed, but was too upset at all the situational changes to sleep. Not getting my nap upset me even more. Fudge, too. He was already on my pillow and giving me a look that said, "Hey, aren't you coming?"

Instead, I got up and paced. Fudge hopped off the bed and followed me back and forth. What a fine pickle I was in. Although I'm not ugly, I don't consider myself more attractive than average and I'd never had a guy stalk me, much less one who could keep me perpetually young with an all-liquid diet. The sight of blood didn't bother me but the thought of actually drinking it gave me a queasy feeling.

Apart from permanently ridding the world of Andy Deland, I had no idea what to do. Omar was a nice guy but I didn't want him or anyone else hanging around for the foreseeable future. I liked my independence too much and fervently hoped either Cassandra's mother or John came up with a solution, and soon.

I knew I wasn't going to sleep so I changed into a caftan. When I'm really upset, I clean. This particular afternoon I emptied my kitchen cupboards, washed the shelves down, washed everything in them and put it all back in an orderly fashion. I checked all the spices and chucked them if they no longer smelled like they were supposed to. I cleared the counters and scrubbed those down. I gave the floor a hands-and-knees scrubbing. When I was finished, the kitchen was sparkling and I'd sweated out all my frustrations.

I decided since the kitchen was so clean, there was no need to dirty it immediately. I called Pizza And More and ordered my favorite veggie pizza for delivery. Fudge would be happy. He loved their sauce.

I was too agitated to write anything regarding romance that night so I turned the tube on as I waited for my dinner to arrive. Turner Classic Movies was having a musical evening and I could lighten my mood with pizza, *Brigadoon* and *The King And I*. It would be a relaxing evening and maybe get me back into the mindset to write a few pages before I went to bed.

CHAPTER 8

When the pizza arrived, I was a good human and put the first piece on a plate down on the floor for Fudge. He daintily picked off all the veggies, set them aside and started in on the cheese and sauce. I dug into mine. I was just putting the leftovers in the fridge when the phone rang. I didn't recognize the Caller ID and let voicemail get it. I'm glad I did. It was Andy.

"Amy, please. Call me back. I really want to talk with you."

Now he had my phone number, too. This was *not* good. I programmed that number into the 'block' function on my phone, then called John.

"It's Amy. I take it you weren't very successful," I said when he answered.

"Unfortunately, no, and he moved out of the house. He didn't show up for an interview today, either. I'm sorry but I don't even know where he is at the moment," he replied.

"So what the hell am I supposed to do? Stake him? Not really my cup of tea but if that's what it takes to get him away from me, I'll do it. I don't want to live the rest of my life being stalked by this guy."

"I have called someone at the Regional Council to deal with him since I can't. It's one thing to seduce a human to feed off them but it's another thing entirely to act like a lovesick calf over food, especially in so public a manner. You know as well as I that we try to keep a low profile. His actions, regardless of his intent, are unacceptable. The Council representative should be here tomorrow. In the meantime, I and a few of my friends are keeping an eye on your place. If he shows up, we'll deal with him."

"You'd better. If he makes a scene again, you're going to lose a client – permanently."

"I have already terminated my arrangement with him as he violated one of the conduct clauses in his contract. If we can't handle him, I will support whatever action you and your friends may take. I'm truly sorry, Amy. I had no idea he'd go off the deep end like this."

"Oh, by the way. Whoever gets him, my number needs to be erased from his phone," I told him.

"Shit. He must have looked at my recent calls when my back was turned. I'll make mention of that to everyone. Good night, Amy. We're trying to watch out for you."

Hopefully only one more night. I called Elinda to let her know what was going on and to apologize in advance for anything that might happen before morning. I was more than pissed that my life had not only been screwed up but made public. It also angered me that it interfered with others' lives, as well.

"Don't worry, darlin'," she said. "After the other night, Marge and I have our vampire arsenal all set up. We talked with the other three tenants *and* Mr. Owens. Everyone is ready if he comes back."

I almost cried. However much I distrusted him, John was actually being a gentleman about all this. Everyone but me was able to do something about my situation, and they were willing to do so. I turned back to my musicals, trying to forget how screwed up everything had gotten in so short a time.

I crawled into bed at the appropriate hour but couldn't sleep. I was too afraid of what might wake me up. Fudge did his best to console me by snuggling close and purring loud. It felt nice but wasn't enough.

Sure enough, around midnight I heard, "Amy!" outside my apartment. I was about to get out of bed, open my door and yell at him to go away when I heard muted, angry voices. I got up and peeked through the curtains.

The light from the streetlamps showed Andy surrounded by four other men, one of whom was John. They all had their arms crossed over their chests and were speaking in low voices. I couldn't hear much, but picked out, "Not only no but hell no" and "You're stepping outside our bounds".

John put his hand on Andy's arm. Andy threw it off. Another, much larger man grabbed Andy by the shoulder, spun him around and threw a punch. Andy's head rocked back but he didn't go down. He assumed a fighting stance which I thought was funny. Andy didn't have the height or the build to take on this guy. The larger man threw a second punch which Andy tried but failed to block. This time he collapsed in a heap on the ground. Three of the four picked him up and started walking away with him.

Even though I hadn't really known what to expect when vamps confronted each other, I had imagined fangs coming out and a lot of hissing. Just a couple of punches was pretty anticlimactic.

John pulled his cell out, dialed a number and my phone rang. "I assume you were watching what went on," he said.

"Yes, of course I was. Please convey my thanks to whoever decked him. I wish I could have been the one to do it."

"He does have a nice hook, doesn't he? Mark used to be a professional boxer, which is why I called him. We'll take Andy back to my house and confine him until the Regional representative arrives later today. He will not bother you again, one way or another. My word on it."

I knew that if someone in the paranormal community gave their word, it was good as gold. I thanked John and hung up. Maybe now I could get some sleep. Nope. My phone rang again.

"That was fun to watch," Elinda's voice said. "I assume your problem has been solved?"

I told her what John had said. "If he gave his word, you're good to go. I'll pack up our stuff and hit the sack. Sleep well, darlin'."

I finally laid my head down and sleep overtook me. When the sun woke me I felt like I hadn't slept at all. Even my usual half-pot of coffee didn't do much to dispel the cobwebs but I had a job to go to. I called Omar to tell him he wouldn't be needed and he sleepily told me Ev had already called him. Word gets around fast.

I dragged myself into the office but even after two more cups of coffee the report in front of me just didn't register. I called Cassandra. After telling her about the previous night, I asked, "You got anything for a pick-me-up? I just can't seem to get going this morning."

"Not really," she replied. "Nothing magical can replace the sleep your body needs. You can drink a cup of peppermint or cinnamon tea. That'll help a little without giving you the caffeine buzz but you really do need to sleep."

"Not in the cards. I've got to get the quarterly reports to the accountant today. I'm coming down for a latte. Go heavy on the cinnamon, maybe it'll help that way."

When I got downstairs, my latte was waiting for me. "You really do look like hell warmed over," Cassandra greeted me.

"Thanks a lot. It's been a long few days with short nights."

"Yeah, sounds like. It's good that someone solved the problem for you. Mom's only suggestion was to buy a sunlamp and keep it in the window in case he came back. But you said you didn't want to hurt him and that would have – permanently. Will Ev let you leave early?"

"He will if he knows what's good for him. It was going to the party for him that got me into all this in the first place. I'm going to finish what I really need to get done and head home. I don't see any reason to spend hours just staring at the computer screen and not being productive."

Ev and his odor wafted in just before noon. "You look like hell," was his greeting.

"It's all your fault, you know," was my retort. "If I hadn't gone to that party for you, this would never have happened."

"I know," he said. "John and I both feel bad about this. But it could have been some guy you met at a mundane party, too, you know."

"Had that happened, the police would have been able to deal with it. Or your or Omar's size would have scared him off. Either way, I'm glad it's over. I'm finishing the reports for Ed and going home, Ev. I need to get some good sleep or I'm going to fall over."

"That's OK with me. Just be back tomorrow, huh? I have to leave for San Francisco in a bit and I'll need to have you available to type up the contract if I come to any agreement with anyone."

I hit my bed about 2:00, woke up long enough to eat a slice of cold pizza and feed Fudge about 10:00 and finally felt human (what a term) the next morning. After all the drama of the last few days, it felt good to get back into my normal routine.

Friday morning dawned dark and gloomy. It looked like we were in for some nasty storms. I walked to work through rain and blustery wind, thankful for my slicker. Sure enough, I'd just started the coffee and fired up my computer at work when the lights flickered and then went out. After a couple of minutes it didn't look like the power was going to be immediately restored, so I went downstairs. (Cassandra had a generator to ensure her freezers and refrigerators kept running. It powered most everything in the deli except the lights.)

"Mornin'," she said. "I thought you'd be down after the power went out. Here's your coffee."

She was alone in the deli. Tommy and Charlie didn't come in until around ten, to start getting ready for lunch. We sat companionably by candlelight, sipping coffee and talking about the events of earlier in the week. My cell phone rang.

"Amy, it's John. I don't know how but Andy escaped our confinement. I thought I'd better call and warn you. With today's weather, he won't have any problems being out and about during the day without taking any precautions."

"What?" I screamed into the phone. "I thought your regional guy was supposed to handle him."

"He is here with me now. We had a long meeting with Andy last night and Max thought he was making progress so he relaxed the wards a little this morning. Apparently Andy, although young, is still strong enough to break through. We're starting the hunt for him, naturally headed your way, but you need to call Ev or someone pronto."

Oh. Shit. I hung up, told Cassandra what was happening and while she went about strengthening the wards over the deli, I tried calling Omar. All I got was his voice mail. I called Ev to tell him what had happened and relate the fact that I couldn't get hold of Omar.

"Since John said he had things under control, I let Omar off. He's probably up north, hunting. I'm going to make some calls. Stay in the deli behind Cassandra's wards until I call you back."

Cassandra looked at me with a very worried expression. "Amy, I'm strong but if he broke through wards set by a vampire *for* a vampire, I'm not sure mine will hold. And I don't know who to call for help on this short notice."

"Go home, Cassandra. He's after me and if you're not around, he won't bother you at all. I'll stay here and deal with whatever happens."

"Not a chance. Neither of us is big enough to deal with him alone but maybe two of us together have a fighting chance. As stinky as it is, stuff all this garlic into your pockets and bra." She handed me a pile of garlic cloves, then took another handful and did the same to herself.

We huddled together at the table, coffee cold and forgotten. A clap of thunder immediately followed by the crackle of lightning shook the building. The storm was right overhead. My phone rang again but it wasn't Ev.

"Something just breached the wards on the building," Elinda told me. "Whatever it is, it's down in your apartment. I've called Mr. Owens. We're going down to investigate, now."

"NO," I screamed. "Stay in your own place. It's that vampire and he's out of control. I don't want any of you hurt."

"Darlin', I've handled more than a young vampire in my time. Don't you worry about us. You just keep yourself safe. I'll call you in a few minutes." She hung up.

This had gone beyond insane. Another thunderclap, another flash of lightning. My nerves were so frayed I jumped with every clap and flash. I could see Cassandra wasn't faring much better. My phone rang again.

"I've gotten hold of Gregory," Ev said through all the static. "He's on his way but according to him, it's going to be about fifteen minutes before he gets there because of the weather. Sit tight."

Tight? I was strung about as tight as I could get. Wouldn't you be if a vampire were stalking you?

All I could do was look out the window, watching the rain sheet down and the near-constant flashes of lightning illuminate the passing cars like I was watching an old-time peep show. Instead of honky-tonk music, the vignettes were accompanied by booming thunder.

All of a sudden, one flash showed not a car but Andy, standing on the sidewalk looking into the window. Although he was obviously soaked to the skin, the weather didn't seem to bother him at all. He saw me, grinned and walked toward the deli door. He stopped and recoiled, like he'd bounced off a vertical trampoline.

His expression changed from a grin to a grimace. He closed his eyes for a moment and when he opened them, they were glowing red. He took another step toward the door and with just a little effort, pushed his way past the wards as if he were walking through nothing more than a waterfall. The red faded from his eyes but the grimace didn't leave his face. The bell tinkled as he opened the door.

"Amy, I'm so glad to see you," he started. "I know if we can just sit and talk, you'll get to know what a great guy I am. We would make a very handsome couple."

I stood up, and Cassandra stood immediately to my left. "Andy, I've told you before that I'm not interested in you. Why can't you understand that?"

Andy turned his attention to Cassandra with a hiss. "This is between me and Amy, witch. Please leave us alone."

"Not a chance, fang-boy. It's my store you're standing in and I'm not going anywhere. Not to mention that it's my friend you're interested in and I'm not leaving her alone with you. By the way, you're dripping all over my floor."

Wow. I don't think I could have managed that much cheek. I was even more grateful for my friend, witchy or not.

Andy moved toward me and grimaced even more. "Get rid of the garlic, Amy. It's not conducive to quiet conversation between adults."

"Adults?" I laughed but took a step back all the same. "Since when is stalking someone who's not interested in you the act of an adult? I'd say it's closer to the actions of a lovesick teenager."

Andy's fangs dropped just a bit. This was not good. "Have it your way. Garlic only hurts, it doesn't kill. We *will* speak so sit down."

Not knowing what else to do until help arrived, I sat back down and trying to be nonchalant, took a sip of my now-cold coffee. My hand only shook a little and I didn't slosh a drop. Cassandra sat back down, too, but pulled her chair close to mine and put her hand on my knee. I could feel a tingle coming from her palm. Andy stood a few feet away, still dripping on the floor.

"Amy, am I not a handsome man? If it's the pale skin that bothers you, I can start going to a tanning salon. I'm rich, too, and can give you everything money can buy. I can control myself well enough to only take sips from you. I promise I wouldn't turn you. We could have a lovely life for several decades."

I tried stalling. "Andy, I guess you're OK-looking for a guy but looks aren't everything. Neither is money. I have no desire to be involved with someone who is in the public eye. I like my life private."

"I could give you that privacy," he pleaded. "You wouldn't have to attend all the parties…" he broke off as the door flew open. Elinda, Marge and Bud (the dwarf neighbor) barged in, a gust of wind adding some more rain to the puddles of water on the floor. The three of them marched over and stood between our table and Andy. Elinda and Marge extended their hands and I think I saw a little sparkle comes from their fingertips.

"Stay away from her, vampire," Elinda growled. "Amy doesn't want you. She is not and never will be yours."

Andy's fangs dropped all the way. "We were having a pleasant conversation until you barged in. Leave us alone and you won't get hurt."

Just then a car pulled to a quick stop at the curb outside, spraying the sidewalk and window with a wave of water. Gregory hopped out and, wading through all the water, ran inside. One look told him what was going on and he, too, extended his hands but from behind Andy. I did indeed see sparkles this time. Cassandra stood, moved to Marge's side and added her sparkles to the mix.

"Binding matrix, now!" yelled Gregory. The four of them extended their arms, palms all facing Andy. I saw the sparkles fly from their palms: red from Gregory, blue from Marge, purple from Elinda and magenta from Cassandra. A mysterious fifth stream of yellow sparkles came from behind me, where the counter was. The candles all blew out like a strong wind had come up in the deli; sparkles meshed into a multi-colored web that surrounded Andy with a twinkling glow and then faded from my sight.

Andy's eyes took on a deathly glow. He hissed, turning this way and that, but couldn't pull his hands out of his pockets or move his feet from where they were firmly planted on the floor. "You will pay for this, all of you," he spat.

"I doubt it," Gregory said. He moved his hands like he was tying a knot, said "done" and the four of them dropped their arms. We all looked over to the counter where Tommy was just lowering his hands and had a very concerned look on his face. "Who's the vamp?" he asked.

"A not-friend of Amy's," Cassandra answered him. "Why didn't you tell me you were a wizard?"

"Wasn't pertinent to the job description."

Cassandra moved over toward the counter and they started talking in low tones.

Gregory looked at me. "I talked with John. He and the council rep are about fifteen minutes away. We would all have been here sooner but there are accidents all over the place with this storm."

I dropped into my chair. I couldn't help myself: the tears started flowing. There was no telling what would have happened. I had been unable to protect myself and all these people had come to my rescue. Gregory stood at the door with his eyes on Andy. The other three crowded around me.

"Yer safe, now and always," Bud's gruff voice penetrated my tears.

Marge put her arms around me and I sobbed into her grandmotherly bosom. "We love you, honey, and wouldn't let anything happen to you."

Just then, the lights came back on. I looked outside and through my tear-blurred eyes, saw that the rain had let up. Cassandra kissed the top of my head and said, "Does everyone drink cappuccino? I think something caffeinated, warm and sweet is called for."

"Does that include me, sweet witch? Your blood smells warm and tasty." Andy gave Cassandra a smile that didn't look very friendly, considering his fangs were fully extended.

"Not a chance vampire," Gregory snapped. "Try to move and the matrix will burn you like sunlight."

"I'll make you a special espresso," Cassandra said. "Heavy on the holy water." Andy hissed.

By the time John, Mark and an older man wearing a trench coat and fedora walked in, we were all sitting at two tables by the window, sipping our cappuccinos. I was still sniffling but at least not sobbing uncontrollably. Gregory had sat down but had turned his chair to keep an eye on the statue that was Andy, standing in the middle of the room.

"Andy Deland, it is the judgment of the Council that you be confined in the Council dungeon for a period of not less than seventy-five years for violation of our Accords," pronounced the unknown man who, although appearing to be in his early sixties, carried himself like a much younger person. He looked at Andy and then at Gregory. "Wizard, I will bind him. When you see mine complete, you may release yours."

Gregory nodded. The Council rep waved his hand up and down Andy once, Gregory moved his left hand to his left and then slashed it quickly back to his right. Andy went rigid and his eyes opened as wide as they'd go. He looked like he was trying to open his mouth to say something but it appeared to be zipped shut.

Mark picked Andy up and put him over his shoulder, like a construction worker carrying a board. It would have been a hilarious sight if not for the circumstances.

"I'll be to the car in a minute," John told the other two men as they exited the deli, Mark taking care not to bump Andy's head on the doorframe.

"I thought vampires couldn't do magic," I asked the group.

"Some of the older ones can," John answered. "A few centuries ago, we didn't have a problem turning a witch or wizard. Something changed about five hundred years ago and we now can't seem to seduce magic-wielders in order to feed off them, much less turn them. But there's a few dozen around the world who can do magic and they're all on or work for the Vampire Ruling Council. It's one of the ways they keep everyone in line. Max is one of the oldest and he happens to live in Kansas City.

"Amy, I can't begin to say how sorry I am about all this. It's rare for a vampire to go rogue and even rarer for one to escape a ward set by Max. But now that he knows what to expect, Andy won't get out again. And the dungeon is in Switzerland, so he'll be far away from you during your lifetime. Gregory and the rest of you, thank you." With that, John left.

CHAPTER 9

"Darlin', we need to go back to your apartment. That kid did a number on your stuff," Elinda said.

"Fudge! Is he all right?" I knew vamps would take an animal's blood if they were desperate.

"I found him under your bed. He's up at my place until we can get yours sorted," Bud told me. "He's not pleased but I thought it'd be better to get him out of there and we didn't think their cats would understand." 'Their' being Elinda and Marge's cats. Oh man. How bad was it?

With the storm's passing, people were back out on the street and customers started coming into the deli. Cassandra and Tommy had to get to work.

Gregory had gotten on his phone as soon as John left. He flipped it closed. "Ev told me to tell you to go home. I'm supposed to forward the phones to his cell the rest of the day," Gregory said. "I suggest you go see what's happening at home and don't worry about the office for a bit. If you need me for anything, just call."

"I'll forward the phones. I have to go back up to shut everything down, get my rain slicker and purse, anyways. But thanks, Gregory. For everything."

Marge would have accompanied me upstairs but my legs just didn't want to cooperate when I stood. I tried to walk and would have fallen over if not for Bud catching me. A clove of garlic fell out of my pocket, which reminded me to get rid of the rest of it, too. Cassandra laughed as she, too, unloaded and put the pile into the compost bin.

"You're in a little shock, I think," Gregory smiled at me. "I'll go forward the phones and bring your stuff back down. Wait here. I'll give you all a ride back to your apartment building so you don't have to walk through the rain again."

We all piled into Ev's limo for the two block ride home. What I saw when we pulled up made me burst into tears again.

My door was off its hinges and all the windows were broken. Mr. Owens, Jack, and Edward (the other mundane tenants) were out in the rain, starting the process of boarding everything up until workmen could arrive to make the actual repairs. I cried even harder when I walked into my home. That creep had pulled everything from the shelves, cupboards and closets, and tossed my furniture around like toys. Anything breakable that Fudge had left alone was now in shards. I turned one of my chairs upright, sat in it and sobbed even harder.

"Amy, I'm sorry. In all my years, I've never had a ward breached before," Mr. Owens said.

"It's not your fault," I replied, trying to choke everything back so I sounded coherent. "He apparently got through others, too. God. I wonder if this is covered by insurance."

"It's not [I moaned] but the Vampire Council will ensure that the damages are covered. I've already been in touch with them," Mr. Owens told me. "Max will be by here later after he's handed that boy off to the enforcers. He'll make you a settlement offer. Don't take the first one, or even the second. They can afford to be more than generous to keep the news of a rogue under wraps."

"How the hell will I know what's fair in a few hours' time? I don't know what needs to be replaced or what needs to be fixed!"

"I'll be here since they owe me money for damage to the building. Don't worry. It'll all get sorted."

During our conversation, Elinda, Marge and Bud had disappeared upstairs. They all came back, Bud armed with trash bags, Elinda with her broom, bucket and mop, and Marge carrying a tray with a large urn and several mugs on it.

"Tea, everyone. Then let's start cleaning up," she announced with a bright smile.

The men righted my furniture, I flipped on the overhead lights so we could see (it was almost pitch black in there as Jack and Edward put up the last board) and they all sat down to a calming cup of tea. I couldn't sit, though. I wandered around, looking at all the books that had been ripped to shreds, my laptop in smithereens and the television with its cracked screen. I knew vamps were fast but he'd done all this damage in less than ten minutes. Even Fudge's food was scattered all over the kitchen floor.

"Bud, can I go get my cat?" I asked.

"Sure. Door's unlocked."

I went out the back door, through the hall and up one flight to Bud's apartment. The smell of his pipe smoke hit me when I opened the door and then something else did, too. Fudge almost flew into my arms. "At least you're OK," I sniffled into his fur. "I'm not sure anything else is, including me."

Fudge purred loudly and snuggled as close as he could to my chest as I walked back downstairs. When we walked back in the door, I saw everyone picking stuff up, looking to see if it was intact and throwing the majority of my belongings into large trash bags. Fudge hopped out of my arms and ran into the bedroom. I followed.

If I was going to clean, I needed something other than office clothes to wear. Picking through the piles of ripped fabric, I found a couple pairs of jeans and a few shirts that were still intact. I changed, carefully hanging my suit in the nearly-empty closet. There was one thing left on the closet shelf that hadn't been moved or trashed – my family Bible. Andy literally couldn't touch it and for that, I was grateful. I started going through the mess. Fudge supervised from the one pillow that had escaped Andy's wrath.

Three hours later, my apartment almost looked like it wasn't lived in. None of the furniture was broken but apart from that, there wasn't much. I had salvaged my jewelry box, most of my jewelry and maybe a quarter of my clothes and shoes. My family pictures were intact but all the frames had been busted. The walls were bare, the bookshelves were empty, no lamp graced any side table and the only things on my desk were the halves of two old books Edward thought could be restored. The kitchen counters were clear and the cupboards were empty, except for my cooking pots, Tupperware and a few spice bottles. I didn't even have a whole plate to eat off of. Twenty lawn-sized trash bags filled the center of the living room, with pieces of broken wall art, the microwave and television leaning against the pile.

Bud and Edward hauled the trash out to the dumpster. "Come have dinner with us tonight," Jack said when the living room was finally clear. (He and Edward alternated cooking nights.)

"Why don't we all have dinner together tonight? Say, at the pub. I think we deserve a night out after all this," Marge said.

"I'm afraid I won't be the life of the party but I could use a drink or three and I'd like to treat you all to dinner," I said. "You've all been so good to me. I'd like to repay you somehow."

"You're on. Add the bar tab to whatever you get out of the vamps. We'll all meet down here at six?" Elinda asked.

Everyone nodded and filed out the door, going back to their homes. Fudge and I were alone in the dark apartment with nothing to do and it was barely after noon. It had been less than five hours since I'd left for work and in that short time, my life had turned upside down. I contemplated going back to the office but didn't want to leave Fudge alone and he wouldn't be happy with the two block walk in the rain.

I laid down on the couch, thinking maybe I could sleep the afternoon away but just as I'd curled up with Fudge, there was a knock on the back door. When I answered it,

Ev stood there with Mr. Owens and Max, the vampire wizard.

"May we come in, Miss McCollum?" Max asked just as I said "Ev, what are you doing here?"

"Yes, of course," I answered Max's question at the same time as Ev said, "I chartered a plane and ran into Max at the airport."

"Hold on. Let's only have one conversation and inside at that," said Mr. Owens.

They all filed in, Ev ducking to avoid the door frame. I took their raincoats and Max's hat and hung them on the wall hooks that had miraculously survived Andy's rampage, although the coats I'd originally hung on them hadn't.

Fudge emerged from the bedroom and stood in the center of the hall, tail fluffed and ears erect, his eyes never leaving Max.

"Unless I miss my guess, you don't normally live in a bare apartment," Max said after he and Mr. Owens sat on the couch and Ev took up a post, leaning against the wall that divided the kitchen from the hallway to my bath and bedroom. I don't think he wanted to brave the ceiling fan to take a seat on one of the chairs. Fudge moved to the opposite side of the hall but kept up his vigilance.

"No. My neighbors kindly cleaned up the mess and if you look in the dumpster, you'll find most of my life in there," I replied. "Andy didn't leave a lot intact. You're welcome to look at what's left."

"I can't begin to express my regret and embarrassment that this happened," Max continued. "This is the first rogue we've had in nearly three decades and it not only happened in my region but I was unable to control him."

"Will someone please explain to me why he wouldn't get it that I wasn't interested in him, even if he were still human, why he was able to get through wards, and then why he felt it necessary to trash my home?" I asked everyone collectively but Max specifically.

"We're not real sure why it happens. It's such a rare event that we don't have a lot of examples to study," Max said. "I can tell you the rogues I've heard of were all young, as Andy was, and we believe never fully accepted their new nature. Then something snaps and they focus on one individual and in some cases, become violent. There was one young man in Greece about three hundred years ago who decided he was going to marry the woman to whom he'd been engaged before he was turned, even though she had aged and was now eighty-five. She had been told he was killed in an accident and the poor lady died of a heart attack when she saw her lover standing before her, looking as if he was still twenty. He went on a rampage through the Acropolis that left the Greek authorities with even more ruins than they'd had before.

"As to why he could get through wards, there are a few vampires who aren't bothered by them as much as others. I'm one of them. Although I felt James' wards [Mr. Owens], were I of a mind, I could have walked through them with only a little difficulty. Naturally, that is impolite and I asked his permission to enter the building. In addition, I have shown him how to construct them so even I would be deterred."

He leaned forward with a stern look on his face. "Andy will *not* bother you again. Of that you may be assured. The place to which he is currently being transported is on a mountaintop with sheer cliffs and only accessible by helicopter. He will be confined not only by the topography but strong wards. We hope he will return to normal with counseling but if not, he will greet the sunrise. It is our way."

Mr. Owens cleared his throat. "About reparations," he said, looking at Max rather pointedly.

"Yes, of course. I presume what you and I had discussed will more than pay for the damages to the building?"

Mr. Owens nodded. "Yes, but I am more concerned with the damage not only to Amy's apartment but the grief she has experienced in the last several days."

"A paid vacation to, say, Hawai'i might be in order," Ev interjected. "I don't see where just replacing all her things will make up for the stress she's been under and I can't exactly expect her to be at her best in the office while she's recovering."

"Ev, I really don't want a vacation. I want my life *back*," I said. "I want my comfy home, my strange job with my goofy boss and my routine."

Ev snorted. "I'm not goofy."

Max smiled. "You are a stronger woman than I gave you credit for. Most mundane women I know would be prostrate with the vapors after being stalked by a rogue and having their home torn apart."

"I don't know about strong. I just want everything to go back to the way it was."

Max asked me how much replacing everything would cost. I answered truthfully that I had no idea. Many of the books that Andy had destroyed were first editions and some of them quite old and rare. He named a figure. Mr. Owens discreetly shook his head and I said I didn't think that would cover it. Max named another, much higher figure and, although Mr. Owens shook his head again, I thought it was way more than fair, so I said yes.

"A check will be FedEx'd to you and should arrive at your office within the week. If there is anything else I can help with, please call me. However, I hope you and I do not have occasion to meet again, unless it's socially. We'd all like to put this unfortunate incident behind us." With that, Max rose, handed me a business card, took his coat and hat and left.

"I've already arranged for the door to be fixed and the windows replaced as soon as weather permits," Mr. Owens said. "If the weatherman is to be believed, that should happen on Monday." He left, too.

Fudge relaxed his vigil and, padding over to where I was sitting, rubbed my legs. I picked him up and held him in my lap.

"OK, Ev. What are you doing here? You're supposed to be in San Francisco."

"Listen, Amy. I know we butt heads a lot and I'm a smelly ogre with a temper. But we've worked together so long that you're like part of my family. I wanted to make sure you were OK. Not to mention that you'd be damned hard to replace and I need you running my office. I'd already finished up what I was going to do out there and was on my way home, anyways.

"Gregory's outside. Can we take you somewhere shopping?"

I would have to start making a very long list. I really didn't know everything I needed to replace at that point but could think of a couple of things: a television for that night and a coffeepot for the next morning. Maybe even a mug to drink from.

"Yeah, thanks. I do need a few things to tide me over until I can get a list made. Discounters Mall out by the freeway should have everything I'll need tonight."

"Come on, then. Your taxi awaits," Ev grinned and waved me toward the door with a flourish.

We arrived back a couple of hours later with the trunk and half of the back seat full. I'd bought a new flat-screen television, a much fancier coffeemaker than I'd had, complete with a selection of gourmet coffee, a new laptop, a full set of dishes, kitchen linens, some new bedding, and one table lamp. Several scented candles would help with the real (and imagined) air in my apartment. I'd also spied some novels I liked in the book section – and on sale, too.

Ev was much handier than I'd ever imagined. Out of the trunk of the limo came a toolbox and while Gregory finished carrying everything in and unpacking the laptop and coffeepot from their boxes, Ev hung the new television on the wall and hooked it up for me.

"Can you come in for a couple of hours tomorrow? I have some contracts that need to be typed," he asked when they had finished hauling the boxes out to the dumpster.

"Yeah, I'll be there," I replied. Anything to get me out of my currently-depressing apartment.

"Good." He opened his arms like he was going to hug me. I shook my head and he just smiled. Gregory winked at me as they left. I had just enough time to shower before the rest of the building's occupants descended on me.

Dinner that night was cheering. As usual, I was the youngest person at the table but I'd gotten used to that. Bud was an unusual dwarf: he had us all laughing with his jokes. Jack chimed in with a few of his own. After a couple of hours, though, I started to yawn.

"We need to get this little one to bed," Bud said. "She's had a long day and we're no spring chickens anymore, either."

Over everyone's objections, I paid the bill. "I thought we agreed this was a way I could thank you all for your help," I told them. "I know there's no way I can truly repay you for what you've done but let me at least do this. And I'm not paying for it, the Vampire Council is."

"Did you get a whopper of a settlement from them?" Elinda asked.

"Nice enough. I won't really be able to replace everything, especially the rare books, but I'll have enough to buy others that catch my eye."

We walked home together and I hugged everyone before they headed up and I headed down. I put food out for Fudge, made up my bed and crawled into it. I was exhausted and asleep before my head hit the pillow.

CHAPTER 10

I woke in the dark to the phone ringing. I mumbled a hello into it while trying to disentangle myself from both Fudge and the sheets. Despite the exhaustion, I hadn't slept well.

"Are you OK?" Cassandra's voice said. "It's after ten."

"Holy shit. I forgot to get a clock at the store yesterday and without the sun I overslept. Thanks for calling. I gotta get moving so I'm there before Ev walks in."

"Too late. He's here already and asked me to call. After yesterday he wasn't sure if you were really alright and thought maybe it'd be better if a girl called you in case you started crying or something. I'll tell him you'll be there shortly, OK?"

"Yeah. Thanks again."

I ducked my body through the shower, pulled a brush through my hair, swiped on some makeup, threw on the one suit I had left – the one I'd worn the previous day which smelled faintly of garlic – and beat a trail for the office. I must have run between raindrops because my hair didn't even feel wet. I took the stairs two at a time (no mean feat in heels) and burst into the office, breathless.

"You didn't have to run. Frisco's two hours behind us. We've got plenty of time to get everything done before anybody there really wakes up," Ev said. "You look like you got some sleep. You OK?"

"Not entirely but I will be. Let me put some coffee on and get some caffeine into my system so I can see the keyboard."

"Already done. Cassandra knows I have no idea how to make coffee the way you like it and that you'd need some. She made a pot for you."

Wow. What friends. I poured myself a cup and put an ice cube in it so I could gulp it down, which I did. I poured a second cup and sat down to work.

Ev had agreed to hire two wizards, both of whom would be relocating to Chicago to service some clients he had set up there. I had to modify our standard contract for both of them, which I did according to his notes. By noon, both were sitting on someone's fax machine in Frisco, the boss was cloistered in his office on the phone and I was starting to think about lunch.

"Hiya." The smell of Brunswick stew accompanied Cassandra through the door. "It's a slow day and Tommy's got the counter so I thought I'd bring your lunch up and find out what happened yesterday from your point of view. I would've called last night but I figured you'd have collapsed into bed early. Ev's already told me what he knows."

I filled her in on what had happened after we'd all left the deli, in between bites of thick, yummy stew and homemade bread.

"You need help making your shopping list? I can come over tonight if you want," she said.

"Sure. I'll order pizza. See you about seven?"

Cassandra nodded and smiled before she went downstairs, taking my now-empty bowl with her.

I did a little more work then called it quits and went home to my dark and dreary apartment. Moving the one lamp I had over to the desk, I fired up the new laptop and started the tedious process of configuring it, loading software and then downloading all my files from the online backup service I used. I cringed when I looked at all the emails I had to answer but decided they could wait just a little while longer. Five hours later I was just finishing up when a brief knock on the door preceded Cassandra's entry. She was carrying a bottle of wine in one hand and a basket in the other.

"Wow. He really did a number, didn't he?" Cassandra said as she surveyed my bare surroundings. "Call the pizza folks. I'm starved."

"What's in the basket?" I asked after I'd ordered our usual.

"Stuff you can probably use … some toiletries, some food for your fridge and some things for me to purify your apartment. I thought you'd want to get rid of the bad vibes."

She was right. The scented candles I'd purchased smelled nice and all, but there was something lingering on the air that didn't feel right.

After we'd devoured the pizza (the three of us, that is), we started making my shopping list. At the top was an alarm clock. I'd need it at least one more morning until the windows had been replaced. Lamps, drapes, clothing, a stereo, a microwave and food completed the list. Everything else I'd pick up online. Shopping wasn't a pleasure for me and I preferred to let my fingers and UPS do the walking.

Once the list was complete, Cassandra had me sit in the living room while she got rid of the bad vibes. The first thing she did was disable the smoke detector in the hallway. She lit a couple of candles after rubbing them down with oil, placing them in the living room and the bedroom. Next came a smoldering bundle of white sage. She walked around the entire apartment, wafting the smoke into all the corners with a huge feather. Her brow was furrowed in concentration as I saw waves of energy come off her and the smoke. It looked like hard work.

Once she'd completed her circuit of the place, she extinguished the nub of the sage bundle in an abalone shell. It was probably a good thing she'd finished. If anyone had opened the door, it would have looked like that microbus scene from Cheech and Chong's *Up in Smoke*. My eyes were watering and Fudge sneezed several times but the smoke was slowly dissipating. Cassandra packed everything back into her basket and plopped in a chair.

"Phew. He left a lot of negative energy. You should start feeling a lot better as soon as the candles burn out, which ought to be in about ten minutes. I need a glass of wine."

We turned the television on and much to her chagrin, I found the baseball game was still going on – it was into extra innings. After I cheered when the Twins finally pulled it out in the twelfth, she re-enabled the smoke detector and got ready to go home.

"We're going to the mall tomorrow. Tommy's letting me borrow his SUV so we've got more hauling room than my little car or a taxi. I'll pick you up at noon."

Ugh. I hated shopping at the mall on weekends but it had to be done. I said goodnight to her with a grimace.

Shopping was *not* fun. I was on a mission to replace what I could in the shortest possible period of time. I hated having to dodge all the mothers with strollers and the teenagers hanging out in clusters right in the middle of the walkways. The mall plus three additional stores yielded most everything I immediately needed. By the time we were done I was footsore and my credit cards were tired.

We unloaded the SUV and then started the process of putting everything away. By seven, all the bags and tags were in the trash and we were exhausted.

"Let's go to the pub for dinner. You cook for a living and I don't feel like it. Let's let someone else cook for us," I said.

"Deal." We headed over to the pub, ate dinner and she took Tommy's car home. They'd swapped vehicles for the day and would swap back on Monday.

Monday passed uneventfully, thank goodness. After the prior week, I wasn't sure I could take any more drama. Although it hadn't quite quit raining, it had only drizzled during the day. When I arrived home after work, sparkling new windows and a very cool-looking steel entry door greeted me. I spent a few minutes hanging the new curtains before napping, and the evening doing Internet shopping for clothes and other things I still needed to replace. I'd be seeing quite a bit of the UPS man in the next week or so.

Tuesday dawned bright and clear with a nip to the air. Perhaps autumn was finally on the way. I vowed to take a ride around the lakes when I got off work to enjoy the weather.

The FedEx guy walked in the door about two with an envelope for me. I opened it and choked. The check was from "The Estate of Andy Deland" and it was for five grand more than Max and I had agreed on. A note accompanied it. In flourished script, it read, "Andy will not bother anyone, anymore. I noticed the two books on your desk. I, too, am a bibliophile and collect old books. This should help you repair those and replace others. Max."

So, something had gone haywire with Andy's incarceration and rehabilitation. A quick Internet search showed me that he'd "died of a heart attack." The scriptwriters on his movie were scrambling to change the storyline. Multiple sites were bemoaning the loss of such a young and talented life. Youngsters' blogs were crying. John was quoted as being devastated at the loss of one of his favorite clients. Honestly? I was relieved. Regardless of the assurances I'd been given, I still had a lingering feeling of wariness.

The Vampire Council sure worked fast. It would have taken weeks to get an estate set up in the mundane world. I hollered at Ev over the intercom that I was going to the bank and would be back in about ten minutes. I wanted to get that money into my account before anyone changed their minds. I had a deposit to make for the company, anyways.

My bike ride after work was glorious. It was a work day which meant the paths weren't crowded, and the cooler weather had emptied the beaches of all but a few hearty souls. I felt totally recharged when I got home and didn't even take a nap. Fudge was not happy until I sat down at the computer. He assumed his supervisory position and was quite pleased when I decided to have a quick tuna salad for dinner, writing between bites. He didn't have to move too far to share!

Happy strolled into the office mid-afternoon on Thursday with a shit-eating grin on his face. Crap. I'd forgotten all about him!

"Good afternoon, Amy," he greeted me with a smile. I smiled back.

"Hi, Happy. What brings you to our little corner of the world?"

"Oh, I just thought I'd share some interesting information with you two. Is Ev around?"

I buzzed Ev on the intercom, told him who was waiting to see him and after his audible gulp, ushered Happy into his office.

"I found out some very interesting information last night," Happy began. "It seems no one has heard that the two of you are married. I also notice Amy is not wearing her stunning wedding ring today. Have you been keeping it a secret from the world, or can it be that you are trying to fool me?"

Son. Of. A. Bitch. I could see from the look on Ev's face that he had the exact same thought.

"OK, we're not married," Ev confessed. "I am quite content with my lifestyle *and* the women I am currently seeing. I truly didn't want you trying to fix me up again. Is that what you wanted to hear?"

"I assumed that was your intention and am not mad at you," Happy said. "Nor do I have any women in mind for you at the moment. I do, however, have the most wonderful man I'd like to introduce to Amy. I believe you would get on famously," he looked at me with a leer.

After the prior week, dating was the last thing on my mind. "I, too, am quite happy with my life at the moment. I have all sorts of opportunities and am not interested in dating right now."

"Ah, but I believe you just have not met the right man. Please, allow me to at least introduce you over cocktails this evening. I promise there will be no strings. I will send a car to your apartment at six. Will that be convenient?"

I looked over at Ev. He just shrugged his shoulders.

"If I meet this person and say I'm not interested, will you leave me alone after that?" I asked.

"I can promise nothing. I love to see people happily married and if I meet someone I think might be a suitable match for you, I would consider myself remiss if I did not at least make the introduction. Please, say yes to this evening."

"Hell, why not. Otherwise you'd probably just show up tomorrow, the day after that and the day after that, until

I caved. However, cocktails only and then I'm heading home. Believe it or not, I do have things to do."

Happy smiled. "Six, then. My car will be out front of your building." With that, he left the office.

"I am going to *kill* you, Ev!" I screamed after Happy had left. "Now he's not only on your case, he's on mine! And how the hell does he know where I live?"

"I'm sorry, Amy, I really am," Ev had turned a dull shade of red. This was an indication that he was sad. "If I knew of a way for both of us to get him out of our lives, believe me, I'd be acting on it yesterday. As for how he knows where you live, I told you he's well-connected. It probably only took him a couple of phone calls or whatever he does to find that out."

"Well, since I have to get ready for tonight, I'm leaving now. I suggest you start working on how to get this creep out of my life. I don't need anyone trying to fix me up with anybody, remember?"

With that, I stormed back into my office, shut down the computer, grabbed my purse and made sure to slam the door on my way out. I covered the two blocks back to my apartment in what would have been record time, except I was slamming my feet with every step and managed to break a heel off one of my shoes. Great. One more log on my fire of ire.

I still had a couple of hours and getting ready wouldn't take that long, so after checking my email (the only thing of interest was a congratulatory note from my publisher on making the top-ten list of ebook downloads on Amazon the previous week), I turned on the television to try to distract myself.

That was a mistake. Afternoon television isn't the most interesting. I've never gotten into soaps, the news is always depressing, and the weather channel was alternating between talking about our nice weather and the hurricane that was bearing down on the Gulf States. Not exactly cheery. You'd think with over 500 channels (according to my cable service) I'd be able to find something distracting, but no.

So, I turned back to the computer and played mahjong until I had to get ready. I could easily distract myself for hours with that game but the little clock down in the corner of the computer screen reminded me that time was ticking away until doomsday – or at least doomshour.

Instead of dressing up, I chose the blandest, most severe business suit I had in my sparse closet, pulled my hair back into a barrette and applied minimal makeup. I wasn't out to impress anyone. Promptly at six, a stretch limo pulled up outside and a gnome (how did he see over the steering wheel or reach the pedals?) tromped down my stairs and knocked on my door. He was dressed in what may have been eighteenth century livery … breeches, tailcoat and top hat. I tried not to laugh at the sight. Just one more indication that Happy really wasn't living in the 21st century.

"Miss Amy, Mr. Happy has asked me to collect you," he squeaked.

I grabbed my purse, locked the door behind me and said, "Let's go." I felt like I was going to someone's funeral – mine.

The gnome opened the passenger door with the remote and after I slid in, closed it from the bottom of the door – which was all he could reach. I could see him through the privacy glass and he could indeed see out the window, although I couldn't see how. Did he grow when he got into the car?

Ten minutes later, he dropped me off at one of the new tapas-and-martini bars that had sprung up all over town. I walked inside, saw Happy sitting with another man and threaded my way through the yuppie crowd to their table. Both men stood as I walked up and Happy helped me with my chair. While I don't mind being treated like a lady, this just got on my nerves. I sat and faced a man who was less than six feet tall, with thinning brown hair and dull brown eyes. There wasn't even any eye candy to look at.

"Amy McCollum, may I introduce James Arthur. Jim, this is Amy," Happy beamed at both of us. "Amy, may I order you a cocktail?"

I said I'd like a glass of merlot, which Happy relayed to the waiter who had mysteriously appeared at the table. I wondered how much money (or something else) Happy flung around to get that kind of attention in a crowded bar. We waited politely for my drink to arrive, which was almost immediate, and Happy continued, "Amy, Jim owns a computer consulting company. I thought you might like to know someone in that line just in case you required service of that type at the office. Jim, Amy, although an administrative assistant, really runs a personal security firm. If your firm keeps on growing the way it has been, you may need a bodyguard at some point!"

I don't remember a lot of the conversation. I probably said something to the effect that I was pretty handy with computers and Jim probably laughed off Happy's suggestion that he'd need a bodyguard. It was obvious neither of us was delighted to be there. I'm sure Jim is a nice guy but when Happy turned the conversation to personal interests, we soon discovered we didn't share a single one. Jim was into action … he skydived, snow- and water-skied, ran his jet ski all over Lake Minnetonka in the summer and was assistant coach for a Pop Warner team. I preferred reading, museums and the theater.

Just as conversation was starting to lag, Jim's cell phone rang. He spoke in almost a monotone, his side of the conversation consisting of mostly 'yes' or 'of course'. Three minutes later he flipped it closed, looked at both of us and said, "My apologies but a client's system has crashed. The tech assigned to the account is out sick and I'm the only other person familiar with this company. I have to leave to straighten out the problem."

"I should be going, too," I said as I stood with him. "Happy, there's no need for your driver to take me home. I have some errands to run on the way so I'll take a taxi."

"Perhaps we're going in the same direction," Jim said. "If so, I'd be happy to drop you somewhere. My car is in the lot." We compared notes and he could indeed drop me at the grocery store a couple of blocks away from home on his way to the interstate.

"Happy, thank you for the drink," I said.

"And the introduction," added Jim.

With that, we made our way outside, Happy watching us leave with a not-too-pleased look on his face.

On the way to the car, Jim asked, "How'd Happy get his hooks into you?"

"Long story, but through my boss," I replied. "I'm going to kill him for getting me into this. You?"

"Same thing. My former boss is stuck with him, too, and when she wouldn't succumb to any of his matchmaking, he turned on me. I'm truly sorry for tonight but honestly, if any computer issues come up, give me a call, OK?"

I took his card as I climbed out of the car.

"Thanks for the ride. I'll call if I need anything." I was glad that encounter was over.

I didn't need any groceries – that was an excuse not to see the gnome again or be beholden to Happy for anything I didn't have to. But to make things look good, I went into the store and grabbed the makings for a salad.

CHAPTER 11

The next morning, Ev asked me how it went.

"Grade-A fail," I told him. "Happy apparently doesn't have the same eye for men for me as he does women for you. Although I seriously doubt it, it would be nice if he learned a lesson and left me alone."

"He'll keep trying. With each meeting he'll learn more about you and try to find Mr. Right. At least that's what he's been doing with me. Really, I *am* trying to think of a way to get him out of our lives. I just haven't come up with anything."

The next couple of months went smoothly. No phone calls from Happy but I assumed it would be just a matter of time before the fix-up began again. I got the next book completely drafted and started on the editing.

Ev managed to find three more wizards and brought them into the fold as guards, immediately assigning them to jobs. I had to work longer hours to keep up with everything. It had reached the point that I had to drop hints about needing some help. But I should have known better than to be subtle. Ev may have been an ogre but he was a typical man. He either didn't get hints, or ignored them. The situation finally came to a head one afternoon when I was trying to finish the books for the accountant, type up a couple new contracts, answer the phone every fifteen seconds (it seemed) and put the preparations for Ev's Halloween party to bed.

"Ev, get your butt out here," I screamed.

He poked his head out his office door and with a look of consternation on his face, said, "What?"

"I've been hinting for some time that I need some help around here and this is the last straw. Either we hire someone to at least answer the phone or you do your own party planning. I know you really haven't noticed, but I've been working ten hour days trying to keep up with everything and I'm drowning."

"Can we afford someone?" he asked.

"If we couldn't, I wouldn't have suggested it." Sarcasm laced my voice.

"Well, if we can afford someone, I'll leave it up to you. Was that all?"

All, he said. The man really was clueless, or possibly blind at times. I'd gotten his permission to hire help. Now all I had to do was find the time to do the hiring!

That night over a glass (or three) of wine, I placed an ad in the paper. It was worded almost identically to the one I'd answered all those years ago, except I only wanted someone part time. That way, we didn't have to offer much in the way of benefits. I used my blind Gmail account to receive the resumes.

After running a week, the ad garnered three whole resumes. I'd have thought in today's economy that any job was better than no job, but there you have it. Only one of the three was remotely interesting so I set up an in-person interview for the next day. I'll admit, I was desperate.

Sally walked into the office promptly at one. If I wasn't secure in my own skin, I would have been intimidated. Put some armor on her, add a sword and a flying horse and she could have been a Valkyrie. Something over six feet tall, blonde hair, blue eyes with that Nordic Ice Queen look. An expensive silk suit, a rock for an engagement ring and what appeared to be real gemstones in her earrings and necklace had me really curious.

I won't bore you with the standard interview questions and answers, with the exception of her reply to my, "Why are you interested in a part time job?"

"My husband travels quite a bit for business and I'm bored with both sitting at home and the social rounds. I was his secretary before we married and remembered all the interesting people who came into his office. I have no need to work but thought with a part time job, I'd get out of the house and meet different people."

Well, she'd certainly meet interesting people here! I asked about dealing with non-humans. She laughed. "My husband is an investment banker and a wizard, I might add. He doesn't discriminate who he raises money for, as long as the project is sound and he gets his percentage. I think I've worked with just about every non-human species there is. They don't bother me."

At that point, Ev came in from lunch and I introduced them. Sally wrinkled her nose as she shook hands with him and after he'd disappeared into his office, said to me, "Now

I understand the scented candles. I thought it was a little unusual for a business office but I just met the explanation."

We talked a little further; mostly I was trying to figure out if our personalities would mesh. I finally decided they would and made her an offer.

"Whatever you offered, I would have accepted," she said. "This looks like an intriguing place to work."

It was my turn to laugh, "I promise, no two days are alike and Ev throws a wrench into the works at least once a day. When can you start?"

Although her answer was 'immediately', I wanted to get the office set up for two clerical types so we agreed she'd start a week later. After she left, I met with Ev about rearranging offices and purchasing new furniture. He was deep in thought about something and answered me again with, "I'll leave it up to you." It's a good thing I was honest. I could have absconded with the company and he probably wouldn't have noticed anything but my absence.

It took some doing but I got two of the dwarf guards to come into the office and help me rearrange everything, moving Ev's personal crap into his basement (where it should have been in the first place) and taking that second office for my own. I found some used furniture that matched the rest of what we already had. Saturday saw me moving files around and by Tuesday, I was ready when Sally walked in at noon.

I greeted her with, "C'mon, I want to introduce you to your source of good drinks and great food." I took her downstairs, introduced her to Cassandra, Tommy and Charlie and got her a glass of iced tea in a recyclable glass.

"Cassandra takes care of us. I know you're only working part time but if you get the munchies and nothing in our cupboards suits, just call down. She'll send one of the guys up with whatever you want."

"Nice arrangement. I wish I'd had something like that when I was working before. It would have made life so much easier!"

We spent the afternoon going over what was expected of her, how I did certain things and brought her up to speed on both employees and clients. She, like me, was a mundane who wasn't fazed by out-of-the ordinary folks. After an afternoon of Ev's breezing in and out past her desk, she even made suggestions as to candle brands. I told her I'd happily buy anything she thought would make breathing easier so we brought up her favorite company's website and ordered a couple of cases of candles whose scents we both enjoyed.

I must admit, having help really made a difference. I hadn't been able to concentrate enough over the previous couple of months to do real justice to my book; the editing process was showing me that. Once Sally was firmly ensconced, life returned to pretty much normal. Fudge was even happy that we had reestablished our routine.

I gave Sally and her husband an invitation to Ev's Halloween party. Two more people weren't going to break the bank and it was an easy way to introduce her to a different side of social glitz.

Ev was between steady girlfriends so as usual when that was the case, it fell to me to play hostess. I stood at his side at the door, greeting the costumed guests as they arrived, taking their coats then directing them to the bar and buffet. Sally and Jack arrived, dressed as Professors Dumbledore and McGonagall – in their bedtime attire. I thought it was clever. Much cleverer than Ev's idea of a costume: he painted his face, hands and legs green, changed to a vest and breeches and announced he was Shrek. (Ev didn't think to use theatrical makeup – he used food coloring. He was green-tinged puce for two weeks. A *really* awful color.)

The highlight of the evening was when John (remember him – the vampire?) decided Sally might make a nice snack. He approached her while Jack was freshening their drinks. I watched with amusement from across the room. I could see him start his 'kiss the hand on introduction' thing, immediately drop her hand with a look of horror on his face and make a beeline for the bathroom. I had briefed Sally on the expected guests before we left work on Friday. I made my way over there.

"So, what did you do to fend John off?" I asked.

She giggled. "Jack is friends with a Catholic priest so we always have a little holy water around. I mixed some in with my perfume and had just finished a wee spritz when John came sauntering up. I don't think he liked what he smelled." I giggled, too.

Jack arrived with fresh drinks, including one for me. "How did you know what I was drinking?" I asked him.

"It doesn't take a psychic to know these things – I asked the bartender," he replied. "What are you two giggling so hard about?"

We told him about John and the holy water. He laughed, too. "That's my girl – always thinking ahead. I'd never have thought to mix it in with perfume. I'd just throw a vial on him."

"Which would have made a mess and spoiled Ev's party. I like my way better," Sally smiled at him.

Even with a long nap beforehand, I started yawning about midnight. Although the party was just getting going for the non-humans, most of us day-type people had already left. I was about to ask Gregory to take me home when in the door walked Happy. Without an invitation I might add. For his costume, he'd added a cape. Otherwise, just the same red suit.

"Good evening, Amy," he greeted me. "I heard through the grapevine about this party and was dismayed that I did not receive an invitation."

"That's something you'd need to speak with Ev about. He's the one that made up the guest list – I just sent the invitations. If you'll excuse me, it's late and I'd like to get home."

"Could I persuade you to have one cocktail with me? There's something I'd like to discuss with you. Or I could come by the office on Monday?"

There's no way I wanted Happy in the office again. I acquiesced to another glass of wine and after we'd found Ev so Happy could greet him (Ev was *not* pleased but tried to hide it), made our way to a corner away from the band so we could hear each other.

"I have another prospective friend in mind for you," he started out.

"I thought the last one would have taught you that your idea of a friend and mine are worlds apart," I told him.

"Ah, yes. Jim was a mistake. I had thought since the two of you were logical thinkers that you may get along. I neglected the social side. However, Anthony is not like that. He is sensitive and shares your intellectual interests. Please allow me to introduce you over cocktails one evening. You never know if the man is right until you meet him, do you?"

"How many times do I have to tell you I *do not* want to be fixed up? I like my life just the way it is so no thank you. Please, do not try again. I find it tiring."

I put my half-finished glass of wine down and turned away. Thankfully, Happy didn't follow. I told Ev I was leaving and had Gregory drive me home. It had been such a pleasant evening until the end. Why did he have to spoil it?

It was later in the year and I got to sleep in until nearly 8:00 Sunday morning before the sun woke me up. Sweet! I puttered around the apartment, not doing much until noon, when I felt it was safe to call Ev to make sure the cleaning crew had arrived and was doing its job. I woke him up but after a moment of listening, he assured me there was enough noise going on downstairs that the crew must be there. He didn't want to be bothered to go down to see if it was indeed the crew or if they were doing what they were hired to do. I hung up, wondering why I'd even bothered calling in the first place.

Fudge and I spent a very pleasant afternoon, curled up on the couch with a book. I was usually lazy the day after a party at Ev's, whether I had a hangover or not. Downtime was deserved after so much work, was it not?

Mid-afternoon on Tuesday brought a lot of commotion out in the reception area. I heard Sally yell, "What the hell?" and another voice say something low, in a calming sort of way. Sally retorted a little more quietly with, "That is *so* arrogant and impolite. Just who the hell do you think you are?" Another low, calming-type response, Sally harrumphed and poked her head into my office.

"What's going on out there?" I asked.

"A demon just materialized in the office. No door, no excuse me. Just popped in like he owned the place. Scared the shit out of me. He says his name is Happy and he'd like to speak with you."

I sighed. "Oh crap. I'm never going to get rid of this guy. I'll give him a minute. Just long enough to tell him to go away – again."

"I can tell him you're busy."

"Nah. He'll just come back again. He's irritating that way. I'll come out and you can hear the entire conversation. He's a pain."

"Good afternoon, Amy. I am pleased to see you again," Happy greeted me when I walked out into the reception area. Sally sat back down at her desk and although it looked like she was typing something, I could tell her interest was focused on us, not her computer.

"I'm not pleased to see you. I thought I told you Saturday night that I really wasn't interested in dating anyone at the moment."

"Ah, but as I've said before, you just haven't met the right man. Please, meet us for cocktails one evening this week. He is only in town until Friday."

"Do you have a boss? Someone I can complain to? I have told you to butt out of my life on several occasions but you not only don't take a hint, you don't take a direct statement. I *do not want to date anyone, much less anyone you choose.* Got that? Now go the fuck away."

"Amy, Amy." He shook his head and tsk-tsked a little. "You spend entirely too much time in front of your computer at home, imagining things that you could actually experience. I am simply trying to assist you in fulfilling your dreams." Happy had a smile on his face that promised consequences if I denied him this meeting.

Now I understood what Ev meant when he said Happy could screw things up personally and professionally. Somehow this guy had found out about my writing. Admittedly, if someone cared to do some research, they could link my given name with my pen name but that was something I didn't want outed to Ev or any of our employees or clients. I liked keeping my two lives separate.

Now what was I going to do? I sighed.

"Alright. One cocktail. Nothing further. Thursday night is best for me."

"Wonderful. I'm sure you and Anthony will get along famously. I'll send my car for you at six?" With that, he vanished. No popping noise or anything, just one second he was there and the next he wasn't. No wonder Sally was startled.

"What the hell was that all about?" Sally asked.

"Got time for a drink after work? I'll tell you what's going on but I'd rather do it elsewhere."

"Sure. Jack's out of town again so I don't have to be home at any given time."

I hung around until five, when Sally was finished for the day. It gave me a chance to get a little ahead of Wednesday's work. We headed over to the pub and bellied up to the bar. Cork slid a glass of merlot in front of me and cocked his head at Sally.

"If he just put a glass down in front of you without asking, I presume you come here often," she said to me after answering Cork's unspoken question with, "Chardonnay".

I'd forgotten Sally didn't live in the neighborhood and really had no reason to trot across the street after work. "Usually about once a week when I either don't feel like cooking or simply don't want to be home. It's close and comfortable."

"So what's up with this Happy guy?" she asked.

I related everything that had happened over the last few months, starting with having to play Ev's wife. Then, with a threat of death if she told anyone, I let her in on my writing life.

"*You're* Deidre O'Shaunessy? I hate to say this but Jack hates you. I spend many nights reading your books instead of something more serious. He prefers more intellectual reading like biographies. I promise I won't say anything but wow. I'm impressed."

"Now you know why Happy said the things he did. I've gone to great lengths to conceal my real identity. Hell, I don't allow my photo anywhere, don't do public appearances or anything that would involve my face, much to my publisher's chagrin. If it were to get out, a lot of people Ev hangs around with would figure out they're some of the characters in my books."

"No wonder they're so lifelike. I had admired your imagination, thinking someone had made all those people up. Now that you mention it, I see several people I've met in your characters. Some of our clients and employees would be pissed, no?"

"Yeah, which is why it's so secret. That knowledge could cause all sorts of problems for Ev and me. Maybe even a lawsuit or two. Although my attorney and editor tell me nothing is close enough to real life for anyone to get twitterpated about, you know these types. They'll call their lawyer at the drop of a hat. If Happy let the cat out of the bag, there would be hell to pay all over the place."

"Man, blackmail at its finest. And because he's a demon, not subject to mundane laws and can't even be killed, you have to keep putting up with his interference in your social life to prevent interference in your business life. Can I ask Jack if he's got any suggestions?"

"Sure, if you can describe the situation without letting my alter ego into the conversation. If Jack hates my books, I don't want to think about how it would color our relationship. He's a nice guy and you're lucky to have him."

"Listen, it's not your books he hates. It's the subject matter. He disdains anything he calls 'without substance'. But I won't say anything to him. As a matter of fact, I can put the whole thing off on Ev. Jack knows how Ev is with women and can draw his own conclusions. I need to go. I'd stay here all night but then I'd be too drunk to drive home, much less answer the phone when Jack calls later this evening. Thanks for the drink and story. I'll see what we can come up with to help."

She left me to my musings. Cork slid another glass of wine in front of me, along with a menu. "Looks like you've had a bad day. But you need to eat," he growled. He wasn't mad. Growling was his normal voice. He sounded like someone who sang bass and was a heavy smoker. But he was right. If I didn't eat something, the wine would go directly to my head and I'd have a hangover tomorrow. I really didn't have an appetite, so I chose some French Onion Soup with a side salad. The bread in the soup and on the side should be enough to soak up the alcohol.

An hour or so later, I made my way home. I wasn't drunk but a little tipsy so I decided to head directly for bed. Maybe I could figure out a way out of my problems in my dreams. Right.

CHAPTER 12

Thursday after my nap (which wasn't much of one – I couldn't calm down from my frustrations with Happy), I changed into a boring pantsuit, once again pulling my hair back into a barrette and putting on minimal makeup. Once again, the gnome knocked on my door promptly at six, his dog-chew-toy voice relaying his instructions from Happy.

This time curiosity got the better of me and I slid onto the seat facing backward in the passenger compartment, immediately behind the privacy glass. That way I could turn my head and look into the driver's compartment. What I saw made me giggle.

The gnome used a remote to open the driver's door and climbed up a small ladder to the top of a box that was held in by the seatbelt. Another click of the remote closed the door. He stood on the box, slipping his feet into straps on the top, which I assumed took the place of a seatbelt. With this arrangement, he could just see above the wheel and out the windshield. The steering wheel was almost as large as he was, especially with the gadgets attached to it and the steering column. It was actually an ingenious solution.

The gnome was driving with the kind of car controls they install for handicapped people.

Twenty minutes later, we pulled up at the door of the Radisson by the Mall of America. (Hmmm. Maybe I should go shopping for a new outfit afterward to calm myself down.) The gnome reversed his entry process and once the passenger door was opened, held the bottom of the door in the same way most normal-sized chauffeurs would hold the handle. "Mr. Happy and his guest are in the bar by the fireplace," he said. "I will be right here when you are ready to leave."

I walked into the bar, and saw that Happy was indeed sitting in a chair by the fireplace. His guest was sitting on a couch, with his back to me. I could see dark curls brushing broad shoulders, which filled a silk suit nicely. A familiar-looking ring graced the hand that draped across the back of the couch. Crap. Double crap.

Happy rose as I approached, as did his other guest. "Good evening, Amy. May I introduce you to …"

"We've met," I cut him off. "Hullo, Tony. Long time."

"Amy. Hi. I had no idea …"

I didn't bother making my way into the seating area, much less taking my coat off and sitting down.

"Won't work, Happy. We dated a long time ago. It didn't work out. Thank you but I'm out of here."

"Wait, Amy," Happy said before I could turn to leave. "I believe I know the source of your problem. It can be overcome."

"Listen," I said. "Tony's a nice guy but his species and mine don't get along during certain times of the month."

"I understand," Happy replied. "However, that would not preclude you from enjoying each other's company the other days of the month."

I got frustrated but took a couple of steps closer to the men, in an attempt to keep the conversation somewhat private in a public place. "I thought your whole shtick was to play matchmaker for permanent arrangements. One mistiming on our part ensures my destruction, and I wouldn't be simply slipping away in my sleep. Again, no thanks."

"It wouldn't hurt for us to try again, though," Tony interjected. "I thought we had a good thing going until that one incident. I now have an app for moon phases on my phone that reminds me in case I don't pay attention to what's happening on the inside."

"You're on this slimeball's side?" I asked him.

"I take offense at your adjective," Happy said. "I am merely trying to ensure that everyone finds their special someone. I take great pleasure when I'm able to match up a couple and they're happy."

"I'm sure you do take pleasure," I said, gritting my teeth. "But I won't retract my adjective. You won't leave people alone when requested to do so and you even issue veiled threats if they don't comply with *your* wishes. That's a slimeball in my book."

"Amy, please, sit with us for at least one drink. It won't hurt you," Tony pleaded.

"No, thank you," I said. "Excuse me, but I have better things to do." With that, I turned on my heel and walked out. I'd gotten about half way to the hotel's front door when

Tony caught up to me. I was walking so fast that his hand on my arm stopped me in my tracks and spun me around.

"Amy, I'd consider it a big favor if you'd come back," he said quietly. "As you mentioned, Happy issues veiled threats and the one he gave me could mean my ruin. This isn't the first time he's tried to fix me up but it is the first time he's threatened action if I don't at least meet his current choice of girl. Since you said something about a threat, I'm assuming it's the same with you. Let's have a drink to keep him calm, huh?"

I looked up into those dreamy brown eyes for the first time in several years and once again, felt myself melt. Damn it, but he was hard to say no to.

"One drink. But in exchange for my presence, I want you to figure out how we can get off this guy's radar. I'm tired of him interfering in my life."

"I don't think there's anyone he's meddled with who's not tired of his interference. However, I don't know anyone else in his sphere of … influence, shall we say? It's not something you go around screaming to the world, you know?"

I did know. But the more people working on the problem of Happy, the more likely it would be that we'd all find a solution. I tried to put a pleasant smile on my face as we walked back into the bar.

"Amy, I am so glad you changed your mind," Happy smiled at me. I took my coat off and sat in the chair farthest from the slimeball and as far as I could get from Tony. I ordered my usual gin and tonic from the waiter. At least I was getting free drinks off this creep but it really wasn't worth the price.

The tension was so thick you could have sliced it. This time there wasn't a lot for Happy to say or do since Tony and I knew each other – rather well. So, he stayed more or less silent while the two of us caught up with each other in a stilted conversation. Tony's cell phone rang about twenty minutes in and we both heaved a sigh of relief when he said he needed to return to his hotel room to deal with a client privately.

"I do hope the two of you will find a way to see each other again. I believe you are well-suited to each other, regardless of the differences in species. I will see you both again soon!" Happy said as we all stood to leave. "Amy, my chauffeur will take you anywhere you'd like to go. As you've figured out, he exists only for my friends. I don't need him."

"Thanks but no thanks," I answered. "I will make my own transportation arrangements."

Tony kissed me on the cheek in the lobby before I turned toward the door and he went in the direction of the elevators. "Think about it, will you?" he said. "For once I agree with that sleaze that we make a good pair."

As much as I didn't like Tony's monthly problem, I had to admit that I enjoyed spending time with him in his human form. "I'll think on it but don't get your hopes up," I told him. "And don't call me. I'll call you."

I had some thinking to do so instead of taking any sort of motorized transportation to the mall, I walked the half mile. Once inside, I headed for the food court and grabbed a couple of tacos to absorb the alcohol. Then I started wandering the mall, only half looking in the windows. I wasn't really in the mood to shop, although I still hadn't quite replaced the wardrobe Andy had managed to destroy.

Even though it was only just after Halloween, all the stores had their Christmas decorations out and PA system was playing holiday music. I got even grumpier. Whatever happened to Christmas rolling out the day after Thanksgiving?

After about an hour of aimless wandering, I finally called Cassandra. I needed a sounding board.

"Hi," I said when she answered. "Are you in the mood for some moody company?"

"I take it you need to talk. Tommy was supposed to come over tonight and we were going to watch a movie but I can easily cancel him. Where are you?" was her reply.

"Aw crap. Don't worry about me. Have fun with Tommy, huh?" I said, maybe a little whiny.

"No. If you called and need to talk, that's more important than watching a movie we can see anytime – even tomorrow. I repeat: where are you?"

"I'm at the Mall of America. I can take a taxi and be there in about twenty minutes."

"Nope. I'm coming to you. We need a bar. I'll meet you in the bar at Rodolfo's in a half hour." She hung up.

I killed the thirty minutes by slowly wandering over to where the restaurant was. On the way, I saw a gorgeous teal silk suit in Macy's window and decided to get it. It would do for the office holiday parties I'd be getting invited to. By the time I got to Rodolfo's, my feet were sore from so much walking in heels. I really shouldn't have hoofed it from the hotel to the mall. Two adjoining seats opened up at the bar just as I walked in. I gratefully sat down and had just draped the suit over the other chair to save it for Cassandra when she appeared.

"Are you saving this seat for someone special?" she asked as she took the suit and hung it from the back of my chair.

"Yep. Best friend's coming to be a shoulder," I grinned. "Drinks are on me so what do you want?"

The bartender came over and dropped a couple of cocktail napkins down before asking us the same question. Cassandra ordered a chocolate martini, I asked for another gin and tonic. I never did develop a taste for martinis.

"So, what do you need my shoulder for?" she asked when the drinks arrived.

I related the recent events with Happy, finishing up with what Tony had said in the hotel lobby.

"Wow. You've certainly got a situation on your hands. Ignoring the issue of Tony for the moment, you need to get this Happy guy out of everyone's lives."

"No shit. I just have no idea how to do it. He's a *demon* for chrissake. He can pop in and out whenever he wants, wherever he wants and I have no doubt he could make good on his threats."

"Listen. I have a great-uncle in England who loves to do research on magic, spirits, elementals and the like. As a matter of fact, that's what he spends most of his time doing. If you like, I can email him to see if he's got any suggestions."

At this point, I was willing to entertain any and all suggestions for getting this guy out of my life. OK, out of everyone's life. But selfishly, I didn't really care about anyone else at the moment. I was wallowing in self-pity.

"On to the subject of Tony," she said after we agreed she'd email her Uncle Morris without going into too much detail to see if he had any ideas.

"Wait. I just woke up. You said you were going to watch a movie at home with *Tommy*?" I said.

Cassandra blushed. I'd never seen her blush. With skin nearly as pale as mine, she did indeed turn radish-red when she was embarrassed.

"We've been sort of seeing each other since the incident with Andy. I've been trying to keep it on the QT since he works for me."

"I can understand keeping it from Charlie and your customers, but me?" I was put out. "I thought we shared secrets. And he's been working for you for several years without you looking in his direction. What changed?"

"I don't know. There was something about the fact that he's a wizard that made me look at him in a different light. I always thought he was attractive and nice but since I know I'm going to live longer than a normal human, I avoid getting involved with them. I don't want the heartache of falling in love and watching someone grow old while I stay relatively young."

"I thought witches could sense each other. So he'd been working for you and you had no idea?"

"Tommy had a problem in his prior job and put up strong shielding so no one would know. I sensed the shield but didn't think much of it because there's no indication of magic behind it. I can sense yours, too, you know, and you're not a magic practitioner. He's good at hiding his capabilities. When he lets his shield weaken, I can sense his strength. He's scary strong!"

She took a sip of her drink. "After his last job, he was afraid I'd get worried about him if I knew he was a wizard. It must be a guy thing. His old boss was also a wizard and apparently thought Tommy would be competition or something. Anyways, after the thing with Andy, we did a lot of talking. I like his cooking, he likes the laid-back atmosphere of the deli and we both dig magic. Not to mention that he doesn't mind watching chick-flicks on occasion. So far it's working well but it's only been a couple of months. I'm reserving judgment."

"Logical to a fault," I told her.

"So blame the Virgo in me. Now, what are you going to do about Tony?"

I had no idea what I was going to do about Tony. I really did like the guy but the fact that he morphed into a monster thirteen times a year creeped me out. I'd already written my heart out about him in my first book but at least there, the wizard's potion worked. I couldn't say the same in real life.

"You don't need a potion to make it work," Cassandra looked thoughtful. "He's obviously figured a way to deal with it or he wouldn't be so successful in the business world. I know a lot of weres are Grizzly Adams types or at least have mountain cabins so when they change they're already in a wild environment. If you really like him, maybe you ought to try again. You know, there's a reason he came back into your life, even if it was through that creep."

"Your sight isn't telling you anything? I could really use some help here. My emotions are all muddled. I don't know what to do." My third drink was taking effect. I was almost in tears.

"I'm not getting any visions about you two, if that's what you're asking. It's time to get you home. I'll do a reading tomorrow night when I'm thinking more clearly and see what the cards have to say. C'mon, pay the nice man and let's get out of here."

I paid the tab, Cassandra grabbed my suit and we made our way to the nearest door. She'd taken a taxi instead of driving so all we had to do was hail the first taxi in line at the stand. That was a good thing. I don't think I could have walked all the way to a car in the parking lot. My feet were killing me.

Cassandra had the cab driver drop me off first even though her house was closer and I gratefully hobbled down the stairs and into the apartment. I went into the bedroom and while I hung up the new suit, took my shoes off. Flat feet felt like heaven. After changing into my pajamas, I grabbed a basin, Epsom salts and bottles of peppermint and eucalyptus essential oils. I made up my soak and took the basin into the living room. After I'd situated myself on the couch, I gratefully sunk my feet into the warm water. Fudge curled up in my lap and we watched television while the foot soak did its thing. Fifteen minutes later I dried my feet and poured the used liquid out. I could walk again.

Happy wasn't to be deterred. The next afternoon I heard Sally swear and say, "Can't you just use the door like normal people?" I only knew one person who didn't come through the door. I sighed and left my desk.

"What the hell are you doing here again?" I asked Happy.

"I thought I would see if you had come to any conclusions about Anthony. It was obvious from your facial expressions last night that you have some feelings for the man."

"You could have used the phone for that. Simply materializing in the office isn't polite. What if there had been a client waiting to see me or Ev?"

"Ah, but I always look before I pop and I assumed you would rather see me here than at your apartment. And there is nothing like a face-to-face conversation to determine how a situation is going."

"In answer to your question, I haven't come to any conclusions. The fact that he changes into a monster and that I've seen that transformation up close and personal gives me the willies. It's hard to become enamored of someone with visions of long, sharp teeth sinking themselves into your flesh. Now, go away. I'm sure you have your ways of finding out if Tony and I see each other again. I have work to do."

"Before you go back to work, I have one suggestion," Happy said before I could even turn around. "I can make you forgot those teeth if you will allow me."

"Let you into my head? No way in hell. I like all my memories intact, thank you. *If* I decide to see Tony again, it will be with full knowledge of his faults. Otherwise, the relationship would be built on a lie and those don't last very long. That wouldn't be in accordance with your plans and hopes, would it?"

Happy pouted. "But it would only be temporary, I assure you. It would help you get over the hump, so to speak."

"No, no, and hell no again. Go away, Happy and do your plotting elsewhere."

"I will see you again. Enjoy the rest of your day." With that and a small smile, Happy dematerialized.

"Man, that guy is getting more than irritating," Sally said. "I'm so glad I'm happily married. Do you know how to shield? If he's thinking about messing with your mind, you ought to learn if you don't."

"Cassandra already taught me the basics a few years ago after she noticed I was getting all jittery at those damned parties. She said it would help with all the paranormal types I was around. Apparently, they put out weird energies."

"That's what Jack says and he taught me years ago, too. But I think you ought to check into shielding against mind attacks. That's completely different than warding off unwanted energy."

"I'll ask Cassandra, then. I'm supposed to talk with her tonight anyways. Thanks for the info."

I walked back into my office and tried to get back to work. I was still having difficulty concentrating. There was too much drama going on in my life and I couldn't quit chewing on it. I finally gave it up and left work a little early.

CHAPTER 13

I ducked into the deli on my way home. I wanted to talk with Cassandra about the shielding issue. As always, she was busy helping customers get their afternoon caffeine and sugar fix so I waited at a table until she had a free moment. She brought a couple of cups of coffee over to the table with her.

"What's up?" she asked. "I was going to call you tonight after I had a chance to do a reading for you."

"I have more immediate issues," I replied, then told her about what Happy had said about making me forget Tony's teeth.

"This guy is really getting to be a major pain in the ass," she said. "Hang on a sec." She left the table and went back into the kitchen. A minute or two later, she came back out with Tommy in tow.

"Tommy's a lot better at shielding than I am," Cassandra said. "I hope you don't mind but I've already told him about your demon problem and just told him about the latest issue."

"No, I don't mind. At this point, I'll take as many people thinking on it as I can get. Do you have any ideas, Tommy?"

"About how to get rid of him, no, but keeping him out of your brain, yes. Shielding your mind is a lot more difficult than simply blocking unwanted energy," Tommy told me. "I think you can do it. You've got a strong mind but it will take some work on your part."

"I'm willing to do whatever it takes to keep this sleaze out of my head. Will you teach me?" I asked.

Tommy looked at Cassandra and she nodded. "Sure. Come over to Cassandra's house about seven. We'll order dinner in and then get to work."

With that, I was content. They went back to work and I went home. I wanted to get another part of a chapter written in my latest book but my mind just wouldn't focus on the characters' lives. I was too caught up in my own at the moment. Once again, I killed a couple of hours playing mahjong and flipping between social networking sites. Just before seven, I walked over to Cassandra's house.

The weather matched my mood. It was late in the year and already dark outside. There was a hint of snow in the air. Unless I missed my guess, we'd be getting an early winter. I shoved my already-gloved hands in my jacket pockets and snuggled down into the collar of my jacket.

As I walked, I became more and more determined to thwart Happy's attempts at interference. Step number one was the shielding. I would do whatever Tommy said, no matter how strange it seemed or how difficult it was. Step number two was figuring out how to get rid of him altogether. I had a lot of people thinking about that problem. Thus far no one had come up with a solution, and if no one did, push come to shove, he could out my writing. I'd have to figure out a way to deal with it. The threats he'd made to others were their problems, although I'd feel bad if Tony lost his business.

I was also curious and would ask Tommy tonight: I didn't think Happy could get through the wards on my building. Otherwise, he'd probably already have visited me at home. Was there a way to shield the office in the same way?

Cassandra had the door open before I could even raise my hand to knock. She had a grin on her face. "We've already ordered pizza and it should be here shortly. Are you ready for a witchy evening?"

"I've never had it described to me in quite that way. Yes, I think I'm ready. Determined, anyways. Hi, Tommy," I greeted him as I hung up my coat. "Hi to you, too, Merlin." I couldn't get away without greeting the true master of the house who had come up to check out my pants and shoes. I reached down and rubbed his ears until he was satisfied with my efforts and walked off.

Tommy had just handed me a glass of wine when a knock at the door announced the arrival of dinner. The guy from Pizza And More greeted Cassandra and seeing me, smiled. "Do you two spend every Friday night eating pizza at one of your places?" he asked. (We'd had the same delivery person for about three years.)

"Not every Friday night. Just a lot of them," Cassandra laughed as she handed him the money and took the boxes out of his hands. "Go on with you. See you in a couple of weeks."

We four promptly devoured the pizzas. (Merlin, just like Fudge, received the first piece.) Talk was minimal since our mouths were full most of the time. Once the boxes had been thrown into the fire roaring in the fireplace, Tommy told Cassandra to go ahead and do her reading. He thought I'd be too tired to absorb what she said later on.

She went into her workroom and came back with a box in one hand and a small piece of black velvet in the other. After spreading the velvet on the floor in front of the fireplace, she gestured for me to sit opposite her. Tommy leaned forward from his spot on the couch.

Merlin crawled into Cassandra's lap. She opened the box and pulled out a deck of cards. They were beautifully illustrated, not cartoon-y like some decks I'd seen, and visibly well-used.

After shuffling the cards a bit, she asked me to cut them, concentrating on my relationship with Tony. I gave the cards back to her and she fanned them out on the velvet. "Still keeping Tony in mind, pick five cards," she instructed. I selected five, handing them to her as I pulled them out.

Cassandra looked at the cards for a minute after she'd laid them all out and then blew out a breath. "Wow. So, let me tell you what I'm seeing."

She pointed to one of the cards. "This first card in the middle signifies what's happening right now. It is the Page of Wands, but it's upside down. We call that reversed. It signifies confusion or indecision. Usually when someone is undecided about something, their entire life is unstable. I knew that already but this confirms it.

"The second card over here to the left of the first is about something in the past that's still having an influence on the present. It is, obviously, The Moon. Normally it means a period of change but in this case, I think we can take it literally. Tony's little problem is made evident by the moon and his problem is what's kept you apart."

She paused for a moment, then pointed at another card. "The third card, to the right of the first is about the future. You drew the Two of Cups, reversed. The suit of cups has to do with love or relationships. This card in this position I'm reading as love with some disruptions along the way. In other words, you and Tony *can* have a relationship but it's not going to be an easy one. If you choose to get involved with him again, be aware that you're going to experience problems. But like in most relationships, you can work through a lot of those problems.

"The fourth card, here, is about the underlying reason for your question. You're a pretty analytical person so you already know why you're asking but the card you drew is the Knight of Swords, reversed. It indicates someone not to be trusted. I'd say that would be Happy. And I'd say you already know not to trust the creep, huh?"

At the mention of Happy's name, my stomach tensed and my fist curled. I took a huge breath to relax myself.

I must have made a noise. A look of concern crossed Cassandra's face but after seeing me relax, she continued, "This last card speaks to the potential of the situation you're asking about. It's the World, reversed. It means that whatever you're working on, in this case, your relationship with Tony, will be delayed. However, the delay is temporary and everything will eventually work out.

"Did I answer you?"

OK, that was a lot to think about but I nodded yes. So, I was supposed to get re-involved with him, it wasn't going to be smooth sailing and oh by the way, we had to get Happy out of our lives. That last was a "duh". I guess it was time to call him and talk.

"Can you concentrate on learning to shield after finding that out?" Tommy asked.

"Yes, I think so. I got the answer I was looking for and I can't really do much else until I talk with Tony. I know he's out and about since it's Friday night so I'll call him tomorrow afternoon." I looked at Cassandra. "How do you feel about having a werewolf in the family?" She laughed. "If you can keep his teeth tucked in, I won't have any problem at all."

I looked back at Tommy. "Now, what do I need to do? Is this something I'm going to have to concentrate on all the time with no room for any other thought?"

"No. Once you get the hang of it, it will be very similar to the basic shielding you're already doing. According to Cassandra, you know how to strengthen your shield at parties or any time you're around a lot of non-humans. You'll do the same when that guy is around. Ready?" Tommy rubbed his hands together. It was time to get down to work.

When Cassandra had taught me to shield, she said to envision a bubble of light around me. The first time I tried,

I almost suffocated myself. Apparently, the bubble was too strong and I'd managed to cut off my air supply! (Who knew that could happen?) She finally got me to imagine a cocoon of screening material. The holes were large on a normal basis and I simply shrunk the size of the holes when I felt it necessary to do so. Sort of like the difference between keeping bees and gnats out of the house.

Cassandra told me she doesn't even think about her shield unless she gets an itchy feeling about something. I'm not that tuned into it. It only took one argument between Ev and one of the dwarf guards to remind me to think about it. Now I do my imagining each morning while I'm doing my stretching and I do the "shrinking" when something in the air at work gives me a warning, or as I'm checking myself in the mirror prior to leaving for a party.

On this particular night, Tommy taught me a different sort of shield. This one was imposed over my normal layer of protection, enveloped only my head and looked like it was a screen made of razor wire with all of the sharp points facing away from me. (At least that's the way I saw it in my head.)

"I have no ability to invade people's minds so I can't test it," Tommy said. "But I can feel it. It's not pleasant. Were I you, I'd tighten the weave to nearly solid when that guy is around. Just try not to suffocate yourself again, huh?"

"OK. I'll work on it," I said. "Now I have another question." I proceeded to ask about shielding the office like my apartment.

"I'm not sure that's possible," Cassandra said. "You and your neighbors have lived in that building for years and you all like and support each other a lot. You've formed a family and that produces love. That love builds up over time and forms its own shield that in our terms is called a threshold. It puts a secondary wall up behind Mr. Owens' wards. Because love is so powerful and the nasties can't comprehend it, they can't go past that wall. I found it very interesting that Andy could get past both wards. He shouldn't have been able to. I've thought about it and the only explanation I can think of is that his obsession is also a form of love and somehow, that allowed him through.

"The office, on the other hand, doesn't have that protection. Sure, you, Ev and Sally like each other but it's not love. Even if it was, there are entirely too many non-family members, if you will, going in and out to allow that love shield to build up.

"With Tommy's help, I've already strengthened the wards on the building to the best of our abilities. We did it mostly to prevent another episode like Andy. It's obvious that isn't keeping Happy away. I'm sorry, Amy, but I don't know anything else to do."

I heaved a sigh. "I trust you guys. If you say nothing can be done well then, nothing can. We'll just have to figure out a way to get rid of Happy permanently. Can we change the subject to something more positive, now? Like, what's up with you two?"

Cassandra blushed again. While she looked good in red clothing, red on her face wasn't attractive at all. Tommy even had the good graces to blush a little.

"I always thought 'Dra was a hot chick. More than that, I liked the way she thought about a lot of things. I just had to wait for her to decide I was worth a second look," Tommy said.

"'Dra?" I was confused.

"She won't let me call her Cass or Cassie, and Cassandra's too much of a mouthful on a regular basis. She doesn't look like a Sandy, does she?"

"Nope." I said and turned to Cassandra. "I never thought you'd let anyone give you a nickname. 'Dra's clever, though and since you haven't punched his lights out, I assume you're OK with it?"

Cassandra blushed even deeper, if that was possible. "Mom will never let me hear the end of it when she hears that for the first time. She's the one who instilled the whole full-name thing into me. But coming from him, I like it. You, on the other hand, may not give me a pet nickname!"

I laughed and told her I'd obey. "So, you mentioned your Mom. I take it that means there's a meeting with the parents in the offing?"

"Yeah. They're biting the bullet and coming here for Yule. Dad doesn't like winter anymore but since I want them to meet Tommy and we can't both be gone from the deli at the same time, they're coming here instead of us going there. Tommy's dad has agreed to come to my house for Yule so it's going to be a party. It'll be the first time since my folks moved that we'll be here for Yule and I'm going to go all out. You'll help me, right?"

"Naturally. I'll even cook stuff if you write out exact instructions for whatever it is."

"Cooking isn't really the issue. As you well know, I like to do that even on my off days and now that I have a really good sous-chef …" She smiled at Tommy and there was more than just friendship in her eyes. "I was thinking more about decorating the house. You know, tree, lights, the whole nine."

"Oh, you want Christmas decorations. That I can do. My folks used to double their electricity bill for the month between Thanksgiving and Christmas. Sure, I'll be happy to help."

Cassandra frowned. "I know you come from a Christian background but we celebrate at the winter solstice – a couple of days before Christmas. The tree is definitely pagan in nature. All the lights and stuff are just plain fun. However, unless you want to get into a very long theological discussion with my dad, don't mention Christmas, OK? He gets all hot under the collar about it."

It was my turn to be embarrassed. "Sorry. I didn't know I was stepping on any toes. But this celebrating at the solstice explains why you always left for Arizona so early and why Tommy always closed the deli around the twenty-first of the month instead of the twenty-fourth. Makes a lot more sense, now. No problemo, though. I'll still help. And I'll try to keep my mouth shut around your dad. Theology never was my strong suit. If you want to get the best decorations, we'd better start shopping now. Sad to say but now that Halloween has passed, it's full-on Christmas shopping season. Do you have any ideas on what you want to do?"

We spent the next hour planning what we would need based on the way she wanted the house to look. Tommy took one look at two women in the throes of a decorating discussion and beat a hasty retreat to Cassandra's workroom. Shortly thereafter I heard some harp music and a lovely aroma wafted its way out of that room. Cassandra interrupted our conversation long enough to tell me that Tommy spent his spare time creating magical oils for one need or another. Her house smelled lovely whenever he was there.

Finally, about eleven we both started yawning. I could sleep in but she had to get up early to open the shop so it was time I was on my way. (Not to mention that Fudge would be looking for dinner.) I went into the workroom to say goodnight to Tommy and he handed me a small vial of oil.

"Dab a drop of this on your pillow each night and on the back of your office chair each morning. It will help you keep that shield up."

I took a whiff of it and it smelled wonderful. I thanked him and said goodnight. Then I hugged Cassandra and walked home.

Halfway home it started to snow. Not heavily, just light flakes, but enough to remind me that the holiday season was fast approaching and for the first time since my folks died, I had somewhere to spend the festive days. And, perhaps, someone to spend them with. It all depended on what Tony had to say.

CHAPTER 14

I slept really late on Saturday. When I finally opened my eyes I discovered why the sun hadn't woken me up at its usually insane hour and why Fudge was still curled up next to me. The sun hadn't been able to break through the heavy cloud cover. There was an inch or more of snow on the ground and it was still coming down. I was right: we were in for an early winter. This was the earliest snowfall I could remember in many years. Days like this I always wished I had a fireplace. There's something about snow and a fireplace that naturally go together. I made do by lighting a lot of candles.

I thought about the previous night as I sipped my coffee and stared at one of the large candles I had going on my étagère. I really did like Tony but were my feelings strong enough to put up with his affliction? Honestly? Yes. I had entertained thoughts of a long-term relationship until that one fateful evening. If we could find a way to deal with it, I thought I could be happy with him.

Happy. Hmm. He was the thorn in everyone's collective side. Not living on that side of the fence, I couldn't think of a way to get rid of a demon so I'd have to rely on my friends to come up with a solution. I could do all the research in the world (if I even had a clue where to start looking) but I wouldn't know what to do with what I found. Since he was seriously into research, I hoped Cassandra's Uncle Morris would find something.

By mid-afternoon I figured Tony would have finally woken from the previous night's revel so I called. I got his voice mail. I almost hung up but then screwed up my courage. "Tony, it's Amy. We need to talk. Call me before Monday, OK?"

I couldn't get into the correct frame of mind to write a romance story when my own love life was so screwed up. I spent the day cleaning. That evening I tried to read but couldn't concentrate on anything. Television was my last bastion and I lost myself in two of the Harry Potter movies. One of the family channels was having a marathon weekend which suited me fine. It was after midnight when I was finally sleepy enough to go to bed. The snow still fell.

The next morning, I was on my second cup of coffee, staring out at a thick blanket of white when the phone rang. Caller ID said it was Tony. I started shaking as I reached for my phone and it had nothing to do with caffeine overload.

"I'm glad you called," he said when I answered the phone.

"What are you doing up so early?" I asked. "It's not even ten in the morning my time. You must have a plane to catch or something."

"Actually, I was in Vancouver when I got your message yesterday. I took the red eye this morning and just arrived home. I thought it best if I was comfortable when we talked. So, what's on your mind?"

"I'm not sure where to start. Tony, I really like you but your species scares the bejeezus out of me. That last time together had me shaking in my boots for days. I don't want a repeat, y'know?"

"Amy, I have tried to apologize. Normally I pay close attention to not only the moon phases but my body's reaction to them. I know when to disappear or at least sequester myself. That has never happened to me before or since. I knew it was the full moon but I wanted to see you. That wizard told me his potion was fail-proof and I wouldn't change when the moon came up that night. Obviously, it didn't work. I would have never even come to the Twin Cities if I'd thought I'd change. It scared me, too. Not only that I was with you but that I was around humans at all that night. It wasn't a pleasant night in my hotel room, and I can tell you that I paid a hefty damage fee when I checked out the next day.

"As I told you Thursday night, I now have a moon phase app on my cell phone just in case I get caught up in something and don't pay attention to my body. I've always planned around the full moon, made sure my schedule is clear and gotten out of town a couple of days before. This is my belt-and-suspenders approach.

I really want to be able to see you the other twenty-some days of the month. I enjoy our time together. Please, can't we try again?"

I was quiet for a moment, trying to sort out my feelings and reflecting on Cassandra's reading Friday night.

"I'd like to try again, too," I finally said. "But there's the large question looming over our heads: Happy. What do we do about him? He'll probably figure he's the reason we're together and ask for whatever payment he generally gets when one of his matches works. I don't want to know his price, much less pay it."

"I'm with you there but I don't know what to do about him. And I don't think telling him he's not the reason we're seeing each other is going to work."

Just then, my computer beeped at me. I had a new email message. While I thought about what Tony had said, I opened my inbox to find an email from Cassandra with the subject line, "Uncle Morris". I told Tony to hang on a minute and opened the message to discover she'd forwarded the following to me:

My dear Cassandra,

What a pleasant surprise to hear from you. I am very glad that you and the deli are doing well.

It wasn't pleasant, however, to read the actual reason for your message. While I will admonish you not to get involved with demons (as if you did not know this already), I will answer your question as best I can from the research I have conducted over the centuries.

There are various levels of demons. The ones seen most often on our plane and in human-like form have been relegated here by their superiors as punishment for some infraction of their rules. One may **call** *a demon in ritual, yes, but these generally do not completely materialise. If the witch or wizard is most careful in calling, they are banished back to their realm immediately upon completion of their* *task.*

I do not know the demon you referenced, but that is not surprising. There are three levels in the demon hierarchy, with **thousands** *in the lowest. I would surmise the one you referenced is of the lowest level. He has only to fulfill his punishment to be reunited with his peers. They generally do not like our realm so they make every effort to return home as soon as possible.*

It may be that his infraction was to fall in love with someone. Love is frowned upon in their realm as an unnecessary emotion. Power is all that counts. His punishment is to play 'Cupid' on this plane (although Cupid probably does not like that comparison). Once he has united a couple in whatever form of marriage appropriate to that species, the two united souls will also become demons. His superiors are always looking for ways to increase their numbers. The more demons they have under their control, the more power they have. He, naturally, has a quota and apparently, hasn't yet met that quota.

I would caution your friend not to become attached to **anyone** *this demon may introduce her to, no matter the attraction, unless she relishes the thought of becoming a demon.*

I can not immediately think of a way to get this demon out of your friend's life without knowing his real name. Should you be able to find that out, I do have a ritual that will banish him back to his realm, at least temporarily. He will be returned here by his superior to fulfill his punishment but as time moves differently there, it will not be for one or two hundred of our years.

If your friend is not human (has an extended life span) and wishes to be 'permanently' rid of this demon, she will need to participate in the spell because she will need the protection the spell will also offer. If he is banished by spellwork, his punishment will undoubtedly be extended for being so caught. He will not be happy and could make her life miserable.

Please give my love to your mother when next you speak with her.

Your Ever Loving,

Morris

I read Morris' message to Tony. "If we can figure out his name, you and I have plenty of witch friends to do the spell. But how do we find out his name?" he asked.

"I know some other folks who are also irritated with Happy. Let me make a few phone calls and spread the word. Maybe with a network we can find it out." I took a deep breath. "Back to us."

"As much as I'd like to hop on a plane and be with you in a few hours," he said, "I think it best that we confine ourselves to the telephone until we figure out what to do about Happy. Since he doesn't appear to use a telephone much at all, it seems to me he wouldn't be able to track electronic conversations the same way he can face-to-face meetings. The energies have got to be different. I'll make a couple of calls, too, to widen the network. There are a few folks out here in the same boat as me. We just need to make sure he doesn't get wind of the fact that someone is searching out his true name. He could make it unpleasant for us all.

"Amy, I can't tell you how glad I am that you're going to give us another chance. That said, I'm bushed and need to catch a few hours of shut-eye before a film premiere tonight. I'll call you in a few days, OK?"

With that, we said our goodbyes. I hung up, feeling more optimistic about things than I had in quite some time. I might have a boyfriend again and I might get an irritant out of my life. I poured another cup of coffee and called Cassandra.

"Hiya. What'd you think about Uncle Morris' reply?" is how she answered the phone.

"I was on the phone with Tony when I got the message. We both think your uncle has a good idea. The question now is Happy's real name. We're both going to put out feelers to see if we can find it."

"Tony, huh? So, you two getting back together?" I heard a male voice warble the old song *Love is in the Air* in the background. Tommy definitely needed to keep his day job. He sang off-key. Then I heard an "oomph", cutting off the song. I assume Cassandra elbowed him.

"Not immediately," I admitted. "We don't want Happy to think he's the one who got us together and exact whatever payment he does. But we will try again, yes."

"Oh, that's so cool. I know you really like him most of the time." She giggled and I heard her say, "Quit that!"

"Listen, go back to your Sunday," I said. "Tell Tommy I said hello and then stuck my tongue out at him. I'll see you tomorrow." I hung up.

Since I'd cleaned the house the day before, I had the entire day to write. Now that I was in the correct frame of mind, I started in on a new book rather than edit. For some reason, the protagonists were a witch and a wizard. If it came out like I thought it would, I was going to be in trouble with Cassandra. Tommy, too. But it was such a fun story!

I took a break around four. I wanted my nap but had a call to make first: to Bella.

"What a pleasant surprise to hear from you! How are you, my dear?" she said after I'd identified myself.

"I'm fine. Well, sort of. I have something you may be able to help with and solving it would benefit you, as well." I related *my* problems with Happy and the gist of Uncle Morris' email.

"Now that *is* interesting news!" she said. "Your friend's uncle may be on to something. I admit that research in the dusty and musty tomes isn't my thing but I know a lot of folks absolutely adore collecting that sort of knowledge. I'll call Adamo and a few other people who have had occasion to dislike Happy. If we come up with anything, I'll let you know."

I'd set the wheels in motion with them and would speak with Ev the next morning. Knowing that things were in the works, I easily fell asleep.

It was still dark when my alarm went off the next morning. It was that time of year, plus the snow was half way up the window. Mr. Owens hadn't gotten around to shoveling and I knew it was going to be a real climb up my stairs to the sidewalk. Fudge and I went through our normal morning routine and I pulled on old jeans and boots under my skirt for the trudge to the office.

The city plows were just clearing the side streets, making hills of snow at all the corners. Some shop owners were already out, scraping off the sidewalk in front of their buildings. Tommy was up early, doing the honors in front of the deli. "You've got a guest already this morning," he grinned.

Man, people before coffee. This day was not starting out well. Mario was waiting outside the office door for me. I couldn't help but stare and ask, "What are you doing here so early? You're normally up until the wee hours."

"I actually got a decent night's sleep last night. Ed's not much of a night owl. I wanted to tell you in person about last night rather than just send in a report. This guy is bizarre!" (Mario was currently following around a new client - one of those rich nobodies.)

"OK but let me put some coffee on, first. You can probably use it and I definitely need it. I used up all my caffeine energy walking over here." I made a beeline for the kitchen.

As soon as we both had a steaming mug in front of us, Mario started in.

"As you know from my reports, the first few days were normal. All I did was follow him from meeting to meeting. But yesterday he said he needed to go up to Alexandria. Why a commodities broker would need to go up there is beyond me but if that's what he wanted to do, that's where we were going.

"We went directly to the museum and he made a beeline for the Kensington Runestone."

He stopped. I know I had a blank look on my face. "The what?" I asked.

"It's a slab of sandstone with runes carved on it," he explained. "It's really controversial. If what it says is true, Scandinavians came to Minnesota a lot earlier than the history books tell us. Some scholars say it's genuine, others say it's a hoax. Anyways, the translation is just about a voyage over here. It's not magical or anything.

"Like I was saying, he made a beeline for the runestone and there was a guy standing by it who turned when Ed approached. This guy, whoever he was, positively screamed magic. Most of us shield but he certainly didn't. They talked for a bit, the guy took out a piece of paper and when the guard wasn't looking, reached *through* the protective Plexiglas which even I can't do. He took a rubbing off the runestone and wrote something else onto the paper, as well. He handed it to Ed who jammed it into a pocket as the guy walked away. We left, too. Two hours each way for a five minute meeting?"

He shook his head. Yet another idiotic activity he had to put up with from our weird clients. "Naturally, I couldn't hear what they said but it wasn't my business anyway. When we got back to the city, Ed told me to take the rest of the day off and he'd see me this morning. That in and of itself is unusual as this guy is scared of his own shadow. I have to damned near tuck him in at night, making sure all the windows are secure and putting a magical lock on the hotel door as I'm leaving. I was curious so just hung out in the hallway outside his door to see if I could pick up anything.

"I didn't hear or feel anything until about an hour later when I felt the snap of a spell going off and heard a commotion inside the room. I barged back in to find Ed naked, painted in what I presume was woad and fighting with a spirit who looked just like a Viking. I banished the spirit and then asked Ed just what the hell was going on. He told me to mind my own business and reminded me that he'd already dismissed me for the day. What could I do? I left. I'm supposed to be back at his hotel in an hour.

"Amy, I've guarded some strange folks but a non-magical person who wants to play with spirits takes the cake. And in the nude? I'm not sure what's going on but I can't protect someone who dismisses me. What do you think I should do?"

You see what I have to deal with at work? No wonder I don't want to quit my day job. The pool of book characters just keeps growing.

"I'll tell Ev what you said. Maybe he knows something we don't. In the meantime, I'd just keep on keepin' on with him. You've only got another three days unless he renews the contract. Unless he makes you too uncomfortable?" I was sure Ev would just snort at this story. He's undoubtedly seen even weirder in his time, but I couldn't imagine what that might be.

Mario shrugged his shoulders, downed the rest of his coffee and left. I wrote myself a note to talk with Ev about it and finally got around to starting my day.

I was surprised that among the many, there was no message from Ed on the answering machine. Apparently, Mario's barging in on his play, or whatever it was, wasn't too big a transgression.

When Ev and his odor finally drifted into the office, I related what Mario had told me.

"Aw, crap," Ev said. "I've heard of the guy. He's an unscrupulous wizard based out of Dallas who preys on non-magical people. I'm not sure how he gets his customers but for a whole bunch of money, he offers spells to fulfill your fantasies. I'm surprised the Wizards' Council hasn't come down on him, although I haven't heard of any nasty outcomes of his spells. Anyways, based on what you said, it sounds like Ed bought one of those spells, wanting to pretend he was a Highlander fighting a Viking invasion. I'll call Mario. I don't think it's anything to worry about."

I logged onto my home computer and added the wizard to my character notes. I could see him fitting into my current witch/wizard love story quite easily!

An hour later, I was buried in payroll when I heard a throat clearing. In my peripheral vision, I saw a red suit standing in front of my desk. Without looking up from my work, I said, "What the hell do you want now?" At the same time, I mentally tightened the razor wire shield.

"Ah, Amy. I had hoped to change your mind regarding Anthony. I can see you have changed your shielding and I think this is an indication that your answer is still 'no'. I would like to know what I can do to convince you that the two of you would make an excellent couple."

"Happy, we've been over this too many times. Tony's species scares me and quite frankly, I like my life the way it is. Go bother someone else. As you can see, I have work to do."

"Then I will continue my search for a mate for you in the human community. I bid you a good day." With that, he dematerialized. I let out the breath I was holding. Ev came into my office.

"Wow. I heard his voice and came to investigate. Did you just completely get rid of him?" he asked.

"At least for now, I hope so," I said. "Hey, while I'm thinking about it …" I told him about Uncle Morris' idea.

"If we can find the name and do the spell," he said, "we'd need to rent a ballroom to hold all the people who are pissed at him. I'll see if my grandfather can figure out who he is. He's been around a long time and knows all sorts of people who know all sorts of stuff. I'm surprised no one else has come up with this idea. I think it's great!

"By the way, I need about a thousand in petty cash. As long as you've got the checkbook out, write me a check, huh?"

I wondered who he had to bribe for what but refrained from asking. I'd find a receipt for something innocuous on my desk the next morning. I dashed off a check and handed it to him.

"Thanks. I gotta go. I'll be out of cell phone coverage until tomorrow."

Ev and Sally exchanged greetings as they passed each other at the door.

CHAPTER 15

Later that afternoon, Sally patched a call through to me without announcing it. That was strange but I understood as soon as I heard, "Hi, Doll. I couldn't wait," on the other end of the line.

"Happy was in here this morning, trying to fix us up again," I said. "Are you sure he can't tell if we talk on the phone?"

"No, I'm not sure about anything when it comes to demons. But since I wanted to talk with you again, I threw caution to the wind. How's your day going apart from an unwanted visitor?"

As much as I'd love to stop everything and just listen to him breathe, I really had work to do. "Tell you what, I'll call you back when I get home. It'll be on two cell phones then, instead of one of us on a landline so it might be even safer. Plus I really do need to get some stuff done before the mailman comes."

"I have a lunch meeting so I'll call *you*. Probably about seven your time, OK? Imagine I'm kissing you goodbye." I heard nothing but the dial tone on the other end. Bastard. Now I had to work while a vivid memory of his kisses swirled around in my head. I squirmed in my chair, mentally slapped myself upside the head and went back to work.

I floated out of my office at four. Sally grinned. "I expect a full report tomorrow … how long you talked, what he said, how he sounded." I grinned back. "Aye, aye, Captain!"

I'm not one to kiss and tell (much) but suffice it to say that we both had to plug our phones in long before the conversation was finished. Thank goodness for unlimited minutes! I floated once again, this time to bed, where I had very pleasant dreams, thank you.

Tony had business meetings all over the country for the next week, so our daily conversations were limited to brief recaps of our days. But the following Monday when he called, he was at home and we had time to chat.

"I know we agreed we weren't going to meet in person until after the issue with Happy was resolved, but I can't wait any longer. This Friday is the dark of the moon so I'm perfectly safe and I've got an idea."

I was growing eager to renew our relationship in person as well, so I said, "I'm listening."

"A friend has a cabin up near the Boundary Waters," he explained. "I've borrowed it in the past and I know for a fact he isn't using it this weekend. This time of year sucks that far north but the cabin is on a road that's always plowed and it's nice and snug. The weather forecast is clear, too. Can you rent a car and meet me there Saturday about noon? I have to be in Chicago on Monday but we can at least have a little over a day together."

I only had to think for a nano-second. "That sounds

wonderful. Do you think we can slide under Happy's sight by getting together so far out of the way?"

"Based on what I know and conversations with a couple of other people, he seems to hang out in the cities. At least we've never heard of him popping up in the countryside, and all the folks I know on his list are also weres. It's worth a shot, anyways. I'm willing to take the gamble if you are."

Oh, I definitely was willing to gamble. Tony gave me driving directions from the Duluth airport, which is all he knew. I looked at a map online to figure out how to skirt the airport and while we were still on the phone arranged for a rental car for Friday night so I could take off first thing Saturday morning.

"How do you and cats get along? Can I bring Fudge or should I get the neighbors to look after him?" I asked.

"Doll, I'm part canine. What do you think? You'd better get the neighbors to help, at least this time. I get along with some cats but I'd prefer to leave the introductions for another time." That made sense. I thought perhaps Fudge was smart enough to recognize that Tony was OK for a dog-type, but just in case he had other ideas, I didn't want the weekend spoiled.

As soon as Tony and I hung up, I called Elinda and asked her to look after Fudge for me. "I'll be happy to, but don't you usually take him with when you go up north?"

Not wanting to spill the beans quite yet, I told a little lie. "I'm not going to the usual place and this new one doesn't allow pets." (For all I know, Tony's friend didn't like cats so maybe it wasn't a lie.)

The next four days passed like four weeks. I didn't say a word to anyone. I trusted my friends completely but I didn't want Happy to find out a damned thing … maybe he listened in on lovers' conversations or something. Both Sally and Cassandra knew something was up and tried to worm it out of me, but I immediately changed the subject. Just like a typical man, Ev was too preoccupied with some problem of his own to notice the change in my demeanor.

I got the car Friday after work and within an hour of arriving home, I had my overnight bag packed and ready to go. You're thinking it was full of sexy lingerie, right? Think again. It was November and I was going even farther into the frozen north. Despite Tony's assurances that the cabin was snug, my nightgown was flannel. He was just going to have to live with it.

It was about a three hour drive so bright and early Saturday morning, I kissed Fudge goodbye and hit the road. I probably could have left at dark-thirty. I was so excited I didn't sleep a lot. Once out of the northern 'burbs, it's a really pretty drive. Easy, too, since it's almost all interstate, running through farm land. The fields were blanketed in white, making everything look pristine. I pulled up to the cabin shortly before eleven and there was a car already in the driveway. Smoke wafted from the chimney. Between that, the trees surrounding the cabin and the drifts of snow cozying up to everything, someone should have made a postcard.

I'd just gotten my bag out of the back seat and shut the car door when the cabin door opened. Tony had a huge grin on his face. He slogged his way down the un-shoveled stairs, took my bag from my hand, threw me over his shoulder and walked back into the cabin. He dropped my bag right inside the door, sat me down and proceeded to kiss my breath away.

"I've been waiting on pins and needles for you to arrive," he said after he let me go. "I hope the cabin is OK."

I looked around. It was straight out of some decorating magazine geared toward the rustic look. The tongue-and-groove walls and ceiling were complimented by a stone fireplace I probably could have stood in had there not been a roaring fire going. It was obviously decorated to a man's taste in browns and greens, yet it all looked quite comfortable even to a feminine eye. The kitchen was open to the great room and looked to have all the modern conveniences. The big-screen television above the fireplace was on, showing a college football game. The view up to the loft over the kitchen and bath showed that to be the bedroom. What were totally out of place were vases of red roses on just about every flat surface, which explained the interesting scent combination of wood smoke and flowers.

"How long have you been here and how did you manage to get all the roses inside without any of them freezing?" I asked.

"I got in a couple of hours ago after overnighting in Duluth. I can't speak to the roses. Those I had delivered by a florist friend in Grand Marais who, presumably, knows her business. I just called her, asked her if she knew about Mike's cabin, which she did, and told her I wanted it covered in roses. She did the rest."

I kissed him again. "You know, I hate to be all un-romantic with this ambiance, but it's lunchtime and I'm hungry. Did you do any grocery shopping?"

Tony walked over to the stove, lifted the lid of a kettle that was simmering there and waved his hand over the top towards me. The smell of chili mingled with the smell of roses.

"I hope chili and French bread suits. It's about all I'm good at cooking. I also hope you don't mind if I leave the television on. I like football and I'm eager to see the second game. Washington is my alma mater and I don't get to see them play very often."

I didn't mind the television; chili and bread would suit perfectly. We ate our lunch on the sofa instead of at the table, each sitting at one end with our legs intertwined in the middle, heads turned toward the television. Tony's chili was a little spicy for my palate and he laughed as he tossed me a second napkin to wipe the sweat off my face. "Did you think to pick up any milk at the store?" I asked. "It's the best thing for knocking spicy heat down to a manageable level."

"Sorry. Milk isn't something I drink on a regular basis. I'll file it away for future reference, though, as well as remembering to tone down the spices the next time I make you chili."

Just before the coin-toss, we cleaned up the kitchen, put the leftovers in the fridge and Tony pulled out the blender. "Want a daiquiri? I'm pretty good at making those, too." He certainly was. He had even picked up some frozen strawberries so I had a pink mustache after the first taste.

"Mmm. Strawberry flavored kisses," he said when he licked away the mustache.

Tony was obviously still a rabid Huskies fan (did I just make a joke?). He cheered and booed along with the crowd and clapped enthusiastically when his team won.

"They've got a good chance of winning the Pac-12 this year. I hope they can keep their winning streak together but the last two games of the season are against their toughest opponents. I'll have to keep up with those on my phone since I won't be in front of a television the next two Saturdays," he said with a sigh. "There are times that I wish I had a nine-to-five desk job."

"No, you don't," I replied. "You're good at what you do and it gives you a lot of freedom. I doubt a normal employer would let you have one or two days off every four weeks."

"You're right. It's just easier to whine. I have all the technology to follow them when I'm on the road but it's not the same as sitting in front of a television, with a good drink in my hand and the lady I love sitting next to me."

I sat up straight and looked at him. "You just used the L word."

At least he had the good grace to blush. "I did, didn't I? I didn't mean to get quite that deep so soon after getting back together but yes, I'm pretty sure I love you. I haven't been able to date anyone else since that time at the Hyatt. No one else has even piqued my interest. So, now that I've opened my mouth far enough to insert my paw, are you heading back to the Cities?"

I thought for a moment before replying. "No, I'm not leaving. I really enjoy our time together when you're in human form, but I'm still undecided how I feel about you in your entirety. I don't want to end up as a snack that you lovingly lick around the edges, you know? And while we've got enough time, why don't you tell me your story? I don't know a lot about you other than you're a good agent, you like many of the same things as I do, you're sexy as hell and now I know you're a Washington grad. While you're on the subject, what does that creep have to hold over you?"

"Shit," he said. "I need another drink if I'm going to do a complete data dump. You want another?"

I smiled and held out my empty glass. "Of course. I may need it to keep calm while you tell your story."

He fired up the blender once more, refilled both glasses and sat on the couch facing me. "There's not a whole lot to tell. I was born in Salem, Oregon."

"I *know* that part, dummy. Get to the good stuff."

"OK, OK. I was turned when I was a junior in college. My roommates and I had gone camping in the northern Cascades, a couple of hours outside Seattle. We'd been to this area several times before. It's fairly isolated, at good elevation and in the right spot, has a beautiful view of Mount Rainier. We were coming back to the campsite after a hike right around dusk, trying to hurry back to get a fire started because we'd heard some wolves howling not too far away. I got separated from Jack and Robby and the next thing I knew, I'd been thrown to the ground from behind. I don't remember anything else until I woke up an hour or so later lying by the fire, with Robby holding a big pad of cloth to my shoulder.

"They'd come back to find me and managed to chase the wolf off. I'd been bitten on the shoulder but Robby said it wasn't deep and was only bleeding a little. They were both thinking we should head back to the city and I should get that series of rabies shots just in case. The funny thing is, I felt fine. The bite on my shoulder only hurt a little and for some odd reason, I wasn't worried about rabies. I talked them out of breaking camp and we finished the weekend out."

He shifted on the couch and took a swig of his drink. "A month later, I was at one of my favorite bars a few steps from campus at moonrise. I'd only had a couple of beers, hadn't been in any arguments and all of a sudden felt like I needed to kill someone. I was chatting with Robby and before I could say anything about how my mood had changed, he looked at me and said, 'Man, your beard is growing weird or something. There's hair all over your face.' I went into the bathroom to look and my nose was starting to turn into a snout and my hands were widening and growing claws. Needless to say, I made a beeline out the back door. I woke up in the park the next morning with only my underwear on and another guy sitting on his haunches, looking at me.

"'Looks like one of the rogues got to you,' he said. I was confused at his statement but he offered me a spare pair of jeans and a sweatshirt, then took me to the local IHOP for breakfast and explained what had happened. He was the leader of the clan in that area. They keep their eyes open for newbies and try to help them understand their new life as best they can. They also hunt rogues when they know about them and he wanted to know where I was attacked so they could deal with him or her."

He paused and looked at me. When he saw I wasn't getting ready to run, he continued. "When I went back to the house, the only person who was concerned was Robby. After all, a college-age guy staying out overnight isn't anything unusual. But he'd seen the beginnings of the change and I didn't have any explanation he'd buy. So I told him what had happened. I also told him there were people who would help me so he and the rest of my housemates weren't in any danger. He seemed cool with it and we're friends to this day. He even jokes that he needs to bring me along when he dates a woman who likes dogs.

"Over the next six months, the clan taught me how to retain *most* of my awareness when I was in wolf form, how to disappear from normal life during that time without raising questions and how to deal with the longer-than-average life span. It's all very civilized and despite the general knowledge of our existence among full humans, we stay pretty much below everyone's radar.

"Errol, the clan leader, became sort of like a second dad to me, especially since I couldn't tell my folks what had happened. They really dislike anything that isn't plain-vanilla human and I didn't want to hurt them. A good opportunity for an internship came up and I stayed in Seattle over the summer, working for one of Errol's friends who had a PR firm. I ran with the clan on Errol's land outside Seattle on the full moons and learned a lot about myself.

"When I graduated and found a permanent job in LA, Errol flew down with me and introduced me to the clan leader in that area. He, in turn, showed me where it was relatively safe to escape to in the hills. Once I'd saved up enough money, I bought a cabin in the Sierras and that's where I usually go although I have access to other places, like this, if the timing isn't right for me to get back to LA."

I asked the question I'd been aching to ask for awhile. "So how old are you really?"

"I'll tell you, but I want to preface it with the statement that age doesn't matter to me. I'm 45. Do you need your drink freshened again?"

I could live with that. Yes, I knew he'd age a lot more slowly but for the moment, age wasn't a factor. "I'm good for now," I answered. "So what does Happy have on you?"

"My were nature. Neither Hal, who is the head of the agency, nor any of my clients know. I've never broached the subject with my clients but I know I get the majority of the non-human ones because Hal gets the willies around them, although as long as they've got the money, he'll take it. He's noticed I get along with them just fine. He wouldn't be happy at all to find out I was one of those types he doesn't like. Hal never questions my whereabouts because I'm on the road so much for clients anyways, and as long as the clients are happy and pay their bills on time, he really doesn't care. Since I'm only in were form for about twelve hours a month and usually during the night hours, it's easy to hide.

"But of course, Happy found out and has threatened to leak the information to Hal. I like my job, I like most of my clients and I have a non-compete so I couldn't take them with me if Hal decided he didn't want me around anymore.

"So, that's my story. I know most of yours but what does Happy have on you?"

I heaved a sigh and let out my deepest, darkest secret. He laughed. "You write romance novels? That's a side of you I never would have thought existed. You're such a practical person!"

I laughed with him then said, "Yeah, but you may not be so cheery about it. The hero of my first novel was based on you."

"Would I recognize myself?" he asked.

"Probably not. Names, places, careers were changed to protect the not-so-innocent."

"So what's the big deal? A lot of people write books in their spare time and some of them, you, obviously, make money at it. Why are you so twitterpated that news might get out?"

I squirmed. "You work with people accustomed to celebrity every day and you have your own share of the limelight. I like my anonymity. Also, so many of my characters are based on people I meet working with Ev that someone might figure themselves out and get pissed. I take great pains to disguise everything but you know how lawsuit-happy people like your clients can get. That sort of hassle I don't need."

"OK, I get it. You know your secret is safe with me. But can I read at least the first book? I'd like to see what you did with me."

Assuming we were going to have this sort of conversation, I'd already packed copies of the first three books in my overnight bag. As I handed them to him, I couldn't help but be a little nervous about his reaction. Sure, they were bestsellers but for some reason, Tony's opinion meant more to me than the royalty checks.

"I'll read them later. This night is for us, not reading," he said, putting the books into his briefcase. "Come on, let's go for a short stroll outside to clear out some of the daiquiris."

Although I'd planned on staying indoors the entire time, I had remembered what it was like at a cabin in winter and brought my boots. Tony retrieved them from the car for me and once I had them on, we walked out into the crisp air.

The sun was almost below the trees and the first stars were winking into existence as he led me around the house to a trail that led farther into the woods. It hadn't been shoveled but it had been tramped down. "The woodpile is just beyond the break and we'll need more for the night. Let's get a couple of armloads, shall we?"

Tony led the way, clearing even more of a path for me. As he reached the break in the trees, he turned, grabbed me and started kissing me passionately. Naturally, I returned the favor. There was a problem, though. The ground was slightly uneven and the difference in our heights started tilting me over to one side. Before he could right us, we fell into a snow bank and broke off our kiss with a laugh. I threw snow his way.

"Now my butt's going to be all wet and it's all your fault."

He scooped up more snow and doused me with it. "It is not. You need to stand still when I'm kissing you." A few more tossed handfuls of snow and we were both soaked.

"We're really going to want the firewood now. Come on and help." He held out his hand and pulled me up out of the snow.

A few more paces led to a neatly stacked pile of split logs. I took an armful (three logs) and Tony carried about three times as much back to the house. We dumped the logs into the holder on the porch, stamped the snow off our feet and dusted each other off before going inside. The warmth from the fireplace felt wonderful! "Get out of those wet clothes before you catch a chill," Tony said. "I'm going to start dinner."

"Won't you get a chill, too?" I grinned at him.

"I'm pretty much immune to that sort of stuff. Haven't been sick at all since I was a junior in college for some reason. My clothes will dry shortly. Now scoot!"

I took my overnight bag upstairs and stripped down to change. I half expected to see his face peering above the loft railing but instead I heard his whistling and the clang of something metal in the kitchen. I put on dry clothes and went downstairs to see what the chef had in mind. I hoped it wasn't anything spicy again.

He treated me to a grilled steak from the broiler, a baked potato from the microwave, a salad and a bottle of my favorite Merlot. I could get used to having someone cook for me and said as much. "Don't get your hopes up too high, Doll. You've just experienced close to the limits of my cooking. You'll get the rest of it tomorrow morning in the form of bacon and scrambled eggs."

We finished the wine on the sofa, watching *Casablanca* on television. Dang. He even likes chick-flicks. It was very comfortable – like you imagine a contented, long-term marriage would be. At the end of the movie, he banked the fire, then scooped me up and carried me upstairs. "The fireplace is the only source of heat in the house. We'll have to keep each other warm," were the last coherent words he said.

CHAPTER 16

I woke to sun streaming through the huge window opposite me, an empty bed and the smell of coffee. It felt very strange not to have Fudge curled up in my hair yet at the same time, very familiar. "Hey sleepyhead, coffee's done," came from downstairs.

I'd neglected to bring a robe or slippers so I pulled on a pair of socks and padded down the stairs in my nightgown. Although Tony had built up the fire, it was still chilly in the house. His were nature was showing, as he only had on pajama bottoms and seemed quite comfortable. He was warm as he snuggled me to him.

"Such sexy nightwear," he said after kissing me good morning.

"It may not be sexy but it's certainly a lot warmer than what I imagine you would have preferred I bring," I retorted. "I don't have a furnace for a metabolism." I grabbed a cup of hot coffee off the counter and took a swig, choking as I burned my tongue.

"Are you hungry?" he asked.

It dawned on me this was the first time we'd actually had a leisurely morning together. Every other time, we'd had to nearly inhale coffee as we were dressing since we either had something planned or he had a plane to catch.

"No, I take awhile to wake up. Give me a couple more cups of coffee before you start talking about food."

We watched the morning news programs in companionable silence punctuated by comments on whatever the story was. The local weather man was predicting a clear day with highs in the twenties. I was planning on leaving mid-afternoon and it sounded like it would be an easy drive back to the cities.

Somehow the news became uninteresting and we ended up back in bed. An hour or so later, I was curled up next to him and my stomach let out a loud growl. "I think you finally woke me up," I said. "What's for breakfast?"

"Slave driver." He untangled himself from me, pulled his pajama bottoms back on and headed downstairs. I rolled over onto his pillow and breathed in his scent. Who knew when we'd be able to see each other again?

Breakfast was indeed scrambled eggs, bacon and toast. As we were cleaning up the kitchen and loading the dishwasher, clouds started rolling in.

"I thought it was supposed to be a clear day?" I said. "I get the shower first!"

When I emerged from the bathroom with a cloud of steam following me out the door, snowflakes were falling fast and thick.

"It started snowing before you even turned the water on," Tony told me. "I'm going to shower and then, as much as I hate to say it, we should hit the road. Otherwise, we may not get out."

I agreed and headed upstairs to start packing my things.

By the time Tony got out of the shower, the wind had picked up and it looked like we were in the middle of a blizzard. He went out to start the cars and even through the wind's howling, all I heard was the grinding of starters.

"Both cars are dead. The driveway is covered over already. Something funny is going on," he said as he pushed the door closed against the wind. He grabbed his phone and looked, then fired up his laptop. "The weather website is still showing clear skies here. Something very funny is going on and I don't like it."

Tony paced, never taking his eyes of what was happening outside the window. I called Cassandra and told her where I was and what was happening.

"Sounds like someone doesn't want you leaving," she said. "Since Tony doesn't have any magical abilities, we have to rule him out. Let me call around and see if anyone can pick up on what's happening. I'll call you back shortly."

I relayed what Cassandra had said to Tony.

"I have a bad feeling about this," he growled.

Have you ever watched a dog pace back and forth when they're in protection mode? They never take their eyes off the threat, their strides shorten, they bare their teeth and they let out a low growl every few seconds. This is what I was watching and it made me very nervous.

"Tony, can you change at the dark of the moon when you're angry? If so, I think you need to calm down for both our sakes."

That stopped him mid-pace. He took a deep breath

and then said, "Yes. If I get really angry, I'll change, regardless of the moon phase. Do you think someone wants that to happen?" Another growl rumbled up out of his throat.

"I don't know what's going on and until I do, I can't even begin to speculate on the meaning behind it all, if there is one. I suggest we wait for Cassandra to call back before leaping to a bunch of conclusions."

Tony resumed his pacing. "I don't like being caged."

"Which is why you have the job you have instead of sitting at a desk every day. If you can't stop pacing, why don't you go get some more wood? It looks like we're going to need it."

"Good idea. I'll be back in a bit." He didn't even put on a jacket as shoved open the door and leaned into the wind.

I stirred the fire as best as a city girl can, threw another log on, turned the television to the Vikings game, poured a glass of wine and sat down to wait. I figured it was going to be awhile before I'd be behind a wheel and thought I'd make myself as comfortable as I could under the circumstances. I didn't really watch the game, though. My mind was on Tony. The longer he was gone, the more worried I got.

The sound of my cell phone ringing made me jump. It was Cassandra's ring tone and I caught it before it got more than a few notes in.

"What did you find out?" was how I answered the phone.

"No good news. There is indeed a spell on the cabin. A friend of mine is a weather wizard and although he can see the spell, he says it's not one he's familiar with and has no idea how to untangle it."

At that moment I heard a "thunk" of logs being thrown onto the pile on the porch and Tony walked in the door. He'd been gone well over an hour and despite the weather outside, he was barefoot and his clothes were ripped to shreds. "I need to change clothes," was all he said as he walked upstairs. I told Cassandra I'd call her right back and followed him up.

"I tried running to blow off some steam," he told me. "I didn't get far. There's a wall of some sort that runs along the boundaries of Mike's property. I ran into it and bounced off. Beyond it the sky is clear as a bell. The wall smells strange, too. Normally magic smells sort of like static electricity. This smells like that but with a tinge of sulfur.

"Thankfully, the closest neighbor is several miles away. Hopefully, no one will notice that we're being buried by snow when everyone else is out enjoying the beautiful day."

I told him what Cassandra had said. "Why in the world would someone want to snow us in here and/or make me change?" he mused.

"I'll give you three guesses and the first two don't count," I said, grimacing.

"Happy. That bastard. He found us and decided to try forcing the issue."

"Got it in one. I'm going to call Cassandra back and then make a couple more phone calls. The issue of finding his real name just moved up to the top of the to-do list."

"Hey," I said when she answered. "We definitely are snowed in and confined. Tony found a barrier along the property lines. Now what do we do?"

"First, I want to say it's a strange spell if you're walled-in and you still have reliable cell service. Most of the time if I do a spell around electronics, something goes haywire. But thank goodness for that. Tommy's been on the phone with a couple of friends. They think they've got a solution but they need to be at the spell's location. Give me directions … we'll be there in about four hours."

I gave her the directions, disconnected from that call and dialed Bella's number. After we got the usual pleasantries out of the way, I described our problem to her. "I hate to sound desperate but I am," I told her. "Getting rid of this guy, somehow some way, has skyrocketed to the top of my priority list. Without any magic of my own, I'm in a deep hole, here."

"Honey, that's awful," she answered. "If you don't mind virtually the whole magical community of the Twin Cities and beyond knowing about your love life and current predicament, I'll put out what I call a code red. We need to banish this guy ASAP."

I relayed what she said to Tony. "At this point, as long as what Happy is holding over us doesn't get out, I don't care who knows about us or our problem. Go for it."

"I'm on it, honey," Bella said after I gave her the OK. "If your friends can't get you out, call me back and I'll see what I can do from here. In the meantime, I'll alert the gang and we'll work even harder to find that demon's true name. I'll call you tomorrow afternoon with a progress report."

Tony had started pacing again.

"If you need to go running, do it," I told him. "Otherwise, pour yourself a glass of wine or fix a drink or something and calm down. We've only got a few hours to hang out before Tommy, Cassandra and their friends get here and we might as well enjoy the time together."

He heaved a sigh, poured a glass of wine and plopped down on the couch next to me. "I really hate not having control of me and my surroundings. I've spent my whole adult life trying to ensure everything goes according to plan and *this* is not according to plan!"

I commiserated. "I know. But since there's nothing we can immediately do about it, I vote for wine and football."

"Regardless of what happens when your friends get here, I'm going to miss my flight. I need to make a few phone calls and rearrange my week."

"Maybe not. Didn't you say you needed to be in Chicago tomorrow morning? If they get us out at a reasonable hour, you can drive and still be there in time for your meeting. It's only about eight hours away and you can skip a little sleep for one night."

"I never thought about that. Whatever happens I need to extend the car a day or so. I can just arrange to drop it in Chicago. Give me a few minutes on the computer to rearrange the flight and the car. I knew there was a reason I loved you!"

He kissed me and dug his laptop out of his briefcase. I turned my attention to the football game.

I stared at the screen but didn't really watch the game. Although I tried to stay calm for Tony's sake, I was a bundle of knots inside. There was just as much at stake for me as for him – namely, my eternal soul if Happy was able to lay claim to us. I had no idea what happened when a person turned into a demon but whatever it was, I certainly didn't want to hang out with Happy and his ilk for eternity!

Tony finished his online work. I borrowed his laptop to extend my rental car another day, as well, and rejoined him on the couch. The game ended and he started flipping through channels to find something else to watch. He found a soccer game being rerun and we stared mindlessly at that. The tension in the cabin was thick with waiting.

Dusk arrived, then dark. Although it was supper time, neither of us had much of an appetite. I choked down some crackers but the thought of a meal (especially since it would be leftover chili with all those spices) didn't appeal.

My cell phone finally rang about 6:30.

"Hey, it's us," Cassandra said. "We're out on the road. Mick and Jerry are going to try to open a doorway in the wall. If they're successful, they won't be able to hold it for more than a few minutes so I suggest you get ready to leave. I'll call you back as soon as I know something." She rang off.

Tony quickly banked the fire and turned out the lights. We put on our warm jackets, grabbed our stuff and headed for the cars. Cassandra didn't say anything about whether the cars would start but we could always hope.

My phone rang again. "Try starting the cars. They've got a hole and are widening it."

I turned the key and my car fired up. Tony grinned and started his. We turned the cars around and headed down the drive for the road. As we approached the end of the drive, I could see two bundled-up figures to either side, in a pose that would make you think they were each holding a heavy drape. I drove out and parked my car behind Tommy's SUV. Tony followed suit. The two figures let go of whatever they were holding and collapsed into the snow.

A groan came from one of them. Cassandra hurried over with a thermos in her hand. "My special espresso. Take a swig," she said. The figure on the ground complied. At the same time, Tommy was repeating the procedure with the other. Both finally stood and made their way back to Tommy's car.

"Tha' was th' worst barrier I've ever come across." A thick Irish brogue came from one of them. "I'm Mick and tho' 'tis not the most pleasant of circumstances, pleased ta meet ya." He held out his gloved hand.

"And I'm his roommate, Jerry," the other said, also holding out his hand.

"You have no idea how grateful we are to you," Tony said as he shook the hands vigorously. "There's a diner that serves good food in town. May I suggest we repair there and dinner is my treat?"

"Aye, I could use some food," said Mick.

"Then follow me," Tony replied. He got into his car, I got into mine and Cassandra surprised me by sliding into the passenger seat. "The boys can drive on their own. You didn't think I'd pass up a chance to get all the gossip first-hand, did you?"

I filled her in as only a girlfriend can do while following Tony's taillights. Fifteen minutes later she knew as much as she was going to know and we were pulling into parking spots in an almost-deserted town. It was, after all, Sunday night, when most decent folks would be winding down their weekend in preparation for the workweek ahead. But the lights of the diner were bright and through the window, we could see a few occupied booths.

The plump lady with salt-and-pepper hair and twinkling eyes behind the counter smiled as we walked in. "Tony, it's been a long time! And I think this is the first time I've seen you with someone other than Mike. You look great! Who are your friends? Here, let me put these two tables together for you."

She said all this as she bustled around, moving tables, chairs and place settings, pushing Tony out of the way when he attempted to help.

"Coffee all around, Gladys. It's been a long day and we all have long drives ahead of us," Tony told her as we all found seats. After a quick glance at the menu board posted on the wall behind the counter, he told us, "Unless you're vegetarians, I'd recommend the meatloaf and mashed potatoes." My stomach, released from its tension, growled in hearty approval of his choice.

As soon as Gladys had put the coffee down and taken orders for six servings of the meatloaf special, Tony looked around the table and said quietly, "I'd love to hear the story of how you did what you did but this is not the place. And since I need to head for Chicago as soon as we're done, I'll have to get it secondhand from Amy. These folks, while as nice as they can be, are about as plain-bread as you get."

Everyone took his meaning and since dinner arrived almost on the heels of the coffee, there wasn't a lot of time for talk, anyways. Tony was right, it *was* good and I, normally of the small appetite, wolfed mine down almost as fast as the boys. Tony and Jerry both ordered seconds before we all had dessert – homemade apple pie topped with homemade vanilla ice cream.

In between bites, Tony filled us in on the diner. "This place has been here for over fifty years. Gladys and her husband, Bob, inherited it from Bob's parents and I suspect their boy, Bob Junior, will take over when they're ready to retire. The menu isn't extensive or fancy but everything is made from scratch. And although this is a podunk little town, they're open from six in the morning until nine at night seven days a week, catering to not only the locals but the log and ore truckers that pass through.

"Mike, my friend who owns the cabin, is a native of these parts and has known the family since he was a kid. I try to come in for at least one meal whenever I'm here. The cooking and company is better than any five-star restaurant."

I couldn't help but agree with him. Watching Gladys move from table to table, she spoke to every customer like they were family. As she cleared the plates, she asked Tony for introductions.

Tony eyed us all and then introduced us, starting with "Gladys, I'd like you to meet my lady love, Amy, and our friends." I blushed. Cassandra grinned and gave me a little kick under the table. "We decided to come up out of the city and enjoy the unspoiled winter at Mike's cabin. I miscalculated the food needs so here we are, getting supper before heading back to civilization."

"Pleased to meet you all. Any friend of Tony's is a friend of ours. You're all welcome here anytime you happen to be in our neck of the woods," Gladys said to the table.

Tony paid the check and we all traipsed out to the cars. After all that food, I didn't really want to move but I knew we all had to head back to our normal lives. As normal as they get, anyways.

"I'm riding with Amy to make sure she doesn't fall asleep," Cassandra told Tommy. "I'll see you at the deli in the morning, huh?" She gave him a quick peck on the cheek and climbed back into my car as Tommy, Mick and Jerry piled into theirs. That left me and Tony standing on the sidewalk.

"Doll, this was *almost* the best weekend of my life," he said quietly. "I don't know what tomorrow will bring but we *will* find a way to spend more time together without interference, won't we?"

"I enjoyed most of the weekend, too," I said, looking up into his dark eyes. "Call me tomorrow night and I'll tell you what happened, what Bella knows and all that, OK?"

He kissed me and I kissed him back. I would have done that for quite awhile if my car horn hadn't sounded.

"I hate to break you two lovebirds up but I have work to do in the morning," Cassandra said out the window.

We sighed, had another quick kiss and then got into our respective cars. I followed him as far as Duluth, where he turned off for his drive through Wisconsin and I continued south.

I glanced to my right. "OK, so tell me about Mick and Jerry. How were they able to open the barrier when no one else you knew recognized the spell?"

"Mick, in case you hadn't figured it out, is from Ireland. According to Tommy, Mick's family specialty is dealing with the Fae – they've been doing it for generations. I'm not sure why he moved here but somehow he and Tommy hooked up and whenever something Fae-ish comes up, Mick is who Tommy calls.

"When Tommy described your predicament, Mick thought it sounded very much like some things he'd encountered back home and volunteered to try his brand of spell-breaking. Jerry is a strong wizard and although he's American, he knows Mick's ways. They sometimes work in tandem. That's all I know. I'm sure I'll get more details tomorrow and I'll be happy to share them with you when I do. So, what are you and Tony going to do, now?"

I told her about my call to Bella and my hopes that her "code red" would light a fire under everyone to find Happy's true name. "Tony and I were together long before Happy stuck his nose in things. Not only do I not want to take any chances but that demon is really irritating a lot of people. I'd consider it a public service to get him off this plane for awhile."

Cassandra agreed. "I'm concerned for my friends, yes, but more so for all the people he's trying to coerce. Uncle Morris' spell arrived in the mail yesterday so once we have the name, we can get the ritual together. Can I call your friend Bella?"

"I don't see why not. I'm not a witch and I don't even play one on TV so I wouldn't have a clue about anything you'd have to do. You can talk shop with her and anyone else you think you need. Her number is in my cell. You're welcome to look it up."

We spent the rest of the drive chatting about our love lives. It was nearly midnight when I dropped her off at her house and shortly thereafter, pulled up in front of my own place. Fudge was standing right at the door when I walked in and promptly turned his back to me with his tail in the air. I was obviously in the dog house for leaving him at home.

"I'll introduce you to Tony just as soon as I can," I told him as I pulled back the covers on the bed. "If you can handle having a dog around, then you can come with the next time."

I set my alarm back a half hour since I had to return the rental car before work and fell asleep as soon as my head hit the pillow.

CHAPTER 17

Even though I'd set the alarm early, I hit the snooze button so many times I nearly didn't have time to drop the rental car before work. The sun was just cresting the horizon when I got to the rental agency. The kid at the drop point hadn't gotten the memo that I'd arranged for the extra day. Thankfully, I had a copy of the confirmation on my cell phone so it only took an extra ten minutes before their courtesy van drove me to the office. Although the place was officially closed, Cassandra was in the deli. She saw me get out of the van, beckoned me through the door and had my coffee waiting on the counter when I walked in.

"I think we both look a little worse for wear this morning," she sighed. "Did you get any sleep?"

"Actually, I slept like a log from the moment I hit the pillow until the alarm went off, although the snooze button got a workout," I said. "Yesterday was more stress than I'm used to. You?"

"I didn't sleep a whole lot. I kept thinking about what would have happened if we hadn't been able to get you out of the cabin, what might happen with Happy, whether we'll find his name, and then I added today's work list on top. I think today's going to be one of those days where I'm a fiendish caffeine addict."

"I thought I was supposed to be the worrier. Can't you just put everything on the back burner, go home and take a nap?

"I wish. We've got a catering job to get out this afternoon and it'll be all hands on deck until we're done. You need to go to work and so do I. See ya later."

I heeded the hint and headed upstairs. After starting my own coffeepot, I sat down to check email, review the reports left on voice mail and all the rest of my normal Monday tasks. The phone was strangely quiet. Ev and his odor wafted in about eleven. He surprised me by stopping at my office door.

"I heard you had a fun weekend. Want to tell me about it?" he asked.

"Huh? How'd you hear about my weekend?"

"A witch friend told me about the code red going through the magical community. She knows about my problem with Happy and when the description went out, she immediately thought of me. Since the alert originated with Bella and we met her together, I put two and two together and came up with you. So what happened?"

I *so* did not want Ev up to speed on my private life! However, anything related to Happy would affect him as well, so I briefly (and I do mean *briefly*) filled him in on Sunday's happenings.

"You and Tony are back together? That's *wonderful!* How are you going to deal with his were nature? What's Happy got on him?"

"Hey, one question at a time," I said. "First, yes, we're seeing each other again but I'm still sorting through all my feelings. Second, what Happy has on Tony is none of your business. I haven't shared your problem with him and I expect you to respect his privacy as well."

He had the grace to look a little abashed. "I'm sorry. It's just that I thought you two made a good couple when you first dated. And I do want to see you happy, you know. Is there any word from Bella, yet?"

She hadn't called and I really didn't expect to hear from her until the afternoon. I told him as much. "Why don't you go into your office to do your own work and leave me to mine. I'll let you know if I hear something and you do the same, OK?"

"You're right. I've got some calls to make. Hey, I need to go to Chicago tomorrow for a couple of days. Can you make my travel arrangements?"

There are days I wish we still had a travel agent. With the advent of the travel sites on the Internet, I'd decided it was easier to book everything myself when our old travel agent retired. That, and it allowed me to keep tabs on Ev. He'd been known to call Marty on his own and then disappear without telling me he was going to be two time zones away for four days. I sighed, said yes, took down the particulars of his trip and added that to my to-do list for the day. On second thought, I put the information on Sally's desk with a note telling her which airlines to use, the fact that Ev always flew at least business class if not first, and hotels Ev liked to stay in with a pointer to the file in the database with all the credit card and reward programs numbers. She could learn to do all that.

I'd just turned my attention back to the pile of bills to be paid when I heard a throat clearing in front of my desk. Since I'd not heard the door or smelled Ev, without looking up I said, "So what can I do for you, Happy?"

"I understand you had a lovely weekend with the handsome Tony," he said with an oily smoothness. "Will you two be setting a date soon? I'd like to ensure my calendar is clear to attend the wedding."

I could feel the blood rising. Violence is rarely a solution to any matter and Happy was probably immune to a kick in the balls (do demons *have* testicles?) but he was certainly putting me on the edge. I finally looked up from my paperwork and said through gritted teeth, "It was a nice Saturday but Sunday left a lot to be desired. Your doing, I suppose?"

"I thought that only a day was entirely too little time for the two of you to sort yourselves out and wanted to provide an excuse for you to not return to your lives so soon. I must say, your colleagues are quite inventive. My friend who set up that spell has never had it broken before."

"As I've said before, I really don't need you or anyone else to help my love life along. As to your question of a wedding date, don't hold your breath. Yes, I like the man — when he *is* a man. The other half of him, I'm not so sure about and it's a big half to contemplate. And in case you've got any other ideas, Tony and I knew each other long before you came along. If we do decide to have a long-term relationship, Ev should be getting the credit, not you."

"Ah, but I was the one that brought you back together. Do you not give me credit for that?"

"I give you credit for being a royal pain in the ass and that's the sum of it. Go away, Happy. I have work to do." I lowered my head back to my work, hoping he'd take that as the dismissive gesture it was. I heard a sigh and then nothing. When I looked back up, he was gone.

A couple of minutes later, I heard the outer door open. Tommy came into my office with my sandwich. "I smell something sulfur-ish. I take it that creep has already been here."

"Ev's in the office but if you're referring to the demon, yes, and that wall or whatever it is wasn't his doing but someone he knows. This is getting worse by the day. If Mick could break the spell, can't he figure out how to get rid of Happy?"

"Mick said the spell was similar to but not quite what the Fae put up. He and Jerry slept all the way home last night and had to call in sick today because the spell modification took almost everything they had. That was just to cut a hole in it, which closed as soon as they let go. They couldn't break the wall completely and for all I know, Mike's cabin is buried to the roofline in snow by now.

"As for the banishment, you know we've got a ritual and all we need is a name. The entire magical community is on it. You'll just have to hang in there until someone comes up with it, I guess."

I heaved another sigh. "I know. I'm just irritated that things have gotten so far out of control. I never did properly thank you and your friends for yesterday and I really do appreciate it."

"Amy, I now consider you a close friend and as such, I'll do whatever I can to help you and by extension, Tony. Who, by the way, seems to be a great guy even if he does howl at the moon on occasion. I don't like bullies and this slimeball counts as one. Mick and Jerry don't like anyone or anything interfering with humans. The magical community has enough of a PR problem as it is. That's why we came up last night. 'Dra and I couldn't do anything but provide transportation and moral support. The other two did all the heavy lifting. But I'll pass on your thanks."

With that, he left to go back downstairs. I took a bite of my egg salad sandwich and went back to work.

Sally came in promptly at one and without even putting her purse down, came into my office. Was I never going to get any peace?

"Apart from the fiasco yesterday, how was it?" she asked with a twinkle in her eye and a grin on her face.

"I take it John got the code red alert, too," I said.

"Yep. The call came in about eight o'clock last night. Of course, he already knew about your problem but this was his notice that he could spread the word to his contacts. By our count, there's now more than a thousand people in the Upper Midwest alone researching. Someone somewhere will know something. So, the rest of the story?"

I told her what I'd told Cassandra the previous evening. In other words, that we enjoyed each other's company but no decisions on how much further the relationship would go. Although I knew she wanted all the juicy details, she wasn't getting them. No one was. I don't write or tell erotica.

"I've added a new item to the list of your responsibilities," I told Sally. "There's a note on your desk about making Ev's travel arrangements. I'm sure it's something you can handle. All we'll have to do is train him to ask you instead of me."

"Oh, I always made John's travel arrangements when I was his secretary. He's got some peculiarities in his wants and after one bad experience with a travel agent, he never let me call one again. I can tell you I spent hours on the phone with airlines and hotels. Now with the Internet, it's a lot faster. No problems. I'll get right on it."

Now could I get some work done? Paying the office bills isn't as easy as just cutting the check. You try reconciling the company credit card statements when you have twenty-five cards on one account, generating several hundred charges each month and then multiply that by four. It takes awhile.

I finally finished reconciling the statements shortly after four. By two, the stress of the day before and a short night had caught up with me. The last couple of hours had seemed like an eternity as I stared at figures. I decided the actual bill payment could slide one more day. I was more than ready for my nap and said as much to Sally as I walked out the door.

"Ev's all set," she said just before I closed the door. "He's leaving here at one tomorrow afternoon and won't be back until after work on Thursday, so you won't have to deal with him for more than a couple of hours. That ought to give you some time to get caught up around here."

I thanked her and closed the door before she said any more. I didn't want to think about work or anything but sharing my pillow with Fudge for a couple of hours.

When I finally woke, it was pitch dark. I was still groggy and had trouble focusing my eyes. Once I did, I saw that the clock read shortly after eight. I probably would have stayed asleep but my stomach reminded me that it was past dinner time. Not to mention that I now had three days' worth of personal email and social media to start catching up on.

I had just finished putting together some tuna sandwiches and chips for me and Fudge when the phone rang.

"It's Bella checking in. Are you OK?" I could hear the concern in her voice.

"A couple of friends managed to get us out last night. Apart from being tired, I'm fine. So what's happening?"

"You caused quite a stir, young lady," she said. "Adamo was the first person I called after I hung up with you and he's agreed to be the collection point for any information. He says he's hearing from wizards and witches he hasn't heard from in nearly a century. Our demon has apparently been more than a little busy. Adamo now has a list of over one hundred people who've had contact with Happy at one time or another, and it's all been interference in their love lives. There are several who think they may know where to search or who to ask so things are looking up.

"In the meantime, I can hear the exhaustion in your voice. Go back to bed. Either Adamo or I will call you when we know something definitive."

I ate my dinner, took one look at the computer and pulled a Scarlett O'Hara. "Tomorrow is another day" and everything that was waiting for me would still be there in the morning. Fudge got his scoop of kibble early and we both headed back to bed.

Sleep, however, just wasn't in the cards. At least not immediately. I'd just laid my head down when the phone rang again. This time it was Tony. I'd forgotten he'd said he'd call.

"Hi Doll. So, fill me in on last night and today."

I yawned. Long and loud. "I'm sorry, I couldn't help it. While I'd love to talk to you for hours on end, I'm afraid I'm going to just fall asleep on you tonight. Can we talk tomorrow night?"

"And I'm the one that drove through the night to Chicago," he teased. "Don't worry about it. I'll call you about the same time tomorrow. Get some sleep. I love you."

I mumbled something back at him, hit the 'end' button and lay down once again. Fudge assumed his normal position at my back and the next thing I knew, the alarm was going off. It was indeed another day.

CHAPTER 18

The next few weeks were routine. Work went smoothly. I spoke with Tony three or four times a week. Flowers arrived on my desk every Monday. But we were both busy and there were no more weekend escapes.

In the evenings, I did my writing. I approved the galleys for book number five, *Things that Go Bite in the Night*. It would hit the shelves sometime in March of the following year. I polished off the manuscript of number six, *Hexy Lexy* and sent that one off to the editor. I was under contract for four more but starting the next one could wait until after the holidays.

Cassandra, Tommy and I shared a table at the pub for Thanksgiving dinner. (Tony was in Salem with his parents, doing the family thing.) Cork put on a wonderful buffet spread. It was great to have a tasty meal and then have someone else clean up the mess. Cassandra and Tommy were gearing up for the holiday party season and despite my efforts to get them to stop talking shop for a few hours, they dragged me into their planning. They solicited my opinion on various recipes they'd used in the deli.

"You're the best taste-tester we've got," they both told me. "We like our own cooking but it's always helpful to have an outside opinion when we decide to tweak something."

I'll admit that it was a perk, being a taste-tester for them. I generally got free munchies all the time as they tested new appetizer recipes and dinner at least once a week when they were working on a main course. Mind you, nothing was really fancy but their stew or soup with homemade bread, or a new pasta salad was better than anything I could put together myself.

Sitting around the pub, we'd just gotten to dessert: apple pie that was good but not nearly as scrumptious as Cassandra's. I was about to take a drink of my coffee when Cassandra told me to put my cup down. I paused a moment, watched her give Tommy a sidelong glance, and then did as I was told.

"We've got something to tell you," she said, and elbowed Tommy.

He looked a little embarrassed, cleared his throat and said, "I've asked 'Dra to marry me and she's said yes."

Now I know why I was supposed to put my cup down. I threw my hands up in the air and whooped. Most of the restaurant patrons turned their heads to look at me. I didn't care. I got up from my chair, ran around the table and hugged them both together.

"That is *awesome*! I'm so happy for both of you. Have you set a date or anything?" I looked over at the bar. "Hey, Cork. We need a bottle of champagne over here." I went back to my chair and now that the major noise had subsided, the other diners went back to their meals.

"No date yet. Not too long in the future, though," Cassandra told me. "Tommy is officially moving into my place next weekend, although most of his stuff is already there and he rarely goes back to his apartment anymore. Then we need to tell the parents and we'll probably do that at the Solstice when everyone is together. But I wanted you to be the first to know and also to ask you if you'd stand witness for me."

I almost started crying. I'd never been in anyone else's wedding before. "But you've got so many friends you've known a lot longer than me and most of those are witches. Why would you want mundane little me as a witness when I don't know a damned thing about weddings for witches and wizards?"

"Because you're my BFF, mundane or not, silly," she said as she came over to my side of the table and hugged me. "Your part is just about the same as it would be in the mundane world. You know, helping me pick out my dress and all that. Don't worry, you'll do just fine."

About that time, Cork appeared at the table with a bottle of champagne and four glasses. "Whatever you're celebrating, I'm in. So, what are we drinking to?" Tommy told him and after the bottle popped its top, Cork poured four glasses. He picked up one and lifting it, said in his gruff voice loud enough for the entire pub to hear, "To Tommy and Cassandra. They've decided to tie the knot!"

The whole bar broke out in applause as we clinked glasses and drank them down. Cork looked sternly at the groom-to-be. "Tommy, I've known Cassandra since she was a little girl. I served her first beer when her grandfather brought her in at age thirteen. You'd best be taking very good care of her."

"Oh, I plan on it. If she'll let me. You know how independent-minded she can be, though," Tommy answered with a grin.

"Oh, aye. That one can be a tad stubborn. But I know you're a good lad and if anyone can handle her, you can. Congratulations, you two. Now if you'll excuse me, I need to get back to work."

Cork went back behind the bar and we turned back to the table.

"So how do witches and wizards get married?" I asked.

"First, we'll go down to the courthouse and make it legal with a judge," Cassandra told me. "Then a day or so later, we'll have a handfasting somewhere; those are generally held outdoors. An elder presides, just like you'd have a priest or minister. The words are sort of similar, too, but no religion is involved and these words are magically binding. Once you say 'I do' in a magical wedding, you really *do*. You can't cheat on your spouse without dire consequences. Then, just like a mundane wedding, we party."

"So, what do I do?" I asked.

"Like I said, just about everything you'd do at a mundane wedding. You help me with all the preparations, sign all the legal papers at the courthouse, affirm your approval of us at the handfasting, and dance the first dance with Tommy's witness — our version of a best man. It's nothing more onerous than a mundane wedding and honestly, a lot more fun."

I turned to Tommy. "Do you know who's going to be your best man, um, witness? Is it anyone I know?"

"No, you haven't met him yet. Hopefully, it'll be my brother, Jamie. He lives in London and only gets back here once or twice a year. I'll call him after we've told Dad. He can't keep a secret and I don't want him spilling the beans when he makes his weekly call home."

I spent the rest of the four day weekend on cloud nine for Cassandra. After all the hell I'd been through the last few months, it was nice to be happy for a change – even if it was for someone else. When Tony called Sunday night, I told him.

"That's wonderful news, Doll. They make a good couple," was all he said. I shouldn't have been as disappointed in his reaction as I was. Guys just don't get into weddings as much as girls do but nonetheless, I was hoping he'd share my excitement just a little.

Before I knew it, the holiday party season was upon us. I didn't see a lot of Cassandra and Tommy as they were buried in the deli, serving customers in between putting together all sorts of party platters. I had my fair share of parties to attend, as well. It was the one time of year that I couldn't beg off any invitations. Everyone expected you at *their* holiday party and wouldn't take 'no' for an answer. I was used to it by this time and my dry cleaner was always happy between Thanksgiving and Christmas.

The weekend before December 21st saw me at Cassandra's house (oops, *and Tommy's*), putting up all sorts of decorations. Tommy hung lights from the eaves while Cassandra and I decorated a Scots Pine nearly twice as tall as me. It brushed the ceiling of the living room because they'd bought a ball-and-burlap tree, intending on planting it in the back yard in the spring to commemorate their first Solstice together.

All the decorations had been stored in a box in the attic and some were quite old. Cassandra picked up one little bauble that looked like a little elf sitting in a rocking chair. "This was handmade by my great-grandfather for my grandmother. Because she was so small, he called her his Little Elf and gave her this for her first Solstice gift. I haven't had a tree up since she died."

"Then it belongs front and center on the tree," I said. She sniffed a little and hung it at what would be my eye level. "Sorry. I can't believe how many memories all these decorations are bringing back."

"Hey, it's no problem. If your Solstice is anything like Christmas, at least the ones in my family, it's all about family and sharing and caring and all that. It's right that you put these decorations up and remember family and good times."

"It's more than that, really, but yes, family is a big part of it. You'll see on the night. It's a pretty powerful ceremony. Mom does a really good job leading it."

"I'm going to be at your thing? Isn't that just for you guys?"

"Aw, c'mon Amy. I've told you several times you're a part of the family now. Just because you're mundane doesn't mean you can't participate. You don't even have to say anything. Just stand in circle with us. It doesn't take long."

I guess I was going to participate in my first ritual or ceremony or whatever they called it, then. As long as I couldn't mess anything up, and Cassandra assured me I couldn't.

Ev decided the afternoon of December 15th that he was going to throw a New Year's Eve party. I almost hit the roof.

"Do you have any idea how difficult it is to plan a party with two weeks' notice?" I yelled.

"Not a big one, Amy, or anything really fancy. I've already got the guest list written out and it's only about a hundred people. I'll bet Cassandra will do the catering, too, if you ask her. I've already called the bartending service. I'll leave the rest up to you."

Thank goodness for computers and the ability to generate invitations on the fly. I gave the list to Sally and told her to get the invitations out yesterday, then headed downstairs.

"You're not going to believe this but Ev decided to throw a New Year's party," I said, catching the deli's hall door so it wouldn't slam against the wall after I threw it open. "Can you guys do the cooking for it?"

"Based on what you've said, our fare isn't what Ev typically serves at his shindigs, is it?" Cassandra asked.

"He seemed to think your stuff is OK for this party because he mentioned you. So, are you solidly booked or can you come up with something?"

"For Ev, we can fit it in. We've only got two parties that night and they're both just appetizer-type stuff."

We sat down with their catering menu and came up with enough finger food for the few hours before midnight and then she called another catering company to do the breakfast thing after midnight.

"This late notice is going to cost, you know," she grinned.

"Don't I know it. But once he gets a hair up his ass about something, he doesn't care about the cost, just leaves it to me to juggle all the money. Do what you need to do and send me the bill. I'll have a count for you by the twenty-eighth, OK?"

She patted me on the back. "Don't worry. I've got your back." I went back upstairs.

"Did you look at the guest list before you gave it to me?" Sally asked when I walked back in the door.

"No, why?"

"Most of it isn't the normal glam crowd. Jack and I are on it, as are Cassandra and Tommy, Cork from the pub and Tony, too. What's he up to?"

I had no idea but I was going to find out. I walked into his office and waited for him to get off the phone.

"What's up with the guest list?" I asked.

"What do you mean?" He shot back.

"Sally tells me it's not your normal rub-shoulders-with-the-rich-and-famous list. She and Jack are on it, as well as Cassandra and Tommy. You've never invited them to any of your parties."

"I was feeling a little nostalgic. I've been watching you the last few weeks and I kind of miss being around normal people. I thought a party with people who *really* liked each other might be kind of fun. But it's not all like that. I've been hearing some interesting rumors lately about some of our clients and a party is the best way to prove or disprove them. So, the guest list is a mix, OK?"

"What rumors?"

"Nothing I'm going to say anything about unless they're true. I'll let you know what, if anything, I find out after the party. Will Cassandra and Tommy cater it?"

"Yes, for you they will. I think they'll be a little surprised to find themselves on the guest list, though."

CHAPTER 19

Cassandra's parents arrived the evening of the twenty-first and I was invited over to the house for dinner. While I knew magical-type people didn't age as fast as normal humans, I had a hard time containing my shock. Cassandra's mother, Celeste, looked like her sister rather than a generation older. Not quite as tall as her daughter, she was just as thin and angular. Her hair was the color of dark honey with nary a strand of gray to be seen. Her father, Marcus, was closer to six feet tall and although his body was starting to show signs of a soft life, his face looked just as young as his wife's. It was he who gave Cassandra her dark hair.

"Amy, we're so glad to finally meet you," her dad said as he gave me a bear hug. "Cassandra should have brought you along on one of her trips years ago."

Her mom also hugged me. "Cassandra has no siblings but from what we've heard, she does now."

I blushed. I'm good at that. I think I managed to stutter out that it was nice to meet them, too.

At dinner I was quiet, not having a lot to contribute to the conversation of catching up on relatives, plans for the next evening's shindig and a heated discussion about the guest list for the handfasting. Celeste wanted to invite several relatives that Cassandra didn't particularly care for and didn't want at the ceremony.

I left shortly after dinner, with the obligatory, "It was nice meeting you and I'll see you tomorrow night". Tommy and Cassandra knew I was a little uncomfortable with the whole family thing and besides, I had a very important – and private – phone call to answer later in the evening.

The following day saw me back at the house just after sundown, bundled up to the point the only thing you could see were my eyes. It was bloody cold, even for December, and I'd been told the ritual would be held outdoors.

"You came prepared," Tommy said as he greeted me at the door. "Thankfully, it's not a long ritual and we'll be back inside before anyone gets frostbite." I could see that Cassandra, her parents and another man I presumed was Tommy's dad thought the same. They already had their parkas on and were pulling robes on over those.

"The spirits really don't care whether we're indoors or out," Marcus said. "But there's just something about being outside under the sky that makes me feel so much better. That's why we go outside no matter what the weather. However, I have to say I much prefer doing the winter ritual in Arizona!"

"I'll echo that sentiment," the other man said. "Hello, Amy. I'm Tommy's Dad, Rhys. We'll all get to know each other once we're back inside, OK?"

Fine by me. The five of them trooped out the back door with me trailing behind. I had no idea what they expected of me. They formed a circle around Cassandra's frozen-solid birdbath. Cassandra pulled me into the circle between her and Marcus and they both held my hands tightly. I looked up to see the moon shining brightly almost directly overhead. I'm sure there were a lot of stars, too, but between the nearly-full moon and the light pollution from the city, I couldn't see them.

Cassandra's mother started to hum. The others joined in. It sounded like at any moment, they'd break out into a Gregorian chant. Although I could *hear* the hum, I also felt it in my chest, as if hundreds of bees all of a sudden swarmed inside my torso. It felt weird.

The humming stopped as if Celeste had given some sort of cue that I missed. I was so discombobulated by the bees in my chest that I forgot to pay any attention to what she was saying. She said something and we all raised our joined hands to the sky while she continued on with her soliloquy. She said something else and our hands came down. Finally she said something that evoked a 'so be it' from the other five. We broke the circle and rushed back into the house.

"So, Amy, how'd you like our solstice ritual?" Marcus asked me as we all shed layer upon layer of clothing. "Short, sweet and to the point, just the way I like them."

I blushed. Again. "I'm sorry, but after I felt all you guys' humming in my chest, I sort of forgot to pay attention to the words."

Marcus looked at Cassandra. "Have you ever tested her?"

"No. Apart from being able to shield which is no big thing, she's never indicated to me there was any ability," came the startled reply.

"Hang on. Test me? For what?"

"If you actually felt the resonance of the hum inside you instead of just hearing it, you probably have a touch of magical ability yourself," Marcus told me. "It may not be very strong or could be strong with development but we'd need to test you to see. We can do that while we're here if you're interested."

"This is all news to me," Cassandra turned on me. "How come you never said anything? We've known each other for *years*."

"I didn't say anything because I don't know what you guys are talking about. So I felt the resonance of the hum. There were five of you doing it, you know."

Marcus put his hand on Cassandra's shoulder. "Honey, she probably had no idea. Remember, she wasn't raised in an aware family." He turned to me. "If this is something you're interested in pursuing, all you need to do is ask. Think on it. In the meantime, I just heard a bunch of stomachs growling. It's dinner time!"

Cassandra and Tommy had outdone themselves for the dinner. There was the usual garden salad with Tommy's "famous" balsamic vinaigrette dressing, rack of lamb with a really interesting rosemary and mint sauce, a sweet potato soufflé, and Crepes Suzette for dessert. Everyone oohed and aahed as Tommy lit the dish and the flames whooshed up and then subsided. He served the crepes quickly so everyone's dish still had dancing flames for a moment or two.

We all helped clear the table, Celeste and I loaded the dishwasher, then Marcus served Irish Coffee in the living room.

"Cassandra got the cooking gene from her mother. I, on the other hand, can burn water but am one hell of a bartender," he quipped.

I could agree with that statement. I'm not usually one for brown liquor but this went down as smooth as could be. Rhys had held off on his questioning but now he asked about the people I worked with. "Tommy's obviously told me a lot about you as you're so close to Cassandra but I'm really curious about your working with an ogre. They usually smell like shit and have such terrible tempers. How do you manage it?" Rhys asked.

I grinned. "Ev's really not that bad. He does make an attempt at hygiene that takes at least the first two layers of aroma off. He travels a lot, keeps to his own office most of the time when he's in town, and I go through a lot of scented candles. As for his temper, he knows better than to yell at me and generally goes for a walk to cool off when things get bad. He deals with humans a lot and has learned he can't really be himself around them."

We chatted some more then I said since tomorrow was a work day, I really had to go home and get to bed. Cassandra and Tommy said the same thing.

"You retired people can stay up all night talking if you like," Cassandra told the older people. "We working stiffs have alarms to answer to."

She walked me to the door. As I layered myself up for the walk home she said, "I hope you enjoyed your evening. I know it was sort of strange for you."

I hugged her. "Yes, it was a little weird but fun all at the same time. Your folks and Tommy's dad are nice people. I'll see you Tuesday morning. My coffee had better be ready!"

I didn't see much of Cassandra or Tommy the next couple of days. They were so busy due to the holiday season that all three parents had come in to help out … Celeste in the kitchen, Marcus and Rhys behind the counter.

Because other businesses did, Ev held to the Christian calendar, so I got Christmas Day off. I happily plugged away at the new book, taking time off to trudge through even more snow for Cork's Christmas Day spread. He gave me a kittie bag for Fudge, who regally accepted the gift of smoked salmon as his due. "Can't forget the four-legged family members, now can we?" Cork said with a wink as he handed me the bag.

Tuesday noon, I heard feet stomping up the stairs before the door slammed open and Rhys came into my office with my lunch in his hands. His face was almost purple with rage.

"Did I do something wrong?" I asked.

"Not you. That damned demon of yours made an appearance in the deli about a half hour ago. I had no idea who he was. When I asked him what he wanted, instead of ordering a sandwich he insinuated that I'd been alone too long and he had the perfect woman to cure the ache in my heart. I lost it. I first asked him who the hell he thought he was; told him no one could replace Bea in my heart, and then shot a "get out" spell at him. He just smiled as the spell bounced off him onto a paying customer, who high-tailed it out of the store."

He took a deep breath but the color remained in his face. "Tommy felt the spell and came out of the kitchen wanting to know what the hell was wrong. That jackass demon of yours smiled at him, then at me and said, 'I can disrupt love just as easily as bring two together. I'll be back.' Then he vanished. It startled so many people that the remaining customers left without buying anything.

"Tommy sighed and told me he was pretty sure that was your demon. Since we didn't have anyone to wait on at the moment, he filled me in on your tribulations with the guy."

Wow. So many expletives from someone I'd been told was as calm as could be in almost any circumstance. I interrupted at this point. "Would you quit calling him *my* demon? Damn, Rhys, I'm really sorry he's interfering with you now, but he isn't *mine*."

"I'm sorry, Amy, it was a bad choice of words. He knew how to get to me. Bea was my soul-mate and when she passed on, I made a vow to stay true to her memory. I have female friends, yes, but I have no interest in dating again, much less anything of a romantic nature."

"What do you suppose he meant by 'disrupting love'?" I asked.

"That worried me, too, since he looked at Tommy before saying it. But I don't know what else to do other than tell Tommy and Cassandra to be on guard and not let little disagreements turn into a full-blown argument." He heaved a sigh. "Eat your lunch. I'll see you when you drop the plate off." With that he left, closing the door behind him much more quietly than he'd opened it.

Sally came in just as I'd finished my lunch. I filled her in on the events in the deli.

"Wow, Happy really gets around, doesn't he?" she rued. "You know, he may be trying to get to you through your friends."

Crap. I'd never thought of that. "I'm assuming Tommy's dad can hold his own with Happy. I can see him doing the same thing Adamo does, meet the woman and then find some reason not to date her, however much of a pain in the ass it might be. But if he screws up Tommy and Cassandra somehow, I'm not sure what I'll do. I guess I just have to hope with all my might that someone comes up with his true name before anything else happens."

Sally agreed and we both turned to our work.

The next evening the shit hit the fan. I was just sitting down to the computer when Cassandra called about eight o'clock. "Come over and bring a couple of bottles of wine with you," she told me.

"What's up?" I asked, dreading the answer. We usually didn't get tanked up on a Thursday.

"I'll tell you when you get here," was all she said before hanging up.

When I got to the house, I swear I saw smoke coming out of Cassandra's ears. She was pacing around the living room. Wait. Pacing isn't the right word. Stomping is a better description.

"What happened?" I asked as I shed my outer clothing and headed to the kitchen to get a corkscrew and a couple of glasses. I spied Merlin under the coffee table – out from under foot but still in a position to keep an eye on his human.

"Tommy. That's what happened. That bastard thought he could just make changes at the deli without asking me. We're not even married yet! It's *my* company. He's just an employee and has *no right* to do *anything* there without talking with me, first."

I handed her a glass of wine. "Take a couple of swigs of this, take a nice, deep breath and then tell me exactly what happened."

She took a swig of wine alright. Half the glass disappeared in one gulp and she resumed her stomping around. "A larger space two blocks down has become available. Tommy thought it was time we expanded and he talked to the owner about leasing it. The first I knew about it was when the guy walked into the deli with a lease in his hand, ready for *Tommy's* signature. We've talked about growing the catering business but I wanted to be able to do it in the current space. I own that building free-and-clear, dammit. I don't want to incur any more expense until the revenue warrants it. Who the hell does he think he is?"

This was *so* not good. And it smelled like Happy. "Wow. First, where's Tommy now?"

"I lost it in the deli. After politely telling the landlord that I owned the company and I wasn't interested in leasing his space at the moment, I went into the kitchen and told Tommy not only was he fired, he could damn well pack up his shit and move back in with his dad. I zapped him in the ass for good measure. His stuff's still here but he's not and that's all I care about. I'll throw his shit on the lawn tomorrow morning."

"No, you won't. At least not yet. Did you ask Tommy about it?"

"I was so pissed I just yelled at him. So no, we haven't talked."

"Did you stop to think maybe it wasn't all Tommy's doing?"

She stopped her pacing and gave me a strange look. "What do you mean, not all Tommy's doing? Mr. Hancock said he was looking for Tommy Llewellyn regarding a restaurant lease. When I asked him, 'What lease?', he explained about the space and the fact that Tommy met with him yesterday about it."

"Did Rhys or Tommy tell you about Happy coming into the deli the other day?" I asked.

"Of course. Happy threatened Rhys on some level but I know Rhys can handle it so I wasn't worried."

"But they didn't mention the fact that Happy said he could disrupt love as easily as bringing two people together, did they? Rhys said Happy looked at Tommy when he said that."

"But Tommy has strong shields. How could Happy make him do something? There's no way he influenced Tommy's thinking."

"Maybe you ought to talk with Tommy to find out, huh? I just don't see him going behind your back on anything, much less anything having to do with the deli."

She finally sat down next to me on the couch, drained her wine and handed the empty glass to me. I duly refilled it … and mine, too. After taking another large swig, she heaved a sigh and calmed down. "I guess you're right. No matter the cause, I need to talk with him. But not tonight. I'll just lose it again."

"So, are you planning on working with a hangover tomorrow? Remember, you're an employee short," I asked, moving from the couch to the chair to prevent being slugged.

"Gods. You're right. Mom and Dad have gone back to Arizona and Rhys probably wouldn't come if I called so it's me and Charlie. And I have to make fifty-two sandwiches for a luncheon tomorrow, in addition to normal stock. I'd better quit now, huh?"

"A couple of glasses aren't going to hurt but I'd advise we stick to just the one bottle or neither of us will be in any shape to think in the morning. I still have to put the finishing touches on Ev's New Year's Eve party in addition to everything else."

At this point, Merlin thought it safe enough to come out and crawl into Cassandra's lap. She absent-mindedly petted him while musing out loud. "If I go in an hour early, I'll be OK. Charlie's supposed to come in at ten and we should be able to get everything together on time assuming counter traffic is as light as it's been during the holiday week. Shit. I'd better shut it down for the night and go to bed if I'm getting up even earlier than normal." She drained her glass, put Merlin on the floor, got up and gave me a hug. "I hate to kick you out but …"

"I know. I need to get going, too. You going to be OK?"

"Not really. Not until I talk to Tommy and find out just what the hell happened. But am I going to go off the deep end? No. Thanks for coming over and talking sense into me. If that damned demon is involved, I will burn his ass to kingdom come when we find his name."

"You and a lot of other people, me included. I wish I had your mojo." I put on my coat and hugged her again. "I'll see you in the morning."

My phone rang on the way home. It was Tony, checking in as he usually did just before my bedtime. "Hi, Doll. How was your day?"

I filled him in on what Cassandra had said and done, getting a little breathless as I trudged through the snow. Damn but I wish more people would shovel their sidewalks!

"So you think," he began, "based on what Tommy's dad said that this is Happy's doing?"

"Yep," I replied. "Knowing Tommy, I just can't see him going behind her back on anything having to do with the deli. That's her baby and he knows it. This smells like Happy cooking up something to get to either me or Rhys. I don't know which and I don't really care. I'll call Rhys at a reasonable hour tomorrow to see what's happening on that end. Those two have to talk, but knowing Cassandra's temper, I think someone with some magical mojo needs to be there in case she loses it again. He's the closest."

"Sounds like a plan. Let me know how things go, OK? And don't get directly in the middle of those two. I don't want *you* being the one zapped, you hear me?"

"Aye, aye, Captain," I laughed. "Fudge is fed and I need to go to bed. I'll talk with you tomorrow."

With that, I hung up and did indeed crawl into bed. I hadn't had *that* much wine but enough that I conked out as soon as Fudge settled himself in my hair.

CHAPTER 20

I stopped into the deli to get my usual latte before heading upstairs. Charlie was behind the counter and in a low voice said, "I don't think you want to talk to her right now. She's in a right snit. Do you know what happened?"

Charlie knew that both Cassandra and Tommy were magical folks, but I wasn't sure how much else he knew so I simply told him they'd had an argument, that I'd calmed her down the previous night and was going to see about getting the two of them to sit down to talk.

"Do it soon. Not only are we short-handed, but she's not concentrating on what she's doing. I kept her from putting too much salt into the mayonnaise a bit ago. I'll try to keep her on an even keel today but it ain't gonna be easy."

I thanked him, told him I'd do what I could and headed upstairs.

After I'd dealt with the most urgent voice and email messages, I called Rhys. Even though it was about nine-thirty, he sounded a little bleary-eyed when he answered the phone.

"Hi, Rhys. It's Amy. I take it you know about the blowup between Cassandra and Tommy yesterday."

"Oh, yes. Tommy came storming in about four o'clock yesterday afternoon, saying Cassandra had fired him over something about a lease, kicked him out of the house and zapped his ass for good measure. He wasn't sure what she was talking about but decided it would be best to get out of her way until she calmed down. Then he proceeded to get rip-roaring drunk and dragged me along with him. He's still sleeping it off. Do you want to speak with him? Should I wake him?"

"Actually, I called to talk with you to see how we can resolve the problem. I have a funny feeling that slimeball demon is involved, trying to get to either you or me through them.

"I got Cassandra calmed down last night and got her to thinking maybe it wasn't Tommy but something Happy did. She and Tommy definitely need to talk but with her temper, I'm afraid of getting them together without someone who can magically pull them apart if things get ugly. Are you up for it?"

Rhys thought a moment. "It'll need to be after the deli closes. Tommy told me Cassandra and Charlie are going to be slammed today with just the two of them. How about you drag her to Cork's after closing and we'll meet you there. It's more or less neutral ground for them and between me and Cork, nothing magical is going to get out of hand."

I agreed to get her there come hell or high water and we set a time of 6:30. That would give Cassandra and Charlie time to get the deli shut down for the night and me time to talk her into it.

I had a difficult time concentrating on work until Sally came in. I was too worried about my friends and the scuzzy creep who was probably interfering with them. I told her what was planned and she had a good idea.

"Let's go down and suggest a girls' night out. If I'm going, too, she won't think you've got something up your sleeve. Jack won't mind if I'm home a little late, especially given the reason."

So, I hollered at Ev that both of us would be out for a few minutes and we trooped downstairs. Thankfully, there were only a couple of customers and Cassandra was at the counter.

"Hey," said Sally. "I hear you're having problems and I think a girls' night out is called for. Are you up for a couple of drinks at Cork's after you close?"

"You know Sally's older than we are and maybe she'll have some ideas. What do you think?" I chimed in.

Cassandra thought for a moment. "It sounds good but it'll have to be an early evening. With only me and Charlie here, it's going to be long days until I can get a new employee."

"Good. Will 6:30 be OK? I know you need to clean up after you close up." Sally was trying to be solicitous.

"That's fine but what will you two do while I'm closing?"

Sally grinned. "Getting a head start on you. We'll meet you there!"

With that, we waved and headed back upstairs. Just as we walked in the door, Ev hollered, "Where have you two been? I can't talk on one line and answer the other at the same time."

I snorted. "Ev, we were gone a total of six minutes. Are you telling me you can't ask someone to hold, answer the other line, ask them if you can return the call, take the number and go back to the first call?"

"Of course I can," he whined. "But it's rude to put someone on hold."

Sally and I looked at each other and laughed. "We're back so it's all good," she said. "Are there any messages for either of us?"

"No. Both are for me. But don't both of you go out at the same time again, huh?"

I was still laughing when I went back to my desk. Ev would never make anyone a good secretary if he couldn't deal with two incoming calls at the same time! I heard Sally calling Jack as I dug back into time sheets and expense reports.

Although I normally left around four, I hung around until Sally was through at five. There's always enough work for me to stay late, I just choose not to most of the time. We bundled up and headed over to Cork's. We made sure to get a table large enough to add a fifth chair without crowding and I gave Cork a heads-up on our plans. "Get them back together however you can," was all he growled out.

Sally and I killed the time talking about the current situation and other weird people we'd met over the course of our business careers, and ate a little dinner to soak up the alcohol. I was hoping I wouldn't be there *that* long but just in case, I wanted to be sure I wasn't going to get plastered by drinking and not eating.

Just before 6:30, Cassandra joined us and right on the half hour, Rhys and Tommy came in. After a moment of looking around, they headed for our table.

"Girls' night out, huh?" Cassandra said as she rose to leave.

"Wait," I said as I pulled her back down into her chair. "Yes, this was arranged but you two need to talk. Most especially, *you* need to listen. Like we talked about last night, things probably aren't as you think they are. Hear what Tommy has to say before going off in a huff. If you leave now, you won't find out the truth. Isn't that what you want?"

She looked at me, as if Tommy wasn't even there. "If you must know, I'm still pissed at him but for you, I'll give him five minutes and it had better be good. Otherwise, I'm out of here and you can spend time with your new friend."

"Cassandra," Sally said quietly. "There are rocky times in relationships. I know. Jack and I have had our differences, too, and some big ones. But if you love each other, you need to *talk* instead of yell at times. Sit down, shut up and listen. I'll tie you in your chair if I have to."

Cassandra glared at Sally, heaved a sigh, put her purse back on the floor under the table and motioned for the men to sit. It was an awkward minute or two before Cork brought beers over for the guys.

"'Dra, I have no idea what you were yelling at me about yesterday," Tommy began after drinking about half his beer in one gulp. "Would you please explain to me without loud expletives or zapping what I did wrong?"

Cassandra related the prior day's events about the lease, the catering, and all. The entire time I could feel something like static electricity building up around her. I was waiting for her hair to start floating like it does when someone puts their hand on one of those static electricity ball thingies. The light overhead flickered.

Rhys reached over and put his hand on hers. "Calm down," he said. "If you can't find your ground, at least release the energy into me and I'll ground it for you. Cork won't like it if you mess up the pub's lighting, or his cash register for that matter."

Cassandra closed her eyes, heaved a sigh and the static field went away. Rhys removed his hand from hers.

She opened her eyes, glared at Tommy and said, "Well? What do you have to say for yourself?"

"'Dra, I swear by the ancestors I did nothing of the sort. I have no idea who this 'Tommy Llewellyn' is that inquired about a lease but it wasn't me. I thought you knew me better than that."

Rhys cleared his throat. "Cassandra, I know Amy mentioned that damned demon to you last night. In the intervening day, haven't you thought that perhaps whatever happened was designed to break you two up? I know my son. He'd never try to interfere in someone else's business, even if that someone was his beloved."

"I have an idea," Sally interjected. "Tommy and Cassandra, why don't the two of you go down to the lessor's office tomorrow and see if, indeed, the guy talked with

Tommy or someone else? If it wasn't him, you've got your answer right there."

"It *wasn't* me and I'm happy to do that. I'd also like to find out just who is impersonating me." Tommy looked pointedly at Cassandra.

"I'll admit the thought did occur to me. But if it wasn't you, who was it and why would they want to break us up?"

"Oh, come on. That damned demon Happy interferes all over the place. Who's to say he didn't think that if you two broke up, either Amy or I would be sad enough – or something – to give into him?" Rhys' voice was calm but you could tell he was upset.

Cassandra heaved another sigh. "I'm too tired to process all of this right now. It's been a long day, I had a short night and I need some sleep. Can we call a truce for the moment? Tommy, you can have your job back because I need you but as to the personal stuff, I just can't think about that while worrying about the store."

Tommy rolled his eyes. "I will come back to work but on one condition: sometime tomorrow, we go together to find out who wanted to sign that lease. I want you to know without a doubt I'd never do something like that. If we go around two or two-thirty, Charlie can handle things for a half hour or so. OK?"

"OK." She turned to me. "I'm not sure whether to thank you or slap you for this. I'm going home, feeding myself and Merlin and going to bed. We'll talk in the morning."

She grabbed her purse and nearly ran out the pub. The remaining four of us looked at each other and heaved a collective sigh.

"I think maybe we got through to her," Sally said. "Since I've now done my part, I'm going home to my happy marriage. See you all tomorrow." She left, too.

"Why would she think I'd ever do anything like that without speaking to her first?" Tommy asked me.

"I have no idea," I said. "All I can tell you is something you well know: that deli is her baby. From what I've heard, her grandparents made a living off it but they never changed the menu, never did catering. I'm not sure but I think she's actually doubled the business since she took over. So anything that affects it deeply affects her.

"What do we do if the building owner says it was you?"

"But it wasn't me."

"I know, but what if whoever it was looked like you?"

"Tommy," Rhys interjected. "You know there are a few Fae out there who can shapeshift and I wouldn't put it past the demon to have found one. If the building owner says it was you, first grab Cassandra's hand and then do a reveal spell. She'll see the truth."

"I know, Dad. I'm just pissed all this is happening and that 'Dra is going through all these changes apparently because of me."

"You're innocent so it'll all work out. As long as we're here, let's have something to eat. You know I don't keep a lot of food around and since you'll be staying with me at least one more night, I guess I'd better be sure you get a proper meal."

I rose. "Listen, Sally and I ate while we were waiting for Cassandra so I don't need dinner and I've got a couple of things I need to do before bed. I'll settle up with Cork for the tab thus far. Tommy, get some sleep tonight. Rhys, thanks for helping."

Cork was very quiet as he processed my credit card. "Everything OK?" was all he said.

"Not completely but hopefully it will be," I replied.

"Me, too. They fit good together. See you soon."

I didn't really have anything on the agenda for the evening but I also didn't want to sit there, get sloshed and rehash the entire thing once again. I'd done what I could for the moment and the rest was up to Cassandra and Tommy. Once home, I tried to immerse myself in a good book for the couple of hours remaining before bedtime but I couldn't really concentrate on it. I spent the night tossing and turning with worry, irritating Fudge who couldn't settle down until I did. Needless to say, neither of us looked our best in the morning. The difference was that Fudge could go back to sleep. I had to work.

Friday morning Cassandra didn't say much when I picked up my latte. I said hi and tried to ask about what she was thinking but she just said, "I haven't made up my mind. I'll let you know when I do." I shrugged my shoulders and headed upstairs.

Tommy brought me a Reuben sandwich for lunch. "Well?" I inquired as he put the plate down on my desk.

"It's strained," he grimaced. "If we can't get things figured out this afternoon, I'm going to have to find another job. Neither of us can work well under these conditions.

And poor Charlie is stuck in the middle, trying to be friendly with both of us. That's not right, either."

"I have faith it'll all work out," I said, trying to speak clearly through a bite of sandwich. I swallowed. "One of you let me know what happens."

"Oh, you'll hear about it. She's either going to come up here and kill you for last night or tell you what an ass she's been. OK, maybe not that last but she'll admit she was wrong."

Tommy left, promising he'd say something if Cassandra didn't. I was only halfway through my sandwich when I heard a throat clearing. "Not again. What now, Happy?" I mumbled around the bite I'd just taken. I didn't care about being polite where he was concerned.

"Isn't it polite to swallow your food before speaking?" he said. "No matter. I just wanted to know if you were thinking about your own happiness with Tony while your friends are fighting."

"So you *did* have something to do with this mess. Why? My relationship with Tony, or any other man for that matter, doesn't have a damned thing to do with my friendships. Or can't you tell the difference?"

"Oh, it has nothing to do with you or Tony. I was just curious as to whether you might see their breakup and become a little more desperate for your own love life."

"So, you're after Rhys, then? Good luck with that. I don't think either he or Tommy will submit to blackmail in that regard."

Happy smiled that oily smile of his. "We shall see," and disappeared. I didn't quite lose my appetite and managed to choke down the rest of the sandwich. That added just one more item to the list of reasons why we had to get rid of that guy. I didn't know Adamo well but it had to be irritating as hell to meet women just to get a guy off your back for a few years. I didn't think Rhys would go along with it to get Cassandra and Tommy back together, but I didn't know *him* that well, either.

3:00 came and went. Sally and I slogged through our afternoon, looking at one another with anticipation whenever I went to the bathroom or kitchen. Ev, of course, sat in his office, oblivious to the drama. Every time the phone rang, Sally answered it after one ring, hoping it would be one of the two with good news.

I left for home at four, Sally telling me to call her if I heard anything. I made her promise to do the same. Being a busybody, I poked my head in the deli door on my way out. Charlie was the only one there. "They left at two thirty and haven't been back. I have no idea," was all he said.

Too agitated to sleep, I passed ten thousand games played of mahjong instead of napping. Dinnertime came and went. I was just about to go to bed when there was a light knock at the door. When I opened it, Cassandra said "hi", pushed her way in and plopped on the couch.

"I'm freezing and I need a cup of tea," she said.

CHAPTER 21

"So what happened?" I asked as I put a mug of water into the microwave to heat and pulled out an Earl Grey teabag, which was all I had left.

"We couldn't find Mr. Hancock. Before I opened this morning, I walked over to the building in question and the 'For Rent' placard with a telephone number was gone. So I had to wait until one of the businesses upstairs opened to get the name of the landlord. I didn't have a chance to get away until Charlie and Tommy showed up for work but when I finally got the number out of one of the receptionists, whoever answered the leasing office phone said there was no Mr. Hancock working for them.

"On top of that, the space isn't set up for food service. As a matter of fact, they leased it yesterday to some retail operation. So, it was all a put-up job."

"Then Tommy's in the clear, right? But if you didn't meet with this Mr. Hancock, where'd you two go this afternoon?"

"Over to a bench by Lake of the Isles to talk. I figured I'd already told Charlie he was going to have to go it alone for an hour or two so we may as well use the time to clear the air."

"And?" I prompted.

"I don't know. Tommy's job is safe because he's good and we work well together but on the personal side, if I don't trust him enough to see through a farce like this, what's it going to be like if something really bad happens? We talked until sunset and I just can't get past the 'what if'."

"First off, you need to give Charlie a bonus. Yeah, I know he's been with you for ages and has worked by himself before but I'll bet you didn't even call him, did you?"

"Yes, I did. About an hour ago. And yes, he's getting a bonus plus two days off next week. He said this afternoon had been slow so wasn't worried that he was the only one there. You know afternoons are mostly coffee and sweets, anyway."

"Not the point and you know it. Back to the problem at hand. Why can't you get past the 'what if'? Before this mess, you said you trusted him implicitly and now you don't?"

"I know. But the deli is my baby and if something happened to it, I'd never forgive myself. Gramma would be pretty upset, too. This just showed me how possessive I am about it and if Tommy and I get married, I'm not sure I'm ready to share it with anyone."

"So who says you have to share? It's your business and has been from the get-go. I thought you two had already talked about all that and he was content with the current arrangement."

She sighed, drained her mug and stood. "We did and he is but I'm still unsure of everything. I need to think but more, I need to sleep. Tomorrow's going to be a very long day and Sunday will be even longer. If I don't call you before then, I'll see you Sunday at Ev's, OK? Thanks for listening."

I hugged her. "Anytime and you know that. Get some sleep. Maybe things will sort themselves out in your dreams."

After she left, I crawled into bed, Fudge settling himself in my hair. I turned out the light, said a little prayer to the universe for my friends and fell asleep.

*****

New Year's Eve finally arrived. It felt a little strange to be going out – I normally hibernated that night to avoid all the drunks and their revelry. Ev had a hostess for the party, his current lady-love ogre, Marianna, so I didn't have to hurry over. I took a cab to his place shortly after nine and after grabbing a glass of wine, started my social rounds.

I hadn't paid any attention to the guest list before handing it off to Sally so was surprised to see Adamo and Bella in attendance. "I thought you two didn't do parties?" I said after greeting them.

"Normally, I hate parties," said Adamo. "However, it was an opportunity to see you and Ev again; and I didn't have anything pressing on the calendar."

"Me, too," Bella said with a smile.

Since I was there as a guest rather than an employee, I hung with them longer than I normally would have at one of Ev's parties. It was fun to not feel pressured to greet everyone with a smile on my face, whether I wanted to or not.

We'd been chatting about twenty minutes when I felt an arm around my waist and saw Adamo's eyebrows rise. No one I knew in the room had my permission to be that close so I shoved my elbow into the stomach I presumed would be immediately behind it.

"Oof," said a very familiar voice. "Is that any way to greet me?"

I turned, put the arm that wasn't engaged with a glass around Tony's waist and, looking up at him with a shit-eating grin on my face told him, "You should know better than to surprise me like that."

A quick kiss told him he was forgiven and then I had to ask what he was doing there. When we'd spoken the night before, he said he was required to make an appearance at some actor's party in a posh suburb of Los Angeles.

"Ev called me last night to see if I was going to be here. And to answer your unspoken question, I didn't say anything about us but he knew anyways. He must pay more attention than you thought. He told me he had an announcement to make and asked if I could figure a way to be here. When I saw whose party I was supposed to be at, it was a no-brainer. But I asked him not to say anything to you. I wanted it to be a surprise and it looks like it was."

It looked like our relationship was going to be made public. I introduced Tony to Bella and Adamo; then he excused himself to go get a drink. He was back at my side in a flash.

"Isn't the skinny chick with the dark hair and apron your friend, Cassandra? I think you've got competition because she said hello to me with a wink."

I elbowed him once again.

We left Bella and Adamo talking to someone else and made nice to the other guests. I was surprised at how many neither Tony nor I knew. Quite a few were old friends of Ev's from his time in Los Angeles. They must have been good friends indeed to have made the trip solely for this party.

About eleven, Cassandra joined us. When I asked about Tommy, all she said was he was done working for the night and had gone home. To his dad's house. Tony, who obviously knew what was going on (I didn't keep secrets) said he'd be the luckiest guy in the room to have two beautiful women to escort. Cassandra elbowed him but I could tell it cheered her a bit. We chatted about nothing, trying to tippy-toe around her issues with Tommy.

According to the huge atomic clock Ev had mounted in the living room for the occasion, it was 11:57 when Ev stood on a chair and boomed, "Everyone. May I have your attention for a moment?"

The room quieted immediately and everyone turned to look at him. "Many of you will notice this isn't one of my normal parties. The reason for that is that to my knowledge, we all, every single one of us, either have a common hatred of a certain demon or are close to someone who has a problem with this guy. I thought a party would be the perfect way to tell you that my grandfather found Happy's real name. My witch friend Cassandra tells me that in a fortnight's time, the moon will be in the correct phase and planetary alignment, whatever that means, to do the banishing ritual. So in a couple of weeks, we should all be free of the bastard!"

You wouldn't believe the amount of noise seventy-something people can make. Tony released his arm from my waist to clap both hands over his ears. His hearing was just as acute as any dog's and even my ears were hurting from the applause, whistles and yelling. It only got louder as the clock dinged and everyone started counting down to midnight.

As soon as we had sung "Auld Lang Syne", Tony leaned down and spoke into my ear. "I didn't get a hotel room. D'you suppose it's time Fudge met me?"

I did, indeed. Gregory appeared at my shoulder. "Ev said for me to give you two a ride home, it being difficult to get cabs tonight and all. If I'm not mistaken, you're ready to go. Cassandra, would you like a ride as well?" She shook her head and said she had her own car. "Then shall we?" One look at Tony's face told me he was as ready as I.

We said our goodnights, grabbed Tony's overnight case and our coats from the bedroom and followed Gregory outside. Snow was lightly falling and made everything sparkle. Or maybe it was just my mood. "Your place, Amy?" Gregory asked with a grin.

"Yes, please. And by the way, Happy New Year to you!" I replied.

Although I was happier than a pig in a poke, I was still a little apprehensive about bringing Tony home for the first time. My dinky little apartment would probably seem like a dump in comparison to his condo and how was Fudge going to react?

Although he'd seen it many times before when dropping me off, Tony surveyed the neighborhood with a critical eye as Gregory turned off Lyndale Avenue. Two more turns and we were on my street.

"Nice and quiet. What I wouldn't give to not hear traffic 24/7."

I gave Gregory a kiss on the cheek when he dropped us off. "Make him give you at least two days off for having to work tonight," I said.

"No worries, Amy. He's already told me to go home after I drop you and that he wouldn't need me for a couple of days. It sounded like he planned on hibernating at the house with Marianna."

The moment of truth had arrived. I unlocked the door and waited for either the assault that greeted me when I came home late or a lot of hissing and spitting. Fudge did neither. When we walked in the door, Tony sat his case down and walked cautiously over to Fudge, who was sitting in the middle of the living room with a quizzical look on his face. He squatted down and held out both hands. Fudge took a quick sniff, looked up at Tony and then over at me.

"He's a part of my life, too," I told him.

Fudge meandered over to me, head-butted my leg, walked over to his food dish and let out a very loud "meow".

"If he hasn't hissed or bit and is more concerned about his food, I'd say you're OK," I told Tony as I made my way to where I kept Fudge's food and poured some into his dish.

"That's my impression, too," I heard but not from the living room. When I turned around, Tony wasn't in sight. "If you're done with the cat, could the dog get some attention?"

I found him sprawled on my bed. It was indeed going to be a good new year.

CHAPTER 22

My phone rang at the crack of noon the next day. Tony and I were only on our second cup of coffee. "Don't you need to sleep in or something today?" I asked Cassandra.

"I left right after you. Must be habit or something, because I was awake at six when the alarm would normally be going off. I've already put all the holiday decorations away and cleaned the house."

"So you called to gloat?"

"No, I called to see how we get all the people that were at the party last night together to do the banishing ritual. Remember, Uncle Morris said anyone that had an extended life span needed to participate to get its protection? There were a lot of non-humans there."

"Without enough coffee in me to think coherently, I'd say it'd be pretty easy – just send out another invitation off Ev's guest list. I can get that back from Sally easy. But I'll need some notice."

"That's no problem. I think I know when it has to be held but I'd like Adamo's input. If possible, I'd also like him to lead the ritual. He seemed to be the oldest magical person in the room *and* he's one of the people affected by the demon. Do you have his phone number?"

I didn't, but suggested she call Bella and hung up. They could sort it out. I wanted to enjoy my holiday.

"Sounds like your friend is getting the ball rolling. Does this mean soon I'll be able to tell everyone you're mine?" Tony nuzzled my neck.

"I guess so, if that's something you want to do. Am I yours?" I snuggled further into him.

"Doll, I haven't met anyone who fits me as well as you. What do you think?"

"I'm still getting used to the idea of seeing someone regularly, and one who gets all furry and scary once a month at that. Can we take it a day at a time?"

His laugh sounded like a big dog's bark. It was deep and gruff. "I don't expect you to immediately change your lifestyle, if that's what you're thinking. I just want to be able to say I'm involved when I'm asked. And I am asked frequently."

"When do you need to leave?" I changed the subject. I had some more thinking to do, but not while wrapped in his arms.

"I have a flight out tomorrow morning. Can you stand me for another day?"

I could and I did. We watched the Bowl games, napped and ordered Chinese in for dinner. But I'll admit that when I kissed him goodbye at the door Tuesday morning, I was really glad to have my apartment to myself again. I wasn't used to having anyone except Fudge around.

January second was the same as every January second. Rich people, for whatever reason, tended to get way too drunk and then in trouble of one form or another every New Year's Eve. Most of my work was just recording incidents in the file for future reference (especially when contract renewals came up) but there were a few phone calls that Ev needed to make to soothe ruffled feathers. Like I said, some folks just didn't take kindly to bodyguards getting them out of a potentially icky situation.

Cassandra called mid-afternoon. "I know this is short notice but can you come over tonight at seven? We need to finalize the plans for the ritual and I'd like you there."

I got a little uncomfortable. "Me? I don't do magic and I wouldn't have a clue what you'll be talking about."

"I know, but you were the one that lit a fire under everyone to finally do something about this guy. Adamo and Bella both think just having you sit at the table will lend value to our discussion."

I heaved a big sigh. Since I was sort of responsible for the mess, I figured I should see it all the way through. I told her I'd be there.

I arrived at Cassandra's shortly before seven. Adamo and Bella were there. Adamo still looked like Gandalf. Bella didn't look like a powerful witch but more like a society matron in an elegant silk pantsuit. Ev was there, too, along with an ogre I'd never met. He looked a little like Ev but admittedly, I had a hard time telling ogres apart if I didn't know them well. The wrinkles and white hair at least indicated that he was much older than my boss. Ev introduced us. "Amy, this is my grandfather, Ragnar. Bestefar, this is my assistant, Amy."

"Ja, Evander's told me a lot about you," he said with a thick Scandinavian accent as he reached down to shake my hand. "I'm very grateful to you for forcing us all to finally take some action."

His hand completely enveloped mine so I allowed him to shake my arm. "I'm pleased to meet you as well," I said as evenly as I could with my whole body vibrating in time to his pumps of my arm. (I found out much later that Ev's grandfather lived in Norway and that *bestefar* is Norwegian for grandfather. Another interesting thing to file away about Ev: he spoke Norwegian fluently. Who'd a thunk it?)

Cassandra handed me a glass of wine just as Adamo cleared his throat. "We're all here so let's get to it, shall we?"

I said hello to Bella as we all found chairs at the dining room table. Ev and Ragnar leaned against the wall. There were no chairs large enough for them, but at least this house was old enough that ceiling height wasn't a problem.

Adamo began. "As you're all aware, Cassandra's great-uncle found us the verbiage to banish Happy, and Ragnar somehow managed to come up with his real name. As pronunciation of the name is crucial, I asked Ev if his grandfather could be in attendance not only at this meeting but at the ritual, as well. Ragnar has graciously agreed.

"We are quite fortunate in that a perfect astrological conjunction happens in a couple of weeks. A banishment can be performed at any time but it's much easier if it's done at the new moon. Aries is the most favorable sign for banishing and it so happens that this month's new moon will be in the sign of Aries. Therefore, we'll schedule the ritual for Saturday the twentieth, in the hour of Saturn or at

8:00 in the evening."

He looked around the room and everyone nodded in agreement.

"Cassandra has graciously agreed to allow us to use her backyard," he continued. "It's perfectly laid out for such a ritual and is large enough to hold about one hundred people. In addition, she tells me the neighbors won't call the police if they see or hear anything of a magical nature." He looked at me. "Amy, I'm assuming you'll handle getting the word out to everyone who was at Ev's the other night." I nodded. "I'll give you the wording for the invitation before we leave here tonight, as well as the addresses of some other people who need to be included. Ev said he'll foot the bill for the printing and postage.

"The ritual itself is fairly straightforward for anyone accustomed to such things. I'm happy to lead it. However, it requires a couple of ingredients I don't currently have in stock. I thought I'd ask the other magical people here if they do. Does anyone have a male mandrake root or black salt?"

Bella held up her hand. "I've got the salt and if Cassandra doesn't have the root, I know where I can get one on short notice."

"Mom's got the root," Cassandra said. "She grows them and I know she's got at least two dried. I'm sure she'll sacrifice one for the cause."

"Good," Adamo said. "Ragnar, is your English good enough to write the name down phonetically? I don't want to say it aloud until the ritual."

"No. I speak English good but I don't read or write it." He looked embarrassed.

"Then we will have to chance saying it aloud. Cassandra, as this is your house, would you kindly protect this room?"

She went into the workshop and returned with a handful of salt. She asked Ev and Ragnar to move closer to the table. She closed her eyes for a second then starting at one end, scribed a circle around the table with the salt. As she got back to her starting point, I felt rather than heard a door slamming shut.

"Thanks," Adamo inclined his head to her. "OK Ragnar, what's the name?"

"Jormundallr."

He wrote something down in the notebook he had in front of him. "Ev, is this right?"

Ev leaned in to look over Adamo's shoulder. "If you can remember that the 'er' you have written is closer to just the letter 'r', then yes. You need to sort of swallow the 'e' part of it."

Adamo grimaced and looked back over his shoulder at Ev. "Tell you what. Just before the ritual, I'll show this to you again and you can remind me."

Ev nodded and moved back from the table a little. He *was* getting better about remembering that humans had sensitive noses.

"Good," Adamo said. "Then Cassandra, if you will kindly break your circle, I think we're done here. I must say, why no one ever thought to spread the word before now is beyond me. Amy, I thank you from the bottom of my heart. This demon has been a thorn in the side of so many people for so many years. And here's the wording for the invitation and the addresses." He tore a couple pieces of paper out of his notebook and handed it to me. "Obviously, time is of the essence. The sooner these go out, the better."

"I'll do it first thing tomorrow morning. At least I think I will. Ev, you don't have anything that can't wait an hour or two, do you?"

He shook his head. "You know I don't get there as early as you do. If there's nothing in the reports that you have to deal with, then I'd say put off everything else until those are done. And Amy, just to be sure, send everything by FedEx overnight. That way we'll be sure they're delivered timely. Now, if you'll excuse us, my grandfather still isn't quite over his jet lag so I'm going to take him home. Cassandra, thank you for your hospitality." Ragnar nodded in agreement.

Ev and Ragnar got their coats and the blast from keeping the front door open long enough for both of them to squeeze through made me move closer to the fireplace. Adamo and Bella were right on their heels and I wasn't far behind but I had a question before I left.

"Cassandra, are you sure Uncle Morris' spell is going to work?" I didn't want to be a doubter but I really had no clue about these things.

"Trust me. His spells are of the tried-and-true variety. Plus, the collective intent of the people who will be gathered will be so powerful, I can't begin to describe it. Have no worries on that score.

"Adamo's read it over," she added. "I'd think if he wasn't sure, he would have changed something and I didn't see him change a thing. Go home so we all can get some sleep. Alarms come early tomorrow!"

Bright and early Wednesday morning, I was at my desk with a cup of Cassandra's cappuccino to keep me going until my pot had finished perking. I pulled the address file for the New Year's party from Sally's hard drive, added Adamo's people and merged it into my FedEx database. Then I printed out a little over a hundred invitations that read:

You are cordially invited to participate in a ritual to banish the demon known in our world as "Happy" on Saturday, the twentieth of January at eight o'clock in the evening. It will be held in the back yard at 2794 Lyndale Avenue South, Minneapolis, Minnesota … please enter through the side gate and dress weather-appropriate.

This banishment may not last beyond one or two hundred years. If you are unable to attend but wish to be included in the protection this spell will offer to non-humans, please send a taglock (strand of hair, fingernail clipping, skin shed) to the address above. We will use this to link the spell to you and will destroy it after the spell is complete.

If you have any questions, contact Adamo at 612.555.7468. Please destroy this invitation after reading it, preferably by fire.

When the clock finally hit 10:00 and I thought she'd be awake and coherent, I called Sally and asked her to stop at the FedEx store on her way in to pick up some more envelopes. When she said she'd just re-stocked the supply, I told her I'd tell her why we needed a lot more when she arrived. I still didn't trust the telephone.

I was just finishing up the year-end payroll when Sally walked in with two boxes of FedEx envelopes and another box of the paper we used for labels.

"So what's up with a huge mailing?" she asked as she dumped them on the floor next to my desk. She and Jack hadn't attended Ev's party and had taken the day before off, so I filled her in on the last couple of days.

"That is so cool! I can look forward to no more materialization in the office. I'll make sure Jack is there to lend his strength. He may not be trying to fix me up with anyone but that guy's just popping in drives me nuts. Not to mention I'd be really happy for both you and Ev."

"Thanks, I think," I replied. "I thought you had to have a vested interest for a spell to work."

"You do and Jack does have a vested interest. You're a friend and Ev's my employer. This whole situation makes me itch. No worries. He'll be there to keep me happy, if nothing else."

We spent the next hour printing labels, stuffing and then sealing the envelopes. We were almost through when Ev finally walked in the door. He looked like he hadn't slept at all.

"So why are you so late and why do you look like hell?" I asked.

"Bestefar – Grandfather. He was looking tired – he should have been tired. I picked him up from the airport just a couple of hours before last night's meeting. That was after one in the morning his time. I thought sure he'd conk off when I got him home, but no. He decided it was time to catch up on my life and then I got a lecture on settling down and starting a family. He even had some pictures of girls in his village he thought I ought to meet. It took me another two hours to explain that I was really quite happy with my life the way it was, that I'd settle down eventually but it wouldn't be with a girl from a podunk town in the middle of nowhere, Norway. The sky was getting light when he finally gave up and went to bed.

"I was headed that direction when my phone rang. It took me a half hour to calm that damned Sarah [blonde singer] down. Apparently, Aggie [dwarf guard] got into an argument with the drummer in her backup band and broke a couple of his fingers. I had to call Aggie and get his side of the story, then find a healer wizard for the fingers – they've got a gig tomorrow night. Finding the wizard wasn't easy. They're in some small town in Alabama. I've had maybe three hours' sleep."

"You've been known not to come into the office at all when you've had a bad night. Why is today different?" I couldn't help but be a little snide.

"Because I wanted to make sure you got all those invitations out and if there was anything I could do to free you up to do that, I wanted to be here. I've got as much riding on this as you do, you know."

"We're done. You can help by hauling all these over to the FedEx office. I can call for pickup but I think it'll be better if we just take them in. Less expensive, too, you know. So drop this pile off and go home and back to bed.

There's nothing we girls can't handle."

"That sounds wonderful. Gregory probably hasn't even left, yet. He went into the deli for something when I came upstairs. I'll get him to help me carry these and we'll be on our way. Thanks, Amy."

He went downstairs and a moment later, came back up with Gregory right behind him, a sandwich held in his mouth. He waved hello, picked up a pile of envelopes with one arm and walked back out, Ev on his heels with the rest. Sally and I were finally back to normal peace, quiet, and breathable air.

"I'm going to cut out, too," I told her. "I've got an editing deadline looming and I haven't even looked at the latest proofs. It's going to be a coffee-instead-of-wine kind of night, I'm afraid."

"Go on. I have a feeling now that the holidays are over, it's going to be quiet for another week or so. If anything comes up that I can't handle, I'll call. You're close by if needed, huh?" She handed me my coat and shooed me out the door.

I'd gotten about two chapters into my editing when the phone rang. It was Sally.

"I think you'd better come back to the office," she said with a tinge of worry in her voice.

"What's up?"

"FedEx just called. The truck that was taking the envelopes to the sorting facility was in an accident. It caught on fire and everything inside, including our invitations, was destroyed."

I about lost my lunch. "Oh. Shit. Do we have enough

supplies to re-do the mailing or do I need to grab a cab and stop at a store?"

"We've got enough of our stuff," she answered. "I've already started reprinting the invitations and will start on the labels next. FedEx is supposed to drop off some more of their envelopes in a few minutes. I need help getting everything done before they come back at seven to pick up the new batch."

I had started pulling my coat on as we were speaking. "I'm on my way," I said as I ran out the door and up the stairs.

This was just peachy. Although he, in theory, had no idea about the ritual, something in the back of my mind said Happy had a hand in this. Maybe I was just being paranoid. Nonetheless, it seriously screwed up my evening.

Sally, true to her word, had the invitations done and labels were starting to spit out of the printer when I burst through the door.

"Calm down," she said. "I've already called Jack to tell him I'll be late. With two of us, it won't take long. As soon as the envelope supply arrives, we can start stuffing."

"This just pisses me off," I growled. "If I didn't know any better, I'd say Happy had something to do with it."

"Maybe, maybe not. Traffic accidents do happen, you know. Either way, we have to re-do it."

Just then, a FedEx guy walked in with an armful of envelopes. "Sorry, ladies. If it helps any, you're not the only ones in this boat. I have more supplies to deliver and I'll be back, say, in an hour?"

Sally took the envelopes from him, thanked him and said an hour would be fine.

"Should we tell Ev?" she asked as she pulled her chair around to the front of her desk so we could work in assembly line fashion.

"No. They're still going out tonight and since I keep the books, he won't know about the extra expense."

At that, she grinned. "Oh, there's no extra expense. FedEx is paying for the pickup *and* crediting the account for $500 to reimburse us for the supplies and extra work."

I smiled back. "How'd you manage that? The pickup I can understand but the credit?"

"I threw a hissy fit. Told them I'd have to make a special trip to the office supply store and was hourly so you'd have to pay me time and a half to recreate the mailing tonight. They don't have to know I work part time or am salaried."

Wow. She was good. We worked in companionable silence and had just sealed the last envelope when the FedEx guy walked back in. I treated her to dinner at the pub, told her to take a couple of days off and trudged home, yawning. Editing could wait another day.

CHAPTER 23

I shouldn't have given Sally those days off. Having some moral support would have been nice.

I was at my desk on Thursday, splitting my focus between answering the phone and trying to get the final proof of my most recent book finished and off to the editor. I wasn't very successful because the majority of my thoughts were directed toward Saturday night. A throat cleared in front of my desk.

I tightened the barbed wire shield. "Hello again, pest," I greeted Happy. I'm sure my voice sounded just like I felt: bored to tears with his efforts and not pleased to see him at all.

"Good afternoon, Amy. I thought I would pop in [he let out a little chuckle] and see how you and Anthony were getting along. If you aren't, I've found a most delightful man, completely human, I might add, whom I believe you should meet. He shares your love of the arts, has a wonderful intellect and sharp sense of humor."

"How many times have I told you that I have no interest in being fixed up with *anyone*?" I blew up. "Despite what you may think, I was and am quite happy being single.

I still haven't come to any conclusions about Tony because not only does he get all furry once a month but I *really* like my privacy and solitude – something you apparently are incapable of understanding since you keep popping in without even announcing yourself, much less making an appointment. Therefore, take your completely human man and your part dog man and get out."

"Amy, I am disappointed in you. It is part of the human psyche to want to love and be loved, is it not? Why do you resist that part of you? It's obvious from your writing that is something you want. I am just trying to ensure you are a completely fulfilled person."

I had been warned quite awhile back to play dumb as to his real intentions. So, rather than tell him he was full of shit, that all this was for *his* benefit, I said, "You don't know me as well as you think you do. I told you to get out and I meant it. If you don't have anywhere else to go, there're chairs out in the reception area where you can quietly sit and twiddle your thumbs. I have work to do."

Thank goodness for the shielding Cassandra and Tommy had taught me. If Happy could read my mind, he'd have found out about the ritual and just how much energy of my own I was going to direct at getting rid of him. He'd also have figured out that I *had* been thinking about my relationship with Tony but had yet to come to any conclusions.

"I will give you a week to think about just how lonely you are, Amy. Then I will be back." Happy went 'poof' once again. I heaved a sigh of relief. I tried to go back to my editing but the focus was completely gone. I headed downstairs.

"Coffee and chocolate. Lots of it," I told Tommy even before the door closed behind me.

"What happened?" he asked as he turned his back to me and toward the espresso machine.

"Happy just paid me another visit."

Cassandra came out from the kitchen just as I got those words out of my mouth.

"Saturday is only two days away," she said as she came around the counter and gave me a hug. "You can make it until then."

"Oh, I know. It's just that this whole situation has me on edge and I have to finish this editing by five or I'll miss my deadline. I'm glad it's quiet upstairs because I've been doing it on Ev's time. Happy's visit just threw me all out of whack."

"Hopefully, this will help." Tommy handed me a double espresso and two of his double-fudge-chocolate-chip brownies.

"Mmmm," I moaned as I bit into one of the brownies. It was so chocolaty and rich, only a chocoholic could love it. I wanted to devour it and at the same time, take itsy bitsy bites to savor it longer. "What was I saying?" I took another bite and moaned again.

They both laughed. "Go back and finish your manuscript. I have faith you can get it done." Cassandra opened the door to the stairs for me. I balanced the plate on top of the cup and walked back upstairs, pausing twice to take another bite of brownie. Tommy knew me well. The first one didn't even make it all the way back to my desk.

I did indeed finish the editing and fired the manuscript off to my editor just before 4:30. Since it was a time for celebration, I treated myself to dinner at Cork's rather than scrounge in my kitchen.

*****

The Saturday of the ritual arrived. I woke early, full of nervous energy. I knew there wasn't anything for me to do but show up. Nonetheless, I felt like I ought to be doing *something*. So, I cleaned my house from top to bottom, even washing the bathroom rugs. I tried to snuggle down with Fudge for my standard afternoon nap but couldn't sleep. The mahjong game got another workout.

It seemed like forever, but it was finally time to head over to Cassandra's. In case you've never visited, January in Minneapolis can be brutally cold or it might be spring-like. You just never know. Thankfully it was the latter so I didn't look like an Eskimo as I left the house.

When I went through the gate to the back yard, I was surprised to see it nearly full. Cassandra had placed torches at strategic points to provide a little light but with no moon, there wasn't much. People were milling around just like they do at a cocktail party. Rhys was in conversation with a woman about his age. I said hello to Ev and his grandfather and turned at a tap on my shoulder. It was Jack.

"Sally told me what was happening," he said. "Even if she hadn't ordered me to be here, I would have come anyway. You're my friend, too. But this guy is really irritating her, too. So you can be sure my full powers will be added, OK?"

I felt better. I didn't want to feel like I'd taken him away from something.

My watch read shortly after 8:00 when I heard Adamo say, "People, please gather in a circle around what would normally be a bird bath. Leave me about three feet of clearance all the way around."

Everyone moved as requested. I made sure I was right at the front. I was shorter than most of the people there and wanted a clear view of what would happen. They'd put a board or something over the bird bath and draped it with a cloth to make a table. Cassandra's favorite cauldron was in the middle, surrounded by four black candles and a silver dish of some kind.

Adamo spoke again. "This is a statement and response ritual. I will say one paragraph and then you'll hear me say, 'repeat after me'. There are four sentences. I will say them one at a time and I want you to repeat them. I'll have another paragraph to say and then I'll slowly raise my wand. Witches and wizards, you know what to do. For you non-magical people, I want you to concentrate all your energy and thoughts on Happy being out of your lives. Direct all that energy toward the tip of my wand. When my hand is all the way up, I want you to push all that energy out and say 'Done' with emphasis. The whole thing is only going to take about ten minutes; then Cassandra has a small repast on the patio for us.

"Is everyone ready? Good. Take the hand of the person next to you or if that's not possible, put your hand on the shoulder of the person in front of you. We must all be connected. Now, focus."

I found myself holding hands with Jack and Cassandra; someone's hand rested on my left shoulder. Although I wasn't *that* surprised to see him, Tommy was on the other side of the circle from us, next to Bella and behind Adamo. The rest of the crowd was a mix of those who appeared human and some types I'd never seen before. The person standing next to Bella was shorter even than me, androgynous and distinctly snake-like, with scales for skin. I was willing to bet the eyes only had slits for pupils, too. I wondered where he/she came from. I could see Ev, his grandfather and a few other ogres towering over the back of the crowd.

Adamo stood tall and cleared his throat. "Spirits of the East, I ask that you watch over our endeavor." He lit one candle. "Spirits of the South, I ask that you watch over our endeavor." He lit a second candle. "Spirits of the West, I ask that you watch over our endeavor." He lit the third candle. "Spirits of the North, I ask that you watch over our endeavor." With this he lit the final candle. I felt a tingling in my hands and a slight pressure in my ears.

"We ask the Universe to heed our collective will.

"Repeat after me: What was dark shall be light." We intoned "what was dark shall be light" as he sprinkled something powdery into the small silver dish.

"Banish this demon from our sight." He added a dark, strange-looking item – probably that mandrake root.

"Crush this spirit from form to dust." He poured something liquid from a glass bottle into the dish.

"Send it back and away from us." He lit a match and set the dish's contents on fire.

We all said our lines right on cue. The entire time, I felt pressure building up, sort of like you feel in an elevator zipping its way from the ground to the fiftieth floor without a single stop. I took a peek at the others I could see around the circle. Every single person's face was a picture of intense focus.

"I call on the powers of the Universe to banish the demon Jormundallr from this realm. [I heard something that sounded like a scream.] Dissolve his unwanted form and send it back to those who sent it to us. Keep Jormundallr from us. [He touched his wand to Cassandra's cauldron, then raised it shoulder high and turned a complete circle. As he came back to his original place, he started raising his wand toward the sky. I saw all sorts of colored tendrils of light tethered from various points in the crowd – including a faint one from *me* to the tip of his wand.] By our will, begone, Jormundallr! And I say it shall be DONE!"

I released my breath and felt a sort of 'pop'; no, more like a 'boom' as I shouted "Done!" along with everyone else. Those tendrils of light combined into one and shot skyward from the tip of Adamo's wand, like a multicolored searchlight. At the same time, the fire that he had lit in the dish flared and went out. I heard a scream again just as the fire extinguished itself. Then something like a little bell rang in my head. Just a "ping" mind you, but something. I felt Cassandra almost lose her balance.

"Are you OK?" I whispered.

"Yeah. Just felt a little dizzy for a moment."

Adamo pinched the flame of each candle with a quiet thank you and then sagged against the makeshift table. Tommy and Bella broke the circle and went to make sure he didn't fall over or pass out.

Everyone else quit holding hands, shoulders, whatever. Cassandra called out, "Hot apple cider and cinnamon cake over here if anyone wants some." Although it may have been spring-like, it was still night, January, and Minneapolis. Hot cider was welcome. Although we all lined up, we let Adamo go first. There were some in the crowd who looked spent but he seemed like he needed it worse than anyone else.

"A little sugar and I'll be fine," he assured me as I raised my eyebrows to him in an unspoken concern for his well-being. "I am not as young as I once was and rituals like this take a toll on the old man. Sweets perk me right up, I promise."

He turned to Tommy. "Would you kindly dispose of the taglocks for me?"

"Sure thing. Here, sit." Tommy gestured to a chair he'd brought from inside the house, then retrieved Cassandra's cauldron from the birdbath/table and poured the contents into the flames in a raised firepit they had on the patio. It smoked a bit and smelled like burning hair, but only briefly, then the usual scent of burning cedar returned.

Some of the people had left immediately, while others stood around talking in low voices. I even saw a business card or two exchanged. It had turned into a cocktail party again. Ev and his grandfather said their goodbyes to me, Ev telling me his *bestefar* was leaving in the morning and he'd see me in the office Monday. The rest of the ogres trooped out after them.

Jack said goodbye, too, telling me Sally would be very pleased with the results of the ritual. I kissed him on the cheek with a "thanks" before he left. Rhys said something to Tommy then let himself out the gate.

"So, is it done?" I couldn't help but ask Bella as we stood around, waiting for the crowd to disperse.

"Oh, honey, is it ever. Didn't you feel at least a little something?" I admitted I felt the release of pressure but nothing else. Bella wasn't a close enough friend for me to share what I felt or knew.

"It doesn't matter. Take my word for it, he's gone, and will be for at least the rest of your lifetime."

I hung around until everyone had left, then helped haul the trash bags over to the dumpster behind the deli's building. For this event Cassandra stooped to using disposable cups and plates but naturally, they were all made of biodegradable materials. Tommy doused the fire while Cassandra and I carried the serving dishes back into the house.

"I'd say that was a spectacular and successful ritual, wouldn't you?" she asked as we washed the serving dishes and put them away.

I shrugged my shoulders. "I guess. If you say so. I still don't know what I'm seeing or feeling. And what about the stuff that was on the birdbath table?"

"Adamo and Bella took the remains from the dish with them. Adamo will dispose of the ashes in the river after he's dropped Bella off. Running water, y'know. [I didn't.] Tommy's clearing the rest of it now."

We'd just finished the dishes when Tommy came in, rubbing his hands together to get some warmth.

"It's warm over by the fire," Cassandra told him. "Why don't you go thaw yourself."

Tommy and I both froze in place and looked at her. She had a sheepish look on her face as she turned to him. "I know I've been an ass these last couple of weeks and I'm sorry. Maybe it was just the stress of wanting the ritual to go perfectly or something. Forgive me?"

Just as he took her in his arms, my cell phone rang. It was Tony. Oh m'god. I'd forgotten about him! "Hi Doll," he said when I answered. "Did everything go alright?"

"Everyone who knows says it did so I guess so. But what about you? You weren't here. How are you covered?"

He laughed. That nice, deep bark of his that I liked so much. "No worries, Doll. I gave Cassandra some of my hair before we left the New Year's Eve party. She said she wanted it for a variety of reasons – to track me in case you got worried or to curse me into oblivion if I ever hurt you. Then she smiled and told me about the ritual and said if I couldn't be there, the hair would tie me to it.

"I'd have given it to her for the first reasons but the last one was OK, too. At that point you didn't have a date for the thing so I couldn't commit. Turns out I couldn't have made it tonight, anyway. So, I take it we're free of the creep. Can I call you mine publicly, now?"

I blushed. Cassandra came up for air long enough to yell, "She's all yours, Tony. Think you can handle her?"

"We'll talk about it later," I said quietly. "I love you."

"Love you, too. Tell Cassandra I can handle whatever you throw at me. Call you tomorrow."

I left the two love-birds-once-again and walked back to my apartment. I felt like a huge weight had been lifted and I slept like a log as soon as I laid my head down. For the first time in a while, I didn't even remember dreaming.

The next morning dawned brightly. It had snowed sometime the night. The light dusting made everything look clean and fresh. It was going to be a wonderful day.

Postscript

Humans are such silly animals, don't you think? My human, Amy, is a witch even though she denies what she sees and feels. Oh, not a real powerful one but a witch nonetheless. Otherwise, I wouldn't have been assigned to her. For five long years, I've been nudging her, trying to get her to acknowledge her abilities but *no*.

If I could speak her language, I'd ask her why she's never succumbed to any of those vampires she meets. She reeks of them when she comes home from those fancy-dress parties and I'm glad when she takes the clothes away to the dry cleaners.

I'd also ask her if she thinks mundanes can see and feel the flow of energy. Perhaps she should ask that smelly ogre of hers if *he* can do that. (I'd also ask her not to ever invite him into the house again. Although I'm finally used to the smell clinging to her when she gets home from work, it's a hundred times worse when he comes to the house. It takes days for his smell to go away.)

At least she's resolved her feelings about the human dog. When she gets jittery, I get jittery. That's not a good feeling for an otherwise calm cat to have. And if she's going to have a relationship with someone, I guess he's better than the others she's brought home. At least he cares for her. As long as he's in his human form when he's here. I don't do full-on dogs.

I spoke with the Familiar Council and asked to be relieved of my assignment. If she's not going to do magic, I don't see why I need to continue hanging out at the computer while she writes her foolish stories. I could be having fun helping another witch who actually *does* magic. They denied my request. It appears this human will need my services at some point.

Soon, I hope. I'm bored.

"Fudge"

ABOUT THE AUTHOR

Deborah J. "DJ" Martin is an accountant, witch, and Master Herbalist. She is the author of four books about herbs.

She left the frozen tundra (Minnesota) many moons ago and now lives in the north Georgia mountains with her husband, their crazy cats and numerous woodland creatures. If she's not clickety-punching numbers for clients or writing, you can probably find her in the garden, visiting her grandchildren or in her recliner with her nose stuck in a book. You can find out more about her at http://www.authordjmartin.com.